Mistress Munn and the Magician

A fantasy novel

by

David Hughes

ISBN 978-1-7393234-5-5

Edited by Sylvia Clare

Published by Clarity Books 2005

Cover design by David Hughes

Printed by KDP

Front cover image: the cover image is an interpretation of a lead badge from the middle ages, found in Germany, designed to ward off evil spirits. Thanks to Malcolm James and his wonderful book The Secret Middle Ages for much inspiration.

My everlasting thanks to my wife Sylvia for listening, reading, editing and supporting me through the trauma of giving birth to this book. You are a wonderful midwife.

Other books by the author

Fiction

The Honest Liars by David Hughes

Julia, by David Hughes – runner up in the isle of wight literary awards for fiction 2004.

Non-fiction

Living the life You Want by Sylvia Clare & David Hughes

Living well with ADHD by Sylvia Clare and David Hughes, illus. by David Hughes

Illustrations

Trust your Intuition by Sylvia Clare illustrations by David Hughes

Who Will I Become? A parenting/ child guide, by Sylvia Clare with Ben Cole, illus. by David Hughes

Heaven Sent Parents by Sylvia Clare & Kelly McKain, illustrations by David Hughes

The Well-Mannered Penis by Sylvia Clare, illustrations by David Hughes

Chapter One

'Cover my face with bees if I am telling a lie'

'What are you talking about Mistress Munn?'

The Magician surveyed the old woman, who was flitting around the room like a frail bird, cleaning as she went. The hair perched on her head, as though she was carrying her own nest, had turned white with age but he knew she dyed it with a boiled acorn tincture. Diminished by time, she had shrunk in stature during his thirty-five years. Her reduction in size had in his opinion been more than countered by an increase in her appetite for gossip. The Magician's sharp brown eyes could not help displaying his inherent distrust of her recent news.

'I am just saying I heard tell that the King has invited Moredeath the Bludgeoner to form a pact by marrying his daughter the Lady Gossamer.'

'Your ears have fallen victim to the words of fools Mistress. Which only goes to prove you should not loiter behind half-closed doors. There is no way the King, codbrain though he is, would invite Moredeath anywhere near his daughter. By all accounts, he is closer to a beast than a man.'

'Well, as I say Magician, this is what I heard, and as my dear old mother would often say 'ears have no tongue with which to lie.' I just thought you ought to know so as you wouldn't be surprised by the news. You know how difficult you gets when people surprise you.'

'What are you talking about Mistress? I am never taken by surprise, and if I were, I would deal with the matter with decorum, as always.'

Whattlewherrit smiled at his ridiculous response knowing she had summed him up perfectly. Mistress Munn laughed.

'Oh yes, of course,' she replied. That was her final opinion on the matter.

The old woman picked up his grubby garment and pulled the odd hair or two off it.

'Have you noticed there is a touch of moon in your hair nowadays Magician? I will guarantee it won't be long before it all turns the colour of snow.'

The Magician looked at her and raised an eyebrow. Why she had to continually remind him he was ageing he did not know. That was Mistress Munn though. Never one to hold back on her inner thoughts.

'I am not old enough for snow to settle on my head yet if you don't mind.'

'Anyway' she said looking at the mud on his clothing 'I see you have been out in the forest again.'

'And?' Replied the Magician.

'Cornelius, 'I pray he is still with us', would not approve.'

'What Cornelius would or would not say is of no relevance. It is three years since his disappearance and there has been no word. I have done what I can.'

Mistress Munn seemed unimpressed, and even though she knew she had hit a nerve, she continued.

'If I can be so bold, you must stop entering the spirits of the creatures so much. Your Cornelius used to warn you against it. No good can come from getting entangled with the nature of a beast. He told you, it can affect your very soul.'

'If you recall Mistress, my reason for doing so of late was actually to seek out Cornelius. What better than the nose of a Bear to taste the evening air, or of a Wolf for travelling many miles in a single day, never mind an Owl to see the forest floor at night?'

'That's as may be, but that is not why you do it now. I may be old, but I am no a fool. I knows you are particularly fond of doing so in the rutting season.'

'What are you suggesting,' protested the Magician.

'Mark my words and speaking as a woman, a man can get fixated upon fighting and lustful things until he can think of nothing else.'

'I can assure you Mistress that my ventures into the forest are purely to keep my practice up to scratch. You never know when I might have need of our animal friends.'

'I am not sure how often rutting is a skill necessary for the practice of magic. I am just saying. That is all,' said the old woman.

The Magician sighed, and keen to change the course of the conversation asked, 'When is this marriage of convenience supposed to be taking place?'

She gave him one of her looks. A look that said, 'oh so now you are taking me seriously.'

'Not one passage of the moon from now, so I hear.'

'This cannot be. If so then how is it no news of this has reached my ear before this?'

The old woman folded her arms and standing as tall as she could which amounted to no more than the height of a donkey's back, stared at the Magician.

'Perhaps you have been out in the forest too much and not around to hear things? As I have already said cover my face with bees if....'

'What else do you know?'

'The Bishop of Nantes is already on his way with his entourage. He is bringing the four holy relics with him. There is to be a week of celebrations culminating in a jousting tournament.'

The Magician could hold back his feelings no longer.

'This cannot take place! It must not! Is that ignorant dolt of a King so stupid that he can't see what will happen? As soon as Moredeath is married to the Lady Gossamer the King himself will meet an inauspicious end and Moredeath will rule the land.'

The Magician suddenly lost interest in the bath where he was relaxing. Its soothing qualities had been overridden by Mistress Munn's alarming news and given way to a strange claustrophobic feeling. He was having one of his visitations and it did not feel good.

'Are you alright Magician?' The old woman could tell he was sensing something. She had been his housekeeper the past thirty years, and she knew when things were not right.

'I need to get out of the tub. Someone is coming.'

Mistress Munn looked at the skinny Magician, dripping wet from his bath and wondered what would become of him. He was an enigma. When he was a child, his father had found him impossible to teach due to his constant distractions and now, when he was nearing middle age, and his father was no longer there, Whattlewherrit was getting even more unpredictable. He had inherited the title Magician but, in all honesty, she admitted to herself, he did not have the temperament nor stature of Cornelius, his father. He spent most of his time out in the forest away from people, avoiding his duty to the King and his court. As she looked at him, she thought it was not surprising that

Whattlewherrit had not inherited Cornelius's nature, for Whattlewherrit, like Cornelius, and indeed all of the Magicians before him, was a foundling

The sad truth of the matter was the whole dynasty of the Magicians of Naze relied upon the foundling wheel, that wicked thief of motherhood. Situated in the wall of the nunnery of the Sisters of Irreverence there lay a horizontal wheel cut into the stonework. Unwanted babies could be placed upon it and when the foundling wheel was turned, it creaked with the weight of the child in its embrace. Then, and only then, a bell rang in the nunnery and the child disappeared forever into the confines of its austere walls. Once every fifty years, if a child was placed on the wheel on a full moon, then that child was taken to become apprentice to the current Magician of Naze. So it was with Whattlewherrit. The prophecy foretold that any child left that way on the right night was blessed to become wise and would master the skills of a Magician.

Mistress Munn could not bear to think of the many nights when Whattlewherrit screamed himself awake as a child with the same dream. 'I hear this creaking like a rusty gate Mistress, and then it all goes dark and it feels as if a part of myself has been sliced away.'
Those were the words the same words he always used. She would comfort him, but she knew that deep down his small soul was crying out for his mother. Perhaps this was so with all Magicians, but she could not help thinking there had been a mistake in his case. There could not have been a least likely candidate for Magician. The child was here, there, and everywhere, from the moment he could walk, driving Cornelius, his surrogate father, wild. Cornelius was a precise and rigid man and could often be heard shouting, 'That boy has been sent to test me, Mistress Munn. He was born under a green moon!'
The young boy's behaviour became worse, the older he grew, causing an unspoken rift between the boy and his father, which was why in her mind, when Cornelius disappeared, Whattlewherrit did little to seek him out, other than entering the spirits of the local forest animals, which she felt he did for his own satisfaction, much to her disappointment and chagrin. Still, that was three years past and nothing could be done about it. It didn't stop her mentioning it, despite his obvious annoyance.
In her heart she knew Whattlewherrit was a good man, it was just that he lived in a world that did not match his temperament or expectations and there

was the rub. Not that she could do anything about it. All she could do was hope he would be careful. His lack of forethought had led him into trouble in the past but back then Cornelius was there to put things right. Now there was no one apart from herself and she knew nothing about magic. She looked out into the chilling night air and sighed.

She was not to know, as she mulled over her thoughts, that half a mile away on the cold waters of the estuary, Sir Sockamore, one of the Knights of Naze sat imperiously in full Knightly regalia at one end of the ferryboat whilst at the other the boatman pulled heavily against the oars. The boatman was fighting the current that swirled around the bay surrounding the Magician's island home.

'Can't you pull harder man?' shouted the Knight across the rising wind.

'I would pull harder if it were a rope around your neck,' he muttered as the wind blew his words leeward.

'What did you say man?'

The boatman spat into the water and in a louder voice replied.

'I said the tide is against us, your lordship. The currents here are strong.'

The Knight huffed and his eyes narrowed, detecting as he had the boatman's lie.

Wouldn't be so hard if you weren't dolled up to the nines with your armour, thought the boatman. If only I had been born to the cock of a lord and not an Innkeeper, I would be sitting where you are, but I wouldn't be so demanding. Sir 'I'm so handsome all the ladies love me' Sockamore. He doesn't even know what they say about him in the local taverns. The whores say he couldn't plug a wormhole with what lies beneath his codpiece.

'Boatman, how long until we get there?'

'I reckons another quarter of the hour your lordship.'

'Good God man, am I to die in this ramshackle boat of yours. Get a move on.'

The boatman said nothing, but his thoughts dwelt on sizzling hot irons being applied to every extremity of the Knight's naked body.

They were heading to the Magician's home, a large tower situated on an island in the estuary of the river Naze. It had been the home of Magicians for hundreds of years. The Magicians of Naze had kept their distance from the Kings of the land by living 'across the water.' Indeed, they were known by many as 'those across the water'. Mention of magic or anything to do with it was deemed to be bad luck.

But no matter where they lived, they were tied to an age-old pledge to serve, something the young Magician fought against whenever called upon by the King. As far as he could see there was nothing positive in the archaic bondage to which some long-lost ancestor of his had unwittingly agreed to submit. Cornelius however had been deeply loyal to the King and had tried to instil into him the virtues of humility, but the Magician could see no advantage to being the servant of a codbrain despot who had the attention span of a Hare on heat. Many a quarrelsome exchange took place on that subject when Cornelius was still around. He was considering this when Mistress Munn interrupted his thoughts.

'I can see a light coming across the water!'
The Magician did not need to be told, he already knew.

'It will be the King's messenger Sir Sockamore, the puffed-up peacock. I sensed his imminent arrival when I was in the tub.'

'Oh lord, then this is bad news, you wouldn't find Sir Sockamore coming out on a night like this unless it were important.'

'He's probably coming to announce the engagement you were telling me about. No doubt the King will want 'his Magician' in attendance at the ceremony. That will be interesting with the Bishop of Nantes there too. No doubt the pompous pontiff will be wearing the Eternal Underpants and decrying magic as evil doing.'
The Magician liked to goad the Bishop, who could not resist responding to his jibes with some reading from the Book of Words followed by the inevitable. 'The great Moyen watches you Magician. He will punish you on judgement day as he will all disbelievers.'

'You needs to be careful Magician. The Bishop is a powerful man. He has had many a man burnt at the stake.'

'The Bishop cannot harm me, Mistress. He knows the King depends upon me and not the church for advice. Do you think the Bishop will be able to advise him honestly on this disastrous plan of his to marry the Lady Gossamer to the Bludgeoner? The Bishop won't say a word because he risks the monasteries and the patronage of the King. I however have nothing to lose by telling him the whole thing is a complete disaster from start to finish.'

9

'Sometimes Magician I think you tread on dangerous ground. Your father told you the same.' Mistress Munn drew a deep breath before adding, 'and you know what I mean.'

'Answer the door Mistress, it is you who are now treading on dangerous ground. I have asked you before not to keep mentioning him. It does no good.'

'Not mentioning him does not mean he has gone away.'

'Please answer the door!'

Mistress Munn reached the foot of the stairs at the very moment Sir Sockamore had raised the huge knocker and was about to let it go. She pulled the thick oak door open with her full force, still seething from the Magician's parting words.

'Yes!?' She called out.

Sir Sockamore stepped back as if confronted by a malevolent apparition. It took him a moment to pull himself together as he pretended he had not been taken by surprise.

'Mistress Munn you were expecting me?'

'I saw the boatman's light approaching the jetty.'

'Ah yes of course, your eyes are as keen as your ears. We must all watch out, mustn't we?'

Unfazed by Sir Sockamore's remark, Mistress Munn replied coldly.

'It pays to keep one's wits about one my lord. with so many scoundrels about nowadays.'

'Indeed. But I am getting cold and bored, I need to see your master.'

And without a word more Sir Sockamore stepped forward and pushed his way past Mistress Munn. He had hardly taken two steps when he was confronted by the Magician, wearing a black robe that brushed the floor. His long damp hair hanging well below his shoulders. He stopped the Knight in his tracks with a simple hand gesture.

'No need to go any further Sir Sockamore, we can transact our business here.'

Sir Sockamore, not used to such lack of courtesy, seemed flustered at first, but soon regained his posture.

'I'd forgotten you were not versed in courtly matters Magician but be it so I have no reason to want to be entertained by someone with whom I have no common understanding of manners.'

'As you can see Sir Knight, I have this minute stepped out of the bath. My understanding of courtly behaviour however is that it requires advanced notice of a visit. Is that not so?'

The Knight shifted uneasily on his heels. He did not appreciate being told how to be courtly.

'But this is an urgent matter on behalf of the King!'

'Then why did you not send a pigeon in advance with a note foretelling your arrival?'

'You know full well why, Magician. Because the last time we did that, it returned as some sort of exotic talking bird that wouldn't keep its mouth shut.'

'I was just trying to advance the future of communication Sir Knight. The written word is so out of date as far as communication is concerned. I will grant you that it was unfortunate that the bird had picked up so many bad habits.'

'I imagine you are referring to the fact the bird called the King 'a pompous codbrain' are you not? And you consider that was just unfortunate?'

'As I explained at the time, that was obviously the bird's opinion and not mine.'

'Enough of this pointless conversation. I have been sent by the King to relay his Majesty's request that you return to the court immediately. I have a boat waiting. He has also asked me to inform you that..' Here he seemed to choke up, 'It is his intention to give the hhhhhhand of the Lady Gossamer to Moredeath the Bludgeoner.'

The distress in the Knight's face was apparent, as was his inability to spit out the words he had to say. The Magician said nothing for a moment. He could spare the man further distress, knowing as he did of Sir Sockamore's infatuation with the Lady Gossamer, but then why should he? Sockamore was a lovesick fool but he also a venomous man who would ruin anyone if it meant his own advancement.

'I always thought she was destined for your hand, Sir Knight?' said Whattlewherrit vindictively.

Sir Sockamore blushed deeply before his embarrassment quickly turned to anger.

'Then you thought wrong, Magician! Magicians should not meddle in politics or matters of love, or it will end up badly for them. Enough of this prattling. The boatman awaits.'

But the time they left the tower, the wind had risen and the temperature of the night had dropped. The waves slapped heavily against the quay wall and their foaming tops broke away, soaking the shore. Everything was restless and uneasy, reflecting the Magician's mind. The small lantern at the prow of the boat bobbed and swayed in the distance, giving barely enough light to cast a shadow and were it not for the dripping tar torches the Knight and the Magician held, they would have had difficulty placing a step in front of them without falling into the thick black water. The journey back to Naze castle would be long and perilous that night, and in the company of the Knight which the Magician despised most. Not that there were many he admired. The land had become drained. Ruled by flaccid men with fat arses who rode carthorses because nothing else could bear their weight. Men who talked of chivalry and whose manners at court were precise and precious but who when they visited the whorehouses reverted to their natural selves. Pretence and hypocrisy ruled the land, whilst the poor bore the strain.

The Magician knew why the King was bringing in Moredeath. He had been so lax in his duties that the bordering lands had become a threat. Skirmishes were regular, and despite their strutting arrogant ways, the Knights of Naze were a sorry lot, not able to defend the land. The King needed someone with whom to build a strong allegiance, but Moredeath was not the right choice. The man was a monster whose father, Deathgrin, had become the most feared person in the known world. Moredeath would destroy the King, roast him on a spit, then feast on him. He had to stop this proposed marriage. Somehow, he needed to persuade the King to change his mind.

'How long back boatman?' Sir Sockamore shouted against the wind to be heard.
        'As long as it takes my Lord.'
        'That's no answer you fool! You must have some idea!'
The boatman lifted a finger at the Knight, then pretended he was testing the wind. He drew breath, then without warning spat into the gale. The gob flew past the Knight missing him by inches.
        'Sorry my Lord. Just finding the direction and strength of the wind.' He shouted
        'Idiot. Can't you see that by the way the flames from my torch are going?'

'I can indeed my Lord but being a boatman is a precise art. The alternative would be to piss into it, but I didn't want to do that. You have no wish to see my cock, I'll vouch.'

'Good God man I swear I will have you on the rack if you do not get on and ferry us to Naze castle within the hour.'

No more was said. The Magician thought the whole exchange amusing but at the same time sad.

As he began to row, the boatman began to sing.

'All day long I tug and haul
The waterman's life is not fair at all
If I'd been born from the cock and ball
Of a wealthy lord I'd have plenty
Room and board and then some more
Money for ale and a good-looking whore
But I'm a waterman simple and plain
Just wedded to my oars in the pouring rain'

Chapter Two

'So you are here at long last. What kept you?' The words of rebuke sat heavy upon Whattlewherrit, who found them offensive having suffered a miserable and dangerous crossing. The dull candlelight of the King's bedchamber reflected bleakly on the remains of a fine goose and a jug of wine that had smeared his rambling beard. He had grown fat from excess food and lack of activity and had to sit well away from the table to accommodate his enormous belly. Whattlewherrit felt sorry for any maidservant who would have to submit to his appetite in the bedstraw. It was well known in the castle that the King took whatever he wanted.

Slobbering like an old dog, his dull eyes barely looked up at the Magician as he ate. Whattlewherrit sensed the mistrust the King had of him. Cornelius, the Magician's surrogate father, had been subservient. But Whattlewherrit baulked against the King's demands, and the King knew it.

'I came as soon as was possible my liege, but you will have noticed that a storm is now raging, and we were but minutes away from destruction in the small boat you sent.'

The King continued his supper, downing whatever came to hand before reaching out for more. His disinterest in the Magician's welfare could not have been more obvious. His bloated face remained fixed on the table and Whattlewherrit had to wait patiently, listening to his greasy chops smacking as he searched the table for yet more food to consume.

'Yes, well, you are here so the boatman did his job well enough,' he said dismissively.

'He did and we paid him for it.' The Magician could not help mentioning the fact but knew the King would have no intention of reimbursing him. The King never paid for anything, not even the ransom demanded for any Knight foolish enough to get captured defending the realm.

'A man deserves to get paid for his good service,' said the King picking a bone from his teeth. 'So, did Sir Sockamore survive the journey?' The King let out a disgusting belch and then chuckled to himself, clearly enjoying the thought of the Knight's discomfort.

'He did your Majesty.'

'And did he convey my message?'

'He did indeed.'

'Good, well then, we are all agreed this marriage is the best possible thing for the future of Naze.'

The Magician drew breath, considering his strategy. He had to try to tell the King how abysmal the whole idea was. His bold words to Mistress Munn seemed paper thin when confronted by the enormous bulk of the King, grunting like a foraging boar.

'Your Majesty I would beg your indulgence for a moment for I would like to speak honestly about the planned betrothal.'

The King stopped mid-mouthful and stared fiercely at the Magician. He did not say a word. His eyes told all, but despite his obvious annoyance he waved his hand to signal the Magician to continue.

'I have serious misgivings about the intended bridegroom.'

The King's face contorted in a hideous manner but the Magician felt obliged to continue.

'Has your Majesty considered the nature of the man and his.......'

Without allowing Whattlewherrit to continue the King slammed his thick fists on the table making the pewter plates jump.

'Damn you Magician! Are you questioning your King? Do you have the impertinence to suggest I have not considered the consequences of the match?'

Whattlewherrit held his ground but was beginning to wonder whether he could handle the King at his worse. In an instant he decided flattery was needed as a balm to soothe the King's anger.

'Your Majesty I am called upon in my role as court Magician to be honest with his Majesty whenever I feel apprehensive about the future. Seldom am I placed in a such position however because your Majesty rules with such considered authority. Indeed, if I reflect upon it, this is the first and only time I have ever felt the need to.....'

The Magician hoped he was on his way to re-establishing the equilibrium when the King violently interrupted him.

'Shut up Magician before you go too far! You are not skilled enough in rhetoric to make me listen to your sycophantic nonsense! I know full well what the opinion of my decision is. Do you think Sir Sockamore approves? That pretentious popinjay thought he was going to bed my daughter and become heir apparent. He was not alone in that desire. Do you think the Knights of Naze aren't all clambering for position in the court. They jostle one another like children at the brazier of a Chestnut seller; but be warned, some of them get too close to the flames and get their fingers burnt. Be careful you do not fall into that trap.'

'Sire I....'

The King farted loudly. 'I need a shit to rid me of my discomfort.'

The King lifted his bulk from the table and lumbered over to the corner of the room where there was an open privy. No more than a board with a hole in it situated in an overhang in the castle walls. He dropped his hose and began farting again. Whattlewherrit tried to avoid the worst of the situation by remaining on the other side of the room.

'Come over here,' demanded the King, 'did you bring the shard?'

The Magician clutched his chest where the shard rested. Shaped like a flint arrowhead, no one would know it was anything more than an ornament should they see it. The King however knew exactly what it was.

'Good. Well I want to take a look at the What Will Be.'

Like cold water penetrating a cloak on a winter's day unease began to crawl over Whattlewherrit's skin. It left him uncomfortable and heavy with the inevitability of his situation. He wanted to object. To say that looking into the What Will Be never brought any good and only ever caused disruption. Cornelius had taught him well in that respect. The words of warning on the day he disappeared stayed with him. 'Beware of looking into the What Will Be.'

'Magician! Wake up from your thoughts and bring out the shard!' demanded the King.

The Magician did as he was told. So much for his brave words to Mistress Munn. Even though he knew in his heart it would do no good, he pulled it out and held the shard on the length of leather used for it to hang around his neck. They both watched as it began to spin of its own accord. Within moments, on the ground at his feet, there opened up a circle of light. And then gradually coming into focus, a picture emerged, lighting up the murky candlelit room. It was a forest. The trees were thick and high and through them a thin path trailed its way into the distance. The King and the Magician heard the sounds of birds and the rustling of leaves, followed by that of a horse, snorting as it breathed in the heavy air and blew it out again. The two men remained silent. Waiting. Then without warning the view changed. They saw the face of a man so fierce and uncompromising that they could be in no doubt this was the Bludgeoner. His jaw was square and thick, and he had a broad forehead that overshadowed his eyes, upon which were dense eyebrows that moved beneath a furrowed brow. He surveyed the forest ahead with the eye of a hunter. Across the man's expansive chest were two leather straps, one holding his sword, the other holding his shield that covered his back like a carapace. No arrow would strike this man from behind and meet its mark, thought the Magician. As for his thighs, they wrapped themselves around the body of his huge horse like thick tree roots that had matured over rocks. The man was enormous and utterly alarming.

'That's him.' There was an edge of awe in the words the King spoke.

They watched as the shard panned out to show the Bludgeoner's retinue. More than fifty men the Magician guessed. All of them having similar brutish features to their master.

'I had not imagined he would be bringing so many of his men with him,' said the King.

The Magician sensed the King's unease but told himself it was all he deserved for such blatant naivety. He was about to suggest they finish the session when the King unexpectedly farted long and hard and Whattlewherrit was hit by the thick putrid aroma of the King's bowels. Whether it was a result of this distraction he could not say but the picture flickered, and something strange occurred. The image changed. They saw a room, unlike any room either had seen before. In contrast to the grey walls of the castle where coloured tapestries were all that brightened the gloom, this room was full of colour but from an unfamiliar light. Small, strange suns shone from the walls. There were peculiar pictures and unrecognisable objects. Furnishings that seemed to be covered in cloth. As if this were not enough to cause confusion, in their minds, in the middle of the room stood a man as naked as the day he was born. Overweight and hairy, he was sporting a large erection.

'Great Moyen!' uttered the King. 'That man's pinklarry is alert for a night's plumping. What is this Magician?'

Whattlewherrit, who was as confused as the King, did not want to think about why anyone's pinklarry would be standing so proud. He felt a terrible sense of foreboding.

'I think I should put the shard away your Majesty.'

'Nonsense Magician we must find out what this is all about,' shouted the King.

The Magician, against his better judgement, held the shard where it was. It was only moments later when a door in the room opened, and a young maiden

17

wearing strange clothes appeared. The second she saw the naked man, her eyes widened and her jaw dropped in shock. She uttered some words, which the King and Magician could not comprehend. It was at this point that the Magician could bear it no longer. He put the shard away beneath his gown and the image disappeared.

'Why did you do that,' demanded the King. 'I wanted to see what happened next!' The King was furious. Had it not been for him having his hose around his ankles, Whattlewherrit was sure he would have struck him. Despite the apparent wrath of the King, the Magician knew he had done the right thing.

'Your Majesty it is far too dangerous to interfere with the What Will Be. You know it is only to be viewed in exceptional circumstances and for the purpose for which one calls it into being. We were enquiring about Moredeath and somehow this man and woman appeared. Something is wrong and if I had not stopped it the What Will Be could have been damaged forever.'

'You are lucky I don't throw you into a pit of dogs for this, and I would do so were it not for the fact I have other plans for you. You have betrayed me Magician, and I shall not forget this.'

Whattlewherrit felt a deep sense of foreboding as the King's eyes continued to bore into him.

The King pulled up his hose, looked down the privy hole and then lumbered back to his seat. A cold detachment had come over him. The Magician knew this of old. One minute violently angry and the next icy indifference. The King's mood swings were legendary.

'You are to go out into the great forest to meet Moredeath and his retinue. You will lead them to Naze.'

This was the last thing the Magician wanted. To be involved in the politics surrounding the Bludgeoner and the King. He knew the Bludgeoner to be as safe as a bear on heat. The man was renowned for his butchery and cruel vindictive nature. In that moment he almost favoured the pit full of dogs. The King continued.

'If I sent a Knight with a party of men, he might mistakenly see it as an act of aggression. You however are not threatening. You couldn't threaten anything. But for all of your inadequacies, you alone know the great forest and its ways. You can guide him into Naze and make sure he arrives safely. We don't want him straying into the Greer swamp not with those......' The King stopped momentarily as if he could barely say the words witches. 'This must not go wrong. He has to marry the Lady Gossammer, whatever happens.'

The Magician took a moment to consider what he had just said. 'This must not go wrong'. He knew about the witches and how dangerous they could be. After all it was but three years since Cornelius had disappeared and there was strong reason to believe the witches were involved. However uncomfortable he felt about the situation he could see there was no point in arguing with the King. Not unless he wanted to be brutally put to death. He knew there was nothing he could do now to stop the inevitable.

Chapter Three

Kenny Catlin leaned backwards in his high-backed leather chair, drawing on a thick cigar. He was fifty-five, mean as a cornered snake, and as selfish as they came. Catlin had built an entertainment empire from nothing. Apart from a $1,000,000 loan from his father. Oh, and all the best schools and an insatiable appetite for money, sex and drugs. The latter enabled him to function on three hours sleep a night.

As he constantly reminded his staff, he was 'a self-made man.' His empire spanned the globe and wherever he walked, doors opened for him. If they didn't, he saw to it the owners of those doors were soon bankrupted. Everything he desired he got. Including his own Caribbean Island, personal jet, New York penthouse, and a fleet of supercars that he managed to regularly wreck.

This was doubtless due to the drugs and three hours sleep a night. The problem with having everything was that it was impossible to find something he wanted and that led to boredom and then frustration. In his case, boredom and frustration inevitably turned to aggression. This particular morning, he was particularly restless. He picked up his cell phone.

'Bailey. When you get this call come over to the house.'

Bailey was Catlin's fixer. If he wanted girls, or drugs, or even revenge, Bailey was his first port of call. What he wanted this morning lay on his desk. There was a photograph of a young woman holding, of all things, a ventriloquist's dummy. She was fresh-faced and extremely beautiful, and her name was Debbie Lamb or as her blurb told him, 'Deborah Deloitte Professional Puppeteer.' Debbie, in her professional capacity, had contacted Caitlin's production company seeking a spot on America's Newest Stars, one of his talent shows. She and her puppet Geeky, so her blurb went, were a cheeky pair who told jokes and sang heartwarming songs. Catlin had seen a short screen test of Debbie and Geeky and it was shit. The jokes were bad, the songs were worse. The dummy, which was supposed to be her geeky twin sister, looked like some sort of demented troll. But for all of that, she was as hot and as innocent as they came, and that was all he needed to know.

Bailey appeared within the hour. Catlin was sitting on a sun lounger by the pool.

'What can I do for you Mr. Catlin?' He asked.

Catlin pointed to the photograph on the coffee table next to his lounger. Bailey picked it up and examined it.

'I want you to make a booking at Klines. Get me my usual room. Twelve o'clock until two. Her details are on the blurb there.'

'Sure thing Mr. Catlin.'

'Just drop her off and see her into the room. I will get there after this morning's meeting at the office.'

'Does she know you want to have 'lunch' with her?' Asked Bailey smiling. Catlin chuckled at the euphemism.

'No, she doesn't yet. But don't worry, she wants to get on the show. These kids will do anything to get on the show.'

Bailey smiled and shrugged his shoulders as if to say that's their choice. With that, he left. Catlin took out some Cocaine, divided it up on the table and sniffed a couple of lines. He was already anticipating having 'lunch'.

The meeting was boring. Everything was boring nowadays especially the script they were discussing entitled, 'The Book of Words.' It was another epic fantasy where demons fight those with superpowers in order to save the world. Catlin was always amazed at how much crap people would pay to see, especially when it had all been done before. But then if he made money out of it, what the hell? The problem with Catlin's life was that no matter how much money he had, how much power, how many cars or yachts, nothing seemed to spark his interest.

He ended up killing someone's career at that particular meeting when they inadvertently made a suggestion he did not like. The demise of their career meant nothing to him As far as he was concerned, they should have kept their mouths shut. In his present state of restless boredom that was enough. He was no more than a Roman emperor giving the thumbs down to the losing gladiator. He had too many sycophants. They became tiring after a while and occasionally needed culling.

When the meeting ended, he got into his Rolls, took a Viagra from the glove compartment and headed off for Klines, the restaurant for the well-heeled of Hollywood. Catlin's arrangement with the management was that whenever he booked, he was given a private room. No one was permitted to interrupt him and any food or drink was to be delivered at a time convenient to Catlin. The arrangement worked well and many a budding starlet had made her entry into

Hollywood via Klines. In Catlin's mind it was a fair exchange. You scratch my back and I'll scratch your.......His phone rang. It was Bailey.

'Miss Lamb is at Klines now Mr.Catlin. Anything else I can do for you?'

'No, that's all for now Bailey.'

'Oh, I thought I ought to mention, she's brought her gear with her. She thinks it is an audition.'

Catlin laughed. 'You mean the doll?'

'I'm afraid so sir. She is very excited.'

'Not as excited as she is going to be,' replied Catlin, ending the call.

Catlin picked up the script and left the meeting. He would take it to Klines. There was nothing like a film script and the possibility of a small part to turn the head of a starlet, especially when she was only expecting to get on his talent show.

On arrival Catlin was greeted like royalty as usual. His car was driven away by a valet and Barry Love, owner of Klines, came out to personally greet him and take him through the restaurant. People stopped eating, conversation died. Only the occasional whispered, 'that's Kenny Catlin,' could be heard. Several 'A' list diners got up from their tables and shook hands with Catlin as he progressed. He took it all in his stride. Such was his celebrity that he outshone even the best-known stars. Catlin was after all 'Mr Hollywood.'

'Your room is ready Mr Catlin,' said Love, as they made their way to the back of the restaurant. 'Your guest is already here.'

'Yes, I have heard.' Replied Catlin.

'When would you like to eat?'

'Oh, in an hour or so. Some Champagne to start with.'

'It is done Mr Catlin, your favourite is already on ice.'

'Good.'

Debbie Lamb was sitting on the red velvet sofa when he arrived. He could tell from her posture that she was nervous. Shutting the door behind him he smiled.

'Debbie,' he said, 'how nice to meet you.'

She stood up and almost curtsied. 'Pleased to meet you to Mr Catlin. I've heard so much about you.'

'Jesus,' thought Catlin, 'this one really is innocent'.

'Have you?' He replied.

'Oh yes, I mean everyone knows you. Even my aunt Pat who doesn't watch TV or films, knew who you were when I told her I was going to meet you.'

'Your aunt Pat eh? Well in that case I am flattered.'

The young woman laughed.

Good, thought Catlin, just put her at ease, and everything will be fine.

'Well I hope you've only heard good things,' he said.

'Oh yes, Mr Catlin.'

'I see you've brought your stage equipment with you.'

'Oh yes. Well, this is an audition isn't it.'

Catlin smiled. 'It certainly is,' he replied sincerely.

'But first why don't we just get to know one another? That way you won't feel nervous. We can have a glass of champagne and you can tell me all about yourself and what you have been doing.'

She seemed reluctant as far as the champagne was concerned and so he said 'if you prefer we also have a Cotes du Rhône here.'

'Oh, I don't really drink Mr Catlin.'

'Just one glass won't hurt Debbie and then I will order up some food and we can talk about your future.' Catlin made a point of dropping the film script on the table.

'Is that a film script Mr Catlin?'

'Call me Kenny,' he said, 'and yes, in fact, it is a script. We are about to start auditioning. He smiled.

'Champagne?'

She looked at Catlin and he saw that moment he had seen so often in the past when against her better judgement she decided to submit.

'Just one glass' she said.

Catlin popped the cork at which she screamed and then giggled. He poured two glasses.

'Can I see your stage prop,' he asked.

'You mean Geeky,' she replied. He smiled and nodded. She turned away to open the case in which the puppet was housed. As she did so he slipped a small sachet of white powder into her drink.

'There,' she said, 'this is Mr Catlin, Geeky.' Catlin's face remained with a rigid smile fixed on it. Inside he was struggling not to laugh out loud.

'Cleased to neet you Nister Catlin.' Using all of his powers of control, Catlin replied, as stiff faced as he could, 'Cleased to neet you too Geeky.'

Jesus Christ, thought Catlin, how is it that people don't see how fucking pathetic they are? Why doesn't anybody ever tell them? And then he thought, because they want to fuck them of course.

'Drink up,' he said, 'here's to you and Geeky, and Hollywood.'

Their glasses chinked and she downed her champagne in one go. He smiled and filled her glass again. He could feel the Viagra beginning to take effect and he slightly shifted his posture to accommodate his growing urge. It did not take long before he saw Debbie looking slightly bewildered.

'Oh, I think that champagne has gone to my head,' she said, 'I am sorry, but I think I need to use the bathroom.'

'Sure thing Debbie, you do that. It's on the right as you go out of the door.

As she left the room Catlin began to undress himself. When she returned, he would be ready. It did not take long. Within minutes the door opened, and she appeared. Seeing Catlin totally naked and with a large erection, her eyes opened wide, and her jaw dropped.

'Mr Catlin, what.......?'

At that moment something devastating happened. It was as though an intense light suddenly filled the room followed by a black hole through which everything plummeted.

Chapter Four

'Well I thinks you should refuse to go,' said Mistress Munn, giving the Magician a rigid stare.

The Magician dismissed her comment with a wave of his hand.

'I have no choice Mistress. Unless you want to see me torn to shreds in the dog pit. Besides there is the oath we Magicians make to the crown.'

'Oath's, my intimates,' replied the old woman, 'how many oaths does the King abide by? Never keeps a one of them if you ask me.'

Despite his annoyance at being told what to do, the Magician knew full well Mistress Munn was only stating the truth. He knew his discomfort was down to the fact he had given way to the King. and she knew it.

'How long will you be gone?' She asked.

'I have no idea, Mistress. The King wants me to lead Moredeath through the great forest and avoid the Greer Swamp. The truth of the matter is he doesn't want any of his Knights straying into the path of the witches.'

'The Bloodly Sisters,' exclaimed Mistress Munn clutching her heart.

'Exactly, The Bloodly Sisters.'

'Oh Magician you beware. I believe it was down to them that your father went missing.'

The Magician did not know what had happened to his father. All he knew was that his father, on behalf of the King, had consulted the What Will Be, just as he had. The very next day he set off for the Greer Swamp, never to be seen again, and leaving behind only the shard and a note telling Whattlewherrit to guard it with his life.

'I know as much as you do about his disappearance Mistress. Everyone knows that it is not advisable to mix with the witches if you can help it.'

'Your father thought he would return, I know it.'

'Then why did he leave the shard? What on earth possessed him to enter the Greer Swamp without the shard?'

'They might have got possession of it. That's why. Can you imagine that? The Bloodly Sisters and the shard? It is too dreadful to contemplate.' She shook her head.

The Magician knew she was right, and it made him pause for a moment. He had always believed his father was a fool to do what he had done but on reflection he began to see another side to his father's disappearance. What had he seen that made him enter the Swamp without even the protection of the shard?

'It won't end well Magician,' said the old woman, 'I have a feeling in my bones.'

The Magician said nothing, but he had a similar sense of foreboding.

'Pack my bags Mistress. I must away on the next tide back to Naze. I will ride out from there as soon as it is light.'

The Magician was deep in thought when she spoke again.

'They say the Lady Gossamer is less than happy with the match.'

'Are you surprised,' replied the Magician. 'Who would want to be married to a twenty stone monster who hacks his way through life with a broadsword and has the manners of a beast on heat?'

'It's the nature of womanhood to suffer.'

'What are you talking about Mistress?'

'We are but meat to the wanton desires of men.'

The Magician began to feel very uncomfortable. He could feel Mistress Munn was about to go off on one of her rants.

'Yes well....'

'It makes my twixt and in-betweens scrunch up to think of what will befall the Lady.'

'Mistress Munn...'

'Twenty stone of ravenous beast enjoying his nuptials.'

'For heavens sake Mistress keep such thoughts to yourself.'

'Men will never know what it is like to be on the receiving end of....'

'Mistress I said enough!'

With that the Magician left the room and sought sanctuary in his study away from Mistress Munn's reminiscences.

The water was dark but still. A far cry from the previous journey he had taken across the water to Naze. Overnight the storm had moved on, but it left a sense of unease in its wake. The boatman sang as usual and seemed oblivious to his passenger, which suited the Magician. He was deep in thought about the journey to come. Not only was he to meet the Bludgeoner, but on the way he was tasked with informing the oldest Knight in the realm, Sir Godfrey of Merrelay that he was summoned to attend the wedding ceremony. Sir Godfrey had long since ceased to attend the court, but his fame remained alive within the Knights of Naze. He was the valiant Knight who had set out many years ago to find the Holy Wine, and who had returned years later, and after many travails, with the wine itself, and had presented it to the King's father. It was the final artefact that proved the great Moyen existed. Alongside the Eternal Underpants, The Book of Words, and The Geeky, the Holy Wine was all that had been missing from the Holy Quartet. However, Sir Godfrey had come back a shadow of the man he had been when he left Naze and from that time onwards, much to the confusion of the court, decided to live the life of a hermit in his castle.

To the Magician, the Holy Quartet was all bunkum, and having had a tankard too many of mead, he had once recklessly expressed these views to the Bishop of Nantes. His remarks only added to the bitter contempt that already existed between them. The Bishop, in his turn had dismissed magic as a pagan thing, or as he put it 'peasant fodder.'

Adding 'only uneducated surfs still believed in magic,' to which the Magician replied he would relay the Bishop's words to the King 'who regularly consulted him'. After much blustering, the Bishop snarled that he would deny the fact they had had any conversation, should the Magician dare do such a thing.

What the Magician despised most about the Bishop and his religion was that he used his power for his own purposes. Followers of the Holy Quartet were amongst the most feared people in the land and yet professed to be the holiest. They used their status for extravagant lifestyles and pursued wicked pastimes, protected by their status amongst the community.

The King, of course, pretended to be a believer in order to maintain his position as head of the church. Income from the church was considerable, and it rested upon the backs of the poor.

In private however, the King's behaviour told a different story. His many infidelities, prior to the queen passing away, were the stuff of legend. He kept none of the vows in the book of words, being greedy, profligate, mean and unkind, just as the Bishop of Nantes himself was. Often the Magician wondered whether he should take some form of action against the church, unmask its hypocrisy and show the people the truth, but he didn't, and this left him at the mercy of his natural inclination to feel guilty about so many things. The Magician realised his intentions never quite matched his actions. Something Cornelius had no hesitation in reminding him of, on a daily basis.

'If you did half the things you are intent on doing, then you would find the magic would work for you and not against you. You spend too much time daydreaming and not finishing your studies.'

Though he hated Corneleus's comments, in later life the Magician was inclined to agree, but there was really nothing he could do about it. No matter how much he wanted to be a good Magician, things always seemed to go wrong at the last minute. As a young boy, words got jumbled up or forgotten. Ingredients were boiled for just too long. Spells were confused for other spells. The list was endless and left him feeling he would never get things right despite the fact he so wanted them to.

Despite his inability to concentrate he had nevertheless been able to acquire a certain level of skill. For the most part he managed to get away with the spells that went wrong. Something somewhere seemed to be on his side, despite his struggles.

Now, with Cornelius gone, there was no one to point out his deficiencies. He only had himself to answer to, and it had become a double-edged sword. He had become his own worst critic. He tried not to show it, but in his head, there was this constant nagging doubt. Could he do better?

Mistress Munn often told him he should be doing more to help others. She had a canny knack of finding a way into his deepest thoughts and voicing them out loud.

There was a jolt followed by, 'we are here' that awakened him from his thoughts. It was the gruff voice of the boatman announcing the arrival of the boat at the town quay. The Magician had missed the bulk of the journey, wandering as he had been in his scattered mind.

'A silver piece' growled the boatman holding out a gnarled hand and turning his head to spit into the river.

The Magician handed him the coin and stepped from the boat to face the bustling crowds in the market on the quay. A foul stench of fish swam in the air, mixed with that of penned animals. Pigs, goats, chickens, rabbits and a variety of other livestock, all with their own distinct aroma. The Magician held his breath. The air was too thick to breath. As he walked by the various beasts, he could sense their fear, and it grieved him. It was a curse Magicians had to bear, that they picked up on the sensitivities of others, and this was particularly true of nature's offspring. Unlike humanity, they were unable to disguise their feelings.

The noises of the street, vendors selling their wares, the dock workers unloading vessels, and the whores shouting obscenities at him from tavern windows, were overwhelming to his senses. This was why he was glad he, and generations of Magicians, had lived over the water. Had he been made to suffer the tumult of everyday street life on a daily basis, he would not have been able to function. The average man saw nothing unusual or discomforting in their surroundings and for all of their wretched drunken lives, they laughed at his ways. Not eating meat, not whoring, not getting pitifully drunk every night was a life only a fool would follow. To them that was a pointless existence. There was even a popular phrase at the time that went, 'why bother living if you have to live like a Magician?'

'Cock and balls broach sir,' said a voice, stopping the Magician in his tracks. He looked at tray of lead broaches each depicting a pinklarry and two plump balls.

'You won't sell him one,' shouted a passing woman, 'that's the Magician's son.' She laughed as she made her way through the crowd.

'Oh sorry sir. I didn't know.....'

Whattlewherrit waved the man away. So, they still thought of him that way, he mused. Not the Magician, but his son. Three years was obviously not enough time for them to come to terms with the fact he was now the keeper of the shard. Perhaps it would always be that way. Perhaps, in their fixed minds, he would always be the Magician's son, and perhaps he would always feel that way.

He shook his head as though it would shake the thoughts away. As for the broaches, he had heard about them from Mistress Munn but had never actually seen them before.

'There are the latest thing. They's wearing them to ward off evil spirits and suchlike,' she said, 'they even think they protects them against the plague. I don't know who came up with the idea that a man's pinklarry could do anything other than cause problems. Just goes to show how stupid people are.'
She looked away as she quietly said, 'but I bought one just in case of the plague.'

The plague was rumoured to be heading towards Naze. Like a distant storm, news of it rumbled in the outer reaches of the land. The Magician knew of it alright but not through gossip. He had consulted the shard and looked into the What Will Be. He had said nothing to Mistress Munn at the time because she found it difficult to keep such news to herself and had a habit of making things worse rather than better. It weighed on his mind but he had other more immediate troubles to deal with. The plague and its consequences would have to take its course and wearing a broach with a pinklarry on it would not, in his view, make a whole lot of difference.

Chapter Five

Geoffrey was standing ready in the stables. The Magician gave his horse a friendly pat and told him they were off on an adventure. More like a suicide mission he thought, but why tell Geoffrey when he wouldn't understand anyway. The horse 'huffered', as he did when trying to communicate and aimed his hoof at the stable door in frustration, banging it loudly.

'Alright Geoffrey, we will be gone soon.'

In the stable, out of the crowds and the smell of the docks, the Magician began to feel a much-needed sense of peace. The warm odour of hay and straw were familiar to him, having spent a great deal of his youth hiding in the stables, trying to avoid book learning. If only life outside were as comforting as this he thought. 'Bang! Bang! Bang!' The horse was having none of it as he hit the stable door once again. He wanted to be on the road.

'Alright Geoffrey, I've already told you we are going.'

Mounted on his horse Whattlewherrit headed out of town above the heads of the milling crowds and their hustle and bustle. He felt the familiar roll of his trusted companion's body beneath him. It had been a long time since their last adventure together and in a strange way he felt exhilarated, despite the purpose of the journey and the heavy weight it placed upon him.

Perhaps thieves and vagabonds lay ahead, or wolves and bears. Who knew? Every day out of Naze itself was a risky business but the raw reality of life on the road far exceeded the dull day-to-day existence of a court Magician. He had the shard, tied as it was by a thin piece of hide around his neck. It gave him the protection he might need in the forests they must go through.

As they went on their way, the Magician thought about Cornelius and how he must have taken the same route to confront the Bloodly Sisters.

The Greer Swamp hags were feared more than anything in the land. So bad was their reputation that it ranked alongside famine and crop failure. Unlike natural disasters though, the Bloodly Sisters always had malicious intent behind their actions. Everything they did was aimed at destroying the natural order of things. This, Cornelius had once explained to him, was why they were so keen on getting their hands on the shard. With the shard in their possession, they could alter the What Will Be with all the catastrophic consequences that would bring. The one and only thing that held them back was their inability to leave the

Greer Swamp. There was a curse put upon them long before the Magician was born that meant they could not leave the swamp unless in the company of another woman and women were forbidden to travel anywhere near the swamp. There had been protests at the time as women demanded their 'right to join their sisters in the swamp', but it had soon been squashed. A proclamation was issued saying that any woman found alone within ten miles of the swamp would be burnt at the stake.

As Geoffrey nodded his way through the ever-thickening woodland, the Magician began once again to wonder what had happened to Cornelius and why he had gone to see the hags. He had foreseen something. There could be no other explanation for it. The What Will Be had shown him the future and he had no choice but to act upon it. Such was the power of the shard and its relationship with the What Will Be. It not only foretold events, but in seeing them, the observer became entwined with them, and became part of them. This was why the Magician had promptly ended the last session with the King. He knew that looking at the naked man and the young woman was now somehow embedded in his future, whether he liked it or not. Not only in his future, the King had seen it too. He was now part of the What Will Be as much as the Magician, which meant the King's future and his own were also intertwined. That disturbed him greatly. He felt he could manage his own future if it proved to be difficult, but he could not manage the Kings. The King was a loose cannon. Unpredictable, dangerous, and potentially fatal. His father had warned him. Did he listen? Of course not. He cursed himself for being so vain as to imagine he had control of anything as powerful as the shard, or, for that matter, the King.

He clutched his chest just to make sure it was there and relaxed when he felt its hard shape beneath his cloak. The shard held the most powerful magic in the land. Without it he would feel naked. It seemed strange to think that until Cornelius had disappeared, he had lived his whole life without it. Since his father's absence however, the shard had become a part of him. Stitched into his very being. He knew how naked his father must have felt going without it to see the witches. So vulnerable and alone. He could not imagine himself doing the same. He did not have that commitment to Naze, or if he was truly honest, the courage to do so.

He had been riding for an hour or so when he stopped to take some food and allow Geoffrey to drink and graze. The rotting fruits of summer still lay in the grass and his horse soon found them beneath a lone apple tree. Crunching up the small fruits, their juices made his mouth foam with delight.

The Magician wondered who had eaten the original apple that caused the tree to grow. He pictured them discarding its core as they walked on their way, never imagining that one day their action would lead to a fine tree growing. Around him on the bushes, the berries of autumn were beginning to show. It would not be long before the land turned cold and hard as the iron on his horse's hoof. Things should be done before winter closed in, and the days shortened. The forest was no place for a man to travel when beasts were hungry, and daylight was short.

The place he had reached was several miles downriver of Naze, one he had visited in his youth when he had spent time avoiding his studies but instead learning all he could about nature. He knew the nearest village was yet another hour away and had nothing of any consequence other than a small Inn and blacksmiths shop to commend itself. After the village there would be nothing other than the odd woodsman's home between there and Sir Godfrey of Merrelay's castle, two days further on. The woods would thicken yet again into forest and the trail become dangerous. He was well aware neither man nor beast felt any hesitation in taking what they wanted when so far from civilisation. At least he had the shard, which was a comfort.

As he sat, he considered the journey ahead and recalled what he knew about Sir Godfrey. Known to men as the hermit Knight, he had mysteriously retreated to his castle, having found the Holy wine. There were rumours about the sanity of Sir Godfrey at that time. Even though the Magician was young when this occurred, he could not help but overhear them. According to the tittle-tattle of the town, something had happened to Sir Godfrey whilst on his crusade. No one quite knew what this was, but he had come back a different Knight, changed in subtle ways. Some said the intensity of his search and the rigours he had undergone had warped his mind. Others that he had contracted some strange disease that had left him too terrible to look at. Still others said even touching the bottle of Holy wine affected the spirit and that he had taken a religious vow to spend the rest of his life in praise of the great Moyen. The Magician's father knew something but would not say, even when questioned by Mistress Munn. She seemed very keen to know about the Knight and pressed him hard for news, but Cornelius always managed to sidetrack her questions.

'The man has been away on a daunting quest these past years Mistress, he deserves his peace.'

When she persisted, he turned to her and asked her why she was showing such an unusual interest in 'this particular Knight.' Mistress Munn huffed and turned away. Whattlewherrit was young at the time, but remembered the conversation and it stuck in his mind. When he had told Mistress Munn he had to call into the castle of Sir Godfrey on his way to finding Moredeath, he could swear she blushed and became flustered, and now, reflecting on all he knew, he wondered if she was better acquainted with the Knight than she cared to say.

'You know what, the more I see of people the less I understand them,' said Whattlewherrit. The Magician's horse continued to graze on the bounty of apples, paying him no attention.

'On the one hand, they behave so predictably, and on the other, they do things you just don't expect.'

The Magician unwrapped his lunch. Dried bread and cheese and some of Mistress Munn's pickles. She came into his mind once more, and he chatted on to the horse.

'Take Mistress Munn for instance. She has secrets and yet cannot for the life of her keep a secret that belongs to someone else. She gossips like a fishwife. She's always spreading rumours. Half of the misinformation in Naze comes from Mistress Munn. I am convinced she knows something about Sir Godfrey, something she doesn't want to share. She has been in my life as long as I remember, and I still don't know her. You would have thought if she knew something about Sir Godfrey, she would have at least told me. It might be important to my journey.'

The horse continued to be disinterested in the Magician's ramblings, but the Magician was used to talking to himself.

'I have a bad feeling about this whole affair Geoffrey. Something is not right. Not just Moredeath marrying the Lady Gossamer but that whole business with the What Will Be. I knew I shouldn't have given into the King but something overcame my common sense. It was as if I had no choice, as if no matter what I intended to do, it was going to be that way, and I had to show him Moredeath. How does that happen? Cornelius of course would have said it was the power of magic. Perhaps he was right after all. Perhaps we are all at the mercy of some deeper magic, of which we know nothing. It is certainly a mystery to me. It is at times like this I wish I had studied more deeply, then perhaps I might know more.'

As he ate, and thought, and ate some more, he looked around him and recalled the endless days when he went searching for his father in that very same wood. Entering the bodies of wolves and deer and birds. Travelling as far as he could. But to no avail. The only place he did not dare venture into was the Greer Swamp. No matter which beast he used as his transport, none would go near the home of the Bloodly Sisters. Each in turn balked at the edge of the swamp and he knew it was too dangerous to go on foot, even with the shard. It hurt his feelings that no one believed he had truly tried to find Cornelius. There was nothing he could do to change their perception of him. Everyone in Naze knew there was no closeness between them and that had coloured their view of his attempts to find him.

Chapter Six

'Mistress Munn, sit!' It was a command and not an invitation. The Lady Gossamer, the King's daughter, had called Mistress Munn to the castle for the purpose of extracting as much information as she could from the Magician's house maid.

'Now,' she said firmly, 'you are well known to be someone who knows the comings and goings of Naze. I am reliably informed that if anything is rumoured, you are often at the root of it.'

'I am sure I don't know....'
The Lady Gossamer interrupted her.

'I am sure you do Mistress. Believe me, as one who is at the centre of the court, I am well informed about the source of the gossip that endlessly percolates the castle. Hence your being here.'

Mistress Munn felt herself shrink. The King was ill-tempered, and the Lady Gossamer could match him in many ways. Her tantrums were legendary, as was her desire for vengeance. Mistress Munn wracked her brains to try and recall which particular piece of gossip the Lady might be referring to. Perhaps the one where she had relayed to a close friend in total confidence that the Lady Gossamer knew what lay beneath every codpiece between Naze and Innesfarn. Or maybe it was the one where she intimated to another close friend that if it wasn't for the King desperately needing a strong ally he would have married the Lady Gossamer himself, he was that debauched. Or perhaps it was...

'Are you listening Mistress? Did you hear what I just said?'

Mistress Munn stiffened in her seat. 'I am sure I did your Ladyship but perhaps you could just repeat...'

'Good heavens woman, are you so old you can't concentrate for two minutes? I said I want you to tell me everything that you have heard about Moredeath the Bludgeoner.'

Mistress Munn felt a sudden sense of relief.

'Well I .....I don't know that much about...'

'Come on woman, before I have you taken to the rack and stretched to cracking.'

Mistress Munn had no intention of being stretched to any length and so began to talk as best she could about what she had heard. She prefaced her comments with a disclaimer.

'What I know is only from tavern talk your Ladyship. So I cannot say that it is all true.'

'Come on woman, just tell me what you know.' It was clear that the Lady Gossamer was in no mood for shilly-shallying.

'Well, if the truth be told, they say that he is a brute. Tall as an ordinary man would be were he astride a horse. His chest is as round as a prize bull. Indeed, not only his chest your Ladyship. I hear tell from a reliable source that his nether parts could well compete with the very same beast.' The Lady Gossamer sat back, her face rigid.

'Go on.'

'Well, it is also said that whereas an ordinary man might pluck one or two fruits a night from the tree of love, Moredeath has been known to devour more than twenty!'

'That cannot be so,' protested the Lady.

'Oh indeed,' replied Mistress Munn, who was now in her element.

'The man you are describing is no more than a rutting beast,' said the Lady Gossamer.

'Indeed he is your Ladyship. I hear tell he can stand proud all night, if'n you gets my meaning. As hard as a pikestaff on a cold winters day I hear tell.'

'Stop! I am not sure I can take more of this news. Are you quite sure you are well informed?'

'I am your Ladyship. I know a merchant, a man who only recently returned from Moredeath's castle who related the same to me not a week ago.'

'Did he say what the Bludgeoner looks like in the face?'

'Well now he did indeed mention a large scar that runs from his ear to his jaw on one side. An axe wound my Lady. Other than that, he could be considered handsome by some.'

'You may leave now Mistress. But if I find your information to be incorrect then you will indeed be cracked. I shall personally pull the levers.'

Mistress Munn left the room, wondering whether she should have kept her mouth firmly shut, but it was too late.

The Lady Gossamer sat brooding. She pulled a small locket from her cleavage and opened it to look at the miniature painting inside. Sure enough the rugged face had a scar running from ear to jaw. Mistress Munn was accurate in that respect. The lady called for her personal maid.

'Get Sir Sockamore at once. Tell him I want to speak to him.'

Sir Sockamore was on the practice field lancing the quintain when the call from Lady Gossamer came. Angry at being disturbed he soon changed his tune when he learnt it was the Lady Gossamer who wished to see him. Sir Sockamore was besotted with the Lady, so much so that he inundated her with love poems praising her beauty, her intelligence and her grace. The arrogant popinjay that he was, he melted every time he saw the Lady and he became no more than a child in her presence. He dismounted and smelling his armpits on the way down decided he would have to bathe before seeing his love. There was no way he would present himself soaked in the sweat of combat and of horse urine. He would look out his finest garb and trim his beard for her. Nothing was too much trouble for the Lady.

'Where is that dull piece of dung!' Shouted the Lady Gossamer. 'I asked you to fetch him an hour ago!'

The Lady's maid shivered in her shoes and apologised, telling her Mistress she had gone straightaway as per her instruction and told Sir Sockamore's knave he was required immediately.

'The jumped up prat of a man, how dare he take his time when I want him. Look at these!' She ranted holding out a sheaf of love poems. Have you ever read such dribble in your life!?'

Let me compare thee to the finest Campion
Alone in a meadow full of common grasses
Like a hermit my longing grows
With each day that passes
I should do anything to be your champion
I kneel at your feet to smell your sweet scent
A woman like you is but heaven sent

'It doesn't even scan. And as for kneeling at my feet and smelling my sweet scent, where on earth does he think his nose is? The man is an idiot, a fool, and he thinks every woman in the land is in love with him. If I didn't have use of him, I would gladly have his pinklarry removed and hung at the castle gates.'

The fury of the Lady Gossamer may well have led to further ranting had it not been for a knock at the door. The maid went to open it and there stood Sir Sockamore in his finest garb, beard recently trimmed, flowers in hand and a childish grin on his face. With impeccable control, the Lady Gossamers face changed, and her voice softened as she welcomed Sir Sockamore into her chambers.

'Sir Sockamore. How good of you to come.'

'My Lady,' he replied, 'I would ride across the hottest desert, ford the deepest river, climb the....'

'Thank you Sir Knight, no need for more,' replied the Lady.

Sir Sockamore's eyes glanced at his love poems, scattered on the table at which she stood. His heart missed a beat.

'Ah, I see you have been reading my poems, my Lady.'

'Indeed sir Knight, they express so well your feelings and your.....' she paused momentarily, 'level of skill in the art of poetry.'

'My Lady, I am honoured that you say so.'

'Given that you clearly wish to be my champion I have a task for you.'

'Anything my Lady.'

The Lady's voice, which up until this moment had been soft and amiable, perceptibly changed, a hard edge tempered her words.

'You have heard of the King's proposal to wed me to Moredeath the Bludgeoner?'

Sir Sockamore's face hardened and his heart sank.

'Indeed, I have my Lady.'

'Well. What if something happened to Moredeath on his way to Naze?'

'I beg your pardon my Lady?'

'Come, come, Sir Knight, you are not naïve enough to have misunderstood my meaning.'

Sir Sockamore was beginning to feel uneasy about the implication of the Lady Gossamer's words, and yet he asked himself would not a man do anything for love? Had he not written such in his poems?

'I think I do understand my Lady, but.......'

'Today I was told by a reliable source that the man I am to wed is no more than rutting animal. A monster who would ravage me each and every night in my bedchamber against my wishes. Is this what you would want Sir Knight?

Is this how 'my pale and tender skin' and the 'red rose of my lips' should be abused? Tell me when you wrote those words that you meant them.'

For a moment he found himself at a loss. He worshipped her in words, indeed he did, and the thought of her pale and tender skin being ravaged by a beast of a man was unbearable, but, and here was a big but, Moredeath the Bludgeoner was a monster. He knew there was no way he could defeat him in combat. Like a dangerous snake, a moment of doubt slithered into his mind. Perhaps his love for the Lady was not quite as overwhelming as he had first believed.

'My Lady, I would of course do anything for you but....'

'Are you afraid sir Knight?'

'Afraid my Lady? I am Sir Sockamore, the King's champion! I am afraid of nothing.'

The words sounded good and true, but inside, Sir Sockamore was beginning to feel something he had not felt before, a strange lack of commitment to love. It was one thing to joust in a fair contest with other men. It was quite another to have your limbs pulled off one by one by an enraged beast.

'Supposing whilst travelling through the woods Moredeath and his men were ambushed? Supposing a band of archers lay in wait, led by a Knight loyal to his future queen? What then? No one would know who or why or how it happened. Moredeath has plenty of enemies. Why would anyone assume it was anything to do with their future King?' The Lady Gossamer touched Sir Sockamore's arm in the way a woman does when she is confirming her trust in a man. He shuddered at the thrill of it.

'Their future King?' The words rang deep in his mind. Was she suggesting what he thought? If he rid her of Moredeath she would marry him?

'What say you, Sir Knight?'

'I say that I am your loyal servant my Lady. I shall call my men together and we will leave tomorrow.'

'Oh, and whilst you are about it, don't forget to dispatch the Magician, he has been a thorn in my side for years.'

Sir Sockamore's eyes lit up. The Magician. He had briefly forgotten the Magician. What he wouldn't give to put a sword through that man's heart! That alone would make his perilous journey worthwhile.

Chapter Seven

Whattlewherrit had been on his travels for two days. The occasional bear lumbering past had caused the shard to twitch, as did the sound of wolves calling to one another beneath the waning moon. These were minor irritations to be expected. Geoffrey, his horse, though skittish, never showed signs of real distress, which he would have, had they been too close. So it was, on the afternoon of the third day, he came to a gap in the trees and saw, in the distance, Sir Godfrey's crumbling pile.

Merrelay castle, once a formidable fortress, had become a sad ruin, slowly surrounded by the forest. Even from a distance it was clear to see where the parapets of several turrets were missing, having tumbled into the moat. It troubled the Magician, and he was not sure why. Even the shard pulsed gently against his heart as if it were uncertain of something. The Magician noticed Geoffrey's ears twitch.

'Something not right here Geoffrey,' he said out loud. The horse turned its head as if to respond to the question and gently huffered.

'I cannot believe that a Knight as renowned as Sir Godfrey is a threat in any way. I have never heard a bad word said against him. Even the King, who is always ready to bring to light the flaws in any man, leaves Sir Godfrey alone. The Magician recalled that Cornelius also held Sir Godfrey in high esteem.

'As honest a man as one can find sitting at the King's table,' he heard his father say, on one occasion, whilst talking to Mistress Munn. However, the closer he got to Merrelay castle, the more he became aware of a strange sensation in his body. At first a slight tingling, not dissimilar to that he felt on cold winter days, when coming indoors and standing by a roaring fire while the feelings came back to his numb fingers and toes. A tingling. Nothing too unpleasant but certainly there. Then, as he approached the drawbridge, it turned into something stronger. A buzzing in his ear, as though he were lying in a meadow in summer, listening to the insects pollinating the meadow flowers. He shook his head. It made no difference. It was then that Geoffrey stopped. The Magician slid forward uncomfortably in his saddle, taken unawares by the horse's refusal to step onto the drawbridge.

'What's the matter Geoffrey? Come on. Step up. We need to get on,' but the horse refused to move. He dug his heels into his horse's sides. Still no movement. For whatever reason, Geoffrey would not budge. He would not step onto the drawbridge. After a few more attempts, the Magician gave up and dismounted.

'I don't know what's the matter with you but I can't stay here all day. You must fend for yourself out here if you aren't coming into the castle.'

He untied his saddle and his bags and carrying them across the drawbridge began to walk towards the castle. Perhaps because of the weight of the load he was carrying, he didn't feel the shard shift beneath his tabard. The Magician had just reached the portcullis when wham! A huge chunk of one of the towers broke away and hurtled down on to the drawbridge, scything it in two with a tremendous roar. The drawbridge shook as it shattered, and the Magician turned to look back at where he had been moments before. Splintered into a thousand pieces, the woodwork had all but disappeared, as rancid water from the moat shot up in a boiling tumult, plastering him in green stagnant slime. He was drenched in the stinking liquid and held his breathe for fear of passing out.

'God's arse,' cursed the Magician, who was in a state of shock, realising that, had the accident occurred seconds earlier, he would have been a dead man. He was considering this, whilst trying to find his footing on what was left of the bridge, when the portcullis began to rise.

'Sire, what terrible thing has happened?' Asked a trembling voice. The Magician turned to look at the squire standing before him.

'Your master seems to have paid little attention to the fabric of his castle that's what's happened. I could have been killed! I nearly was.'

'I am so sorry Sire. Please come in and let me find you fresh clothing and a bath.'

'Is Sir Godfrey here,' asked the Magician.

'He is always here Sire. But whether he will see you is another matter.'

'Tell him the King's Magician is here with an urgent message. He will see me.'

'I will do my best. But for now, follow me, and I shall see to it that your garments are cleaned and you are able to bathe.'

Whattlewherrit was taken to a room on the first floor of the castle where a tub was brought and part filled with cool water. It was then topped up with boiling water from the kitchens so that it reached a reasonably pleasant temperature. The whole procedure took the best part of an hour, during which the Magician sat shivering on the edge of a bed in a warm but scratchy blanket. Once in the tub he dunked his head under the water and sat for a moment as it dampened the outside world. He was trying his best to get over the shock of his recent encounter. When his breath ran out, he raised his head above the water and gasped a long luxurious breath. He rubbed his eyes and looked around the room.

Someone, or something, was watching him. He could sense it. It did not take long to see the rat, perched on the window ledge. It was staring at him, its head slightly to one side, as though trying to work out who he was. His first thought was that he didn't want a rat in the room, his second was that he didn't want a rat looking at him in such a curious way. In a moment of annoyance, he picked up the closest thing he could find and threw it at the rat. The rat jumped, and the back scrubber, which he had thrown, clattered to the floor, having missed it completely.

'What is this place,' he said to himself. 'Tumbling turrets, festering moats, rats! Is there nothing good about it?' Then there was the sound. That sound of insects in a summer meadow. A humming and buzzing that barely caught the ear but was definitely there nonetheless, ever-present and extremely confusing. He would stay but one night. Any longer he told himself would be far too risky.

That evening, as the sun dropped low, one of Sir Godfrey's servants appeared and told him Sir Godfrey would see him and that he was to follow him to the banqueting hall. When they arrived, they found the banqueting hall empty but for a huge table that might have once sat twenty or more people on each side. A huge log fire roared at one end of the hall, but seemed to be drawing out heat rather than providing it, so that the Magician shivered. The room smelt slightly dank. Its candle lit interior was lined with aged tapestries. It maintained a dull look despite the efforts of the numerous waxy lights trying their best to brighten the gloom.

'Please sit,' said the servant, 'Sir Godfrey is on his way.'

The Magician took a seat towards the head of the table and contemplated the gloom. Ever since arriving at the castle he had this feeling of discomfort. Not just because of the incident at the drawbridge, or the rat, or even the cold. There was something not quite right about Merrelay castle.

He was thinking this when he heard a door at the end of the room creak open and a figure appeared. Small and thin, the man stooped, as if heavy weights were upon his head. His face was narrow and his high cheekbones showed through his thin skin. Beneath his nose, a moustache drooped almost to his chin, so that it was impossible to make out his lips. However, it was his eyes that struck the Magician most. Like those of a tired old dog, they had a sadness of expression that told of a thousand woes.

The Magician stood as the old man shuffled his way towards the head of the table. He had not expected Sir Godfrey to look so old and worn, and tried not to show his surprise.

'I apologise for the accident that occurred upon your arrival,' were his first words. 'I believe you must be young Whattlewherrit?'
The Magician nodded. He thought it sounded strange to be called 'young.'

'I knew your father well. It was extremely unfortunate, what happened to him, disappearing like that. He deserved better.'

'Thank you, Sir Godfrey, I appreciate your thoughts on both matters.'

'I have ordered some food, but we can talk whilst we wait.'

The old Knight's gaze seemed fixed upon the candle flame in front of him, the light dancing in his watery eyes gave them a hint of expression they otherwise would have lacked.

'So tell me young man, what can the King want with an old Knight like myself?'

'He has betrothed his daughter to Moredeath the Bludgeoner in an alliance he hopes will protect the borders of Naze.'

The Magician was about to continue but the Knight interrupted.

'Holy Moyen,' he cried. 'The Bludgeoner? What kind of madness is that? The man will destroy the King and take the land for his own.'

Suddenly the old man was totally animated, his face taught with rage.

'Exactly my thoughts sir. Indeed, I expressed the same view to his Majesty and barely came away with my head.'

The old man huffed. 'I have been away too long to know the comings and goings of the court but I know enough about Moredeath and his father, Deathgrin, to say without hesitation, this is a disaster waiting to happen. But I interrupted you Whattlewherrit, what is your purpose with me?'

'The King wants you to attend the ceremony. The Bishop of Nantes will be there with the Holy Relics and you of course found the Holy Wine. The King wants you to be there to share in the joy of the occasion.'

'Joy? My horse's arse. There won't be any joy from my point of view I can assure you of that. And what does the Lady Gosammer think of the arrangement?'

'Sire, I know nothing of that. I am not familiar with the tittle tattle of the court. I leave that to my housemaid Mistress Munn.'

As soon as the words left Whattlewherrit's lips, the old Knight began a coughing fit so violent that the Magician feared for the old man's life. A servant appeared, offered the old Knight a glass of wine and eventually managed to calm the fit. It was minutes before Sir Godfrey was able to speak again.

'I do apologise young man, something caught in my throat. Ah, I see the food is arriving, let us not talk about it anymore. I shall consider the King's request,' was all he said.

That night the Magician was in his room reading by candlelight when once again he felt eyes upon him. Sure enough, as he scanned the room, he saw two red dots in the corner, reflecting the light from the candles. It was the rat. The Magician grasped the shard, muttered a spell, and within the blink of an eye found himself inside the creature.

He had merged with it, as he had done with so many beasts in the past. They were unaware of his presence. He was but an ethereal passenger. His essence was inside the rat, and was about to go on a journey.

The rat dropped from its perch on a shelf and skirted the room, hugging the walls for protection. It was fascinating for the Magician. He could experience every movement. He felt the rat's sensations as if he were the creature himself and yet remained conscious of his being a separate entity. He was experiencing being a rat, just as he had experienced being an eagle, a dog, a stag, and so many other creatures during his lifetime. He could smell what the rat smelled, hear what the rat heard, feel what it felt, and what a different world that was.

The creature scuttled through the corridors of the castle at great speed. Up and down staircases, in and out of doors, until it came to a great oak door under which it sneaked, making its way into a room in which a solitary candle dimly burned. There, sitting on the side of a huge four-poster bed, sat Sir Godfrey. The rat ran towards the bed and, much to the Magician's surprise jumped up. The Knight looked down at the rat with his sad watery eyes.

'Mortimer!' He cried 'Where have you been lately? I hope you haven't been spying on our guest again. I don't think Whattlewherrit wants a rat in his room.'

The Magician felt a flood of satisfaction seep through him as the old Knight stroked the rat. These weren't his feelings though, these belonged to the creature he now inhabited.

'Hah,' breathed the old Knight, 'what a mess Mortimer, what a dilemma. I knew it would come to this at some stage. You can hide away for a thousand years and still the past will catch up with you. Why did I think it would all go away? Why was I so naïve? When he mentioned Mistress Munn, my Beth, I almost choked. How I have tried to forget her. I don't think Whattlewherit knew why I was coughing though.'

The Magician's mind was spinning like a top. Why was he calling Mistress Munn by her birth name? And why would Mistress Munn's name have affected him so?

'And then Whattlewherrit he started talking about the wine! If that jumped up fart of a man the Bishop of Nantes, only knew the half of it, he would have me hung drawn and quartered. Oh Mortimer, what should I do, what should I do?'

The old man's cries of anguish were genuine. Whattlewherrit suddenly understood that whatever had happened in the past was clearly a terrible burden to him. But what was it?

'Forgive me Mortimer, I must pray. You may stay with me but I cannot pay you attention now. I have to confess.'

With these words the old Knight got up from the bed and went over to his praying stool and, with a loud crack from each knee, knelt down and clasped his hands together.

'Great Moyen, forgive your humble servant, Arthur Godfrey. It has been too long since I sought your mercy. Tonight, I had a visitor from the King, the son of the old Magician of Naze, once my dear friend. He has come to bring me to my reckoning. I knew it would happen one day. What can I tell you that you in your all-powerful wisdom do not already know? When I found the Holy Wine, it was my intention to bring it back to Naze. I had no thought of anything other than offering it up to the King, the final mystery of the Holy Quartet. But I was a weak man. Having to cross the Desert of Nameless Souls, my thirst became so powerful, it overcame me. I drank from the bottle. Yes, I drank from the Holy

Wine. But I have paid dearly for it. There is no such thing as death for me or for Beth, who, upon my return, I tricked into drinking some too. Believing as I did then that if I was to become immortal, I wanted her to join me. What can I say? I have lived with a broken heart. The guilt, the shame, the endless nights of regret, have plagued me ever since, but I have never confessed to anyone other than you. There's the rub. In order to rid myself of the burden I need to confront my peers and own up to my failure. They have falsely showered me with praise and gratitude, not knowing how I tricked them. Replacing what I had drunk, and sealing the bottle again was a wicked crime. I am an abomination to the name, 'Knight of Naze'. Forgive me great Moyen and help me to face the inevitable.'

The Magician was stunned. Sir Godfrey thought he was immortal? This couldn't be. The Holy Wine was a joke as were the other holy relics. Despite his long-held views, a moment of doubt seeped through his senses. And Mistress Munn, Sir Godfrey's 'Beth', was she really his lover and had she also drunk from the Holy Wine? It was all too much to understand. He needed to get back to his room at once. He visualised holding the shard. All of a sudden it was as if something tore him from the body of the rat and he flew back into his own frame.

Chapter Eight

The following morning dawned with a clear sky, and to Whattlewherrit's annoyance, the sound of clipping. The Magician raised his weary body from the hay mattress and listened. Sure enough, there was an annoying 'clip' 'clip' 'clip' outside. His curiosity overcame his lethargy, and he made his way to the window to see what it was.

Down below, at the top of a set of very tall stepladders, a servant was perched, holding some instrument, and cutting a shape into a tall shrub. The garden, where he was working, had numerous statuesque hedges and shrubs formed into exotic creatures and bird shapes, the like of which the Magician had never seen before. Geometric designs formed the basis of the layout, between which were small walkways, with seats every few yards. It was one of the strangest things the Magician had ever seen, and he was curious to know its purpose. Clearly it was not for growing food, so why was it there? Why on earth would anyone spend time shaping trees and plants into patterns? It just didn't make sense.

He turned away from the window, thinking that nothing made sense in Merrelay castle. Just at that moment there was a loud juddering and everything in the room went dark as a huge chunk of the castle parapet hurtled past the window. The Magician turned back to where he had been moments before, to witness a scene of devastation, and hear a very loud 'God's arse!!!' coming from the gardener, who was now lying on his back in the middle of the once pristine shrub that was no more than a twist and tangle of twigs.

'I hate this damnable place,' he cried out as he lifted himself up, brushed himself down, and stomped off.

The incident sealed the Magician's previous intent to leave early that morning. Despite wanting to cross examine Sir Godfrey on what he had heard whilst in the body of Mortimer the rat, he had more urgent tasks to undertake. Moredeath was constantly on his mind and there would be time at the wedding celebrations to find out from both Mistress Munn and Sir Godfrey what the business with the Holy wine was all about.

They parted at the portcullis, the Magician thanking Sir Godfrey for his hospitality and the old Knight wishing the Magician well.

'If you have a mind to lose the Bludgeoner in the Greer swamp, I would say nothing about it to anyone.' He chuckled and the Magician caught a fleeting glimpse of the light-hearted man Sir Godfrey had clearly once been.

'Would that I could Sir Godfrey but you know as well as I that in the end, all misdeeds find their way back to the door of the miscreant.' The Magician looked the old man straight in the eye. Sir Godfrey's eyebrows twitched slightly in recognition of the barbed nature of the comment.

'Perhaps I have underestimated you Whattlewherrit,' said the old man, 'perhaps you are more perceptive than I thought. It strikes me you may be more your father's son than I imagined.'

The Magician found the old man's comment disturbing. Comparing him to Cornelius was not something that sat well with the him. There were so many things about Cornelius he did not want to be, and each time anyone referred to him as his father, a dull pulse of guilt echoed through his body. The same old questions came to mind, 'where is he, and is he still alive?'

Having navigated what was left of the drawbridge, the Magician found Geoffrey contentedly grazing, as if nothing had happened the previous day. He saddled up and they were on their way. The further from Merrelay castle they travelled, the less the annoying buzzing in his ears became. He was glad to have left that place, with its dereliction and decay, and the old man whose guilt seemed to be leaching the very strength from the walls.

'I hope your night was good Geoffrey,' he said as the horse plodded on through the dappled light of the trees. 'Mine was disturbed.' The horse, as always, said not a word in reply.

'My mind is stretched by what I heard and saw at Merrelay and I now see Mistress Munn in a different light. Women are in themselves a mystery, as any man would tell you. But she is not an ordinary woman. She may gossip and fiddle about with domestic matters, as would any other, but beyond that, there is something not quite right about our Mistress. The strange thing is Geoffrey, the more my mind seeks answers to Mistress Munn, the more it gets lost. As if there is a tangle of confusion somewhere, a knotted ball of inconsistency that denies being unpicked. How is it for example that one minute she can be with the Lady Gossamer and the next with me? It is as if there are many Mistress Munns.....

Yet when I come to question her about it, her replies seem so reasonable. She makes out it is I who have got things wrong. I am the one who is mistaken or who has misunderstood. Then comes a moment when for no reason whatsoever, the matter no longer seems worth pursuing. As if something outside of myself plugs the barrel of thought and nothing else is forthcoming. When I get back to Naze, our Mistress is going to have a lot of things to answer.'

Chapter Nine

'People just don't go missing,' Detective Bullmeyer eyed the room from which Kenny Catlin and Debbie Lamb had disappeared. 'Especially famous people like Mr Catlin.' He was talking to Barry Love, the owner of Klines.

'You say he arrived at twelve o'clock sharp?'

'That's right detective.'

'And you showed him to this room?'

'I did.'

'And what about...' the detective checked his phone 'Miss Lamb?'

'She was already here.'

'What time did she arrive?'

'Oh, about 11.40. She was early but that wasn't a problem. We expect Mr Catlin's lady guests to get here before him.' The detective tapped something in his phone.

'This is a regular thing? Mr Catlin entertaining young ladies in this private room?' Barry Love shifted uneasily on the spot.

'Look detective, I have a good business here. People come not only because of the food and the ambience, but because I am discrete. My clients, as I am sure you are aware, require privacy. I don't want to....'

'Listen up Mr Love, I will only say this once, two people have gone missing. One of them is very famous. Discretion is fine for day-to-day comings and goings, but this isn't normal. We could be talking kidnap. We could be talking murder. You get the picture?'

The detective stared the restaurant owner in the eye.

'Kidnap and murder! Surely not, I mean this is just a mistake isn't it? It's got to be. There has to be a simple explanation.'

'You think so? So why were Mr Catlin's clothes scattered all over the room? All apart from his boxer shorts of course. Is it usual for someone to leave the restaurant without their pants, or their socks and shoes? And what about Miss Lamb? Where is she? According to Mr Catlin's assistant Mr Bailey, she arrived here with a case of some sort containing a ventriloquist's dummy of all things. Where is that?'

'I don't know detective. I mean I left them both straight after Mr Catlin arrived. There's a bell,' he pointed to a switch on the wall. 'Mr Catlin forbids anyone coming to the door unless he has rung the bell. It's agreed. It's why he comes here.'

Mr Love was beginning to sweat profusely.

'So let me get this straight. Mr Catlin brings young women here to your establishment to wine and dine them?'

'That's right.'

'But because he is famous, he requires a degree of privacy whilst eating?'

'That's right.'

'So does he have sex with them here?'

'What!?'

'He doesn't fuck them? You know have sex with them, you know what men and women do?'

'I...I can't......'

'You can't what Mr Love? Imagine him doing that?'

'Look I need to speak to my lawyer.'

'You do that Mr Love. But when you do, don't forget to mention that when we did the forensics on this room we found a few things he or she might be interested in. The glass with Miss Lamb's DNA on it, contained traces of Rohypnol.'

'I don't know what.....'

'I am sure your solicitor will know. It's commonly called the date rape drug.'

'Oh shit...'

'Ah, I see you are getting the picture at last. Not only that but there are traces of Cocaine on Mr Catlin's clothing. Mr Catlin, it appears, was using it. We aren't sure about Miss Lamb. So when you have a chat with your lawyer make sure you tell them how far in the shit you are.'

'Look, I didn't know any of this! I wouldn't...'

'You wouldn't be an accessory to rape? You wouldn't turn a blind eye to Mr Hollywood doing his thing in your restaurant? You realise it doesn't stop with the disappearance of Mr Catlin and Miss Lamb? You need to think back Mr Love because I've got a feeling this is going to bring up a whole lot of trouble. Just saying.'

Later that day, Detective Bullmeyer sat in the interview room with another suspect. This man was a totally different ball game altogether.

Marcus Bailey, Kenny Catlin's fixer, was well known to the police. They knew about him but couldn't get to him because of the influence Catlin had over those in authority. Catlin ran the town. His power, be it coercive or patronising, allowed his employees a free hand when it came to illegal activity. He had the best lawyers. He had access to the top echelons of society and he had files, lots of incriminating files, which meant that no one who was anyone was going to give him problems. Bullmeyer knew this and that was why he sat staring at Marcus Bailey with a fierce sense of frustration. He read out the normal stock interview blurb to Bailey and his lawyer. Bullmeyer's partner, Detective Lucille Dullich sat passively at his side.

'So Mr Bailey, a few questions about the day Mr Catlin disappeared. Can you tell me where he was before he went to Klines and what he was doing?'

Bailey drew a slow breath as if considering whether he should answer. Then he tipped his head to one side slightly, and smiled. Not a good sign, thought Detective Bullmeyer.

'So, Mr Catlin had a meeting that morning at the studios. There's a big project they were discussing, a new film.'

'Go on.'

Bailey made a gesture with both hands open as if he didn't really know any more, but he did continue.

'I don't get involved in that stuff. I mean I am Mr Catlin's assistant but not in that way.'

'What was the film called?' Bailey sniffed.

'Oh I don't know, something about a book.'

'The book of words?'

'Yeah, that sounds about right. Mr Catlin didn't talk to me much about the industry but he was asking me what I thought about it because I have kids you know. They watch this fantasy crap. He thought I might know whether they would watch something like it. It was about some quest and you know all that mystical shit where people fight evil. It's all the fucking same to me.'

'So that morning, he had a meeting. Do you know what happened at the meeting?'

'Not really. As I say, I don't get involved.'

'Did you know he fired someone at the meeting?'

'Oh yeah, I guess he mentioned that, but it was just some minor jerk.'

'So you don't think this minor jerk could have had anything to do with Mr Catlin's disappearance?'

Bailey laughed.

'What's so funny?'

'Oh, come on are you fucking joking? So, Mr Catlin fires this dude and goes to Klines straight after the meeting with another person...'

'Miss Lamb?'

'Sure, Miss Lamb, and this guy manages to know where Mr Catlin is going, and not only that, gets into Klines, which I can tell you, you don't do without an invitation, and then he manages to somehow get both of them out of the restaurant with Mr Catlin just in his shorts! If he managed to do that, I want to meet him and shake his hand.'

Detective Bullmeyer was not serious when he asked the question. He had thought it improbable and impossible right from the start but he needed to get Bailey to think he was a fool. It was a tactic he had used before and more often than not, it worked on arrogant suspects.

'So what do you think happened then?'

Bailey sat back in his seat and gestured once again that he didn't know anything.

'Am I wrong to think that one of your main jobs for Mr Catlin is protection?'

Bailey's eyes narrowed. His solicitor leaned towards him and told him he didn't have to answer the question.

'Depends what you mean by protection.' He replied.

'I mean making sure Mr Catlin was given privacy, ensuring no one bothered him.'

'You could say that.'

'What else do you do for Mr Catlin? Do you provide him with drugs?'

Bailey's solicitor leaned over once again but didn't have the chance to say anything.

'No I don't. That sort of thing, it's illegal isn't it?'

Detective Bullmeyer expected the reply but continued.

'So you don't know anything about Rohypnol or Cocaine?'

'No, should I?'

'What about Viagra?'

Bailey laughed out loud again. 'I don't need it. Ask my wife.'

'Alright, well before you go, Mr Bailey, apart from his photogenic face and beach-ready body, does Mr Catlin have any other distinguishing features?' Bullmeyer sat back enjoying his moment of sarcasm.

'Why do you want to know that?'

'Because unfortunately Mr Bailey, sometimes we don't find victims of violent crime in one piece.'

Bailey thought for a moment and then said, 'he has a tattoo. Across his groin, which says 'welcome to the club.'

Bailey could see Bullmeyer was confused.

'It's what's they call a double entendre'

Bullmeyer still looked confused.

'Anyone that gets that far with Mr Catlin has so to speak 'joined the club?' Ok? But he's talking about his dick as well, see?'

'Ok, well I think that is all for today,' said Detective Bullmeyer, 'thank you for your time, Mr Bailey.'

When Bailey and his solicitor had left the room, Detective Bullmeyer turned to his colleague.

'Well, that was a waste of everyone's time.'

She nodded and then asked him whether he thought Bailey was involved.

'I don't think he is. He supplied the drugs, I have no doubt about that, and he is complicit in the meetings at Klines over the years, but I don't see a motive in him getting rid of Catlin. After all, he has a good life working for Catlin. He gets well paid, he gets free lawyers when he needs them, he even gets health care. Why would he give that up?'

'Kidnap, blackmail. Maybe he could make a lot more from that?'

'I don't think so. Why do it when the kidnap victim is with someone? Why not do it when he is driving Catlin somewhere, or at his home? And it's not Bailey's forte. He is a criminal ok, a thug, but he's not stupid. He knows he would be top of the suspect list if anything happened to Catlin.'

'What about the guy Catlin sacked that day? You were asking about him.'

'Oh, that was just a red herring to divert Bailey. What Bailey said summed it up well enough. It was too soon after the meeting where he was sacked. Who thinks about kidnap or murder twenty minutes after your life has gone down the pan? And why take both of them? And more to the point, how? The more I think about it, the crazier it gets. You've seen the CCTV at the restaurant. There's no sign of either of them leaving. Where the fuck did they go? You know what?'

'What?'

'I think it all went wrong. I think he drugged the girl, and something went wrong. He got the body out of the place with the help of Mr Love the manager and Bailey. Let me put a scenario to you. Catlin slips Rohypnol into her champagne glass and she loses consciousness. He starts to do the business but something happens, maybe she wakes up and struggles, maybe he gives her too much and she has a heart attack. Now he has to get the body out of the restaurant. He calls Bailey and together they somehow manage to leave where the CCTV can't pick them up.'

'Why didn't you say that to Bailey?'

'Oh, he's too smart to give him the low down on how I am thinking. I want him to believe I'm a total dickhead. I want him to believe he is in control, only that way can we build a case that is going to put him and Catlin away forever.'

'Where do you suppose Catlin is now?'

'Probably sunning himself abroad on his yacht whilst his minions mop up his mistakes. He will come back, claiming they were both kidnapped and denying any responsibility for Miss Lamb's disappearance, you mark my words.'

Chapter Ten

The forest was getting thicker by the mile. The further from Merrelay castle they travelled, the fewer the well-trodden paths there were, and the harder it was to see ahead, such was the density of the canopy. The shard was getting twitchy. The Magician could feel it underneath his tabard. Just a soft vibration now and again but it was there. nonetheless.

'I have a feeling our meeting with the Bludgeoner is not far off,' said the Magician to his horse. 'By my reckoning he should have entered the forest two days ago and our paths will cross this day.'

Just by saying it, the Magician felt uneasy. He was no diplomat and had no skill when dealing with the likes of the Bludgeoner. He held onto the shard and in a moment of humility, asked it to help him over the coming days. It brought to mind Cornelius telling him he was too careless.

'To get anywhere with magic you must first admit you know nothing. Even when you have been practising for years you must always look at yourself and say 'I am at the beginning of the journey'.'

What did that mean to a young man, on one hand rather full of himself, and on the other deeply insecure? At the time it was mumbo jumbo. However, as the years went on and especially after Cornelius disappeared, Whattlewherrit thought he was beginning to understand. He was not in control, as he had imagined in his youth. Far from it. And here he was, a fine example of it, heading into a meeting with the most dangerous man ever to set foot across the borders of Naze.

'What a horses arse the King is Geoffrey. No disrespect meant to you of course.'

Then thinking it still mattered to his horse he said, 'No he is actually a Boar's arse, a full-blown, soiled Boar's arse, and I hope he reaps the rewards of his decision for many a year.'

The Magician was talking to himself like this when the shard went crazy, as did Geoffrey the horse. It reared up, then refused to put a foot further. He had come to the edge of a clearing which was as long as a jousting field and twice the width. The sun, which had been hiding most of the way due to the canopy of the trees, lit the spot with an intensity that meant it took a moment to readjust his eyes. As he did so, what he saw sent a shiver through him. Across at the opposite edge clearing, standing stock still, was the biggest horse he had ever seen and sitting on the horse was the biggest rider. The man was immense. The men following him on foot looked tiny when compared to him. The Magician looked at him. He looked back at the Magician. It was a brief standoff. The Bludgeoner heeled his horse's flanks and it walked out of the shadows of the forest and into the clearing, followed by his retinue. The Magician prodded Geoffrey and he too reluctantly began to walk into the open.

'What have we here,' boomed out a bullish voice, 'What rag bag of a man dares to approach Moredeath?'

The Magician was offended. He was definitely not a rag bag of a man.

'I am Whattlewherrit, the King of Naze's Magician. I have been sent to escort you to Naze.'

'The King sends me this,' he said looking down to his men. 'Why didn't he just send me someone of importance, like the keeper of his piss pot.'

Moredeath's men laughed loudly.

'I have travelled two days to meet you......' the Magician had no chance to finish his words.

'You little turd of a man. What do you think you can do to help Moredeath? Protect me from Wolves? Save me from Bears? I break them in two and feed them to my dogs! And, if you do not get out of my way, I shall do the same to you!!'

The Magician could see that his diplomatic skills would be fully put to the test, and he was about to do so, when it suddenly sounded like a heavy rain was falling. The sky grew dark. Thousands of arrows were winging their way towards Moredeath and his men. They didn't stand a chance. The Magician grabbed the shard, uttered an incantation and everything exploded into a fierce ball of light.

Moredeath the Bludgeoner had never been on a bus before. The shock of being at one moment in a forest glade in Naze and the next in a large box full of strange looking people overrode his natural inclination to kill someone. The brain of a man from the twelfth century, used to basically doing half a dozen things i.e eating, sleeping, marauding, molesting, murdering, and mutilating, with the emphasis being on the four 'm's', was finding it hard to understand why everything was moving by him whilst he was sitting still. Furthermore being on the top deck he was looking down on the world passing beneath him, and what a strange world it appeared to be. Nothing was recognisable. His brain raced as it tried to comprehend the incomprehensible. His hands clasped the handle of his axe, his thick knuckles turning white as tried to think. What had happened? He was on his horse with his men ridiculing the little shit of a Magician when arrows began to fall and....

'Are you Conan the Barbarian?'

It was the voice of a small boy sitting behind him. He was leaning over the seat, looking at the Bludgeoner intently.

'I don't think you look like him if that's who you are supposed to be.'

To the Bludgeoner the words made no sense. The language he spoke was similar but so many of the words sounded foreign, just like everything around him.

'My dad does a better Conan than you. He goes to the gym, and he would beat you any day.'

Moredeath looked round to see a woman next to the child staring at something in her hands, oblivious of the child. He summoned up a wad of sputum, rolled it on his tongue and spat it at the child. A thick mucous lump splattered on the boy's T-shirt, who let out a yelp. Moredeath turned away and grunted. At that moment the boy's mother looked up from her phone and screamed.

'You little shit, look what you've done! You're disgusting. You only put that on this morning. You wait till we get off this bus, I'm going to give you a good seeing to!'

The bus was a chartered one, heading for the Squirrel Hills Country Park where, amongst other activities, there was to be a re-enactment of mediaeval combat by a group of local enthusiasts. A number of those travelling on the bus were doing so in authentic mediaeval costumes, something that was confusing the Bludgeoner. So many things were strange and yet he could see traces of his world. Hardened as he was to battle and fearless as he was, his instinct told him to act as though nothing unusual was happening. Let your enemy show their hand before you act was his motto. And so it was that, when the bus stopped, and people started to get off, he followed suit. Bent almost double to squeeze his enormous frame through the bus, he made his way down the stairs and out into the open air where crowds of people were walking towards the entry gate. He looked at the promotional banner at the entrance and grunted.

It depicted a jousting session and armed combat. Things were looking familiar at last. At the gate the ticket collector waved him through. 'Free admission to participants,' he said looking at Moredeath and backing off at the same time. There was no way he was going to ask him for money.

Squirrel Hills Country Park was basically a huge basin gouged out of the hillside by thousands of years of weathering. Twenty or more acres of grassland surrounded by trees. As the Bludgeoner walked through the woods, he could see down below the tents, the amusements, and the crowds of people milling about. What caught his attention however was the joust taking place. Two Knights on horseback were galloping towards one another, clashing to the tremendous roar from the watching crowd. The Bludgeoner's eyes narrowed as he saw the Knights turn once again, to face one another. Things were beginning to get even more familiar. Whatever the Magician had done had turned his world upside down but not entirely. Inside he raged. His temper burned like a forest fire. He was going to kill the Magician as soon as he could find him, and, in the meantime, anyone that got in his way. Stomping down the hill he growled as he continued to watch the re-enactment.

'Ladies and gentlemen' said the announcer over the intercom, 'give a huge round of applause for the Forest Knights re-enactment team and their jousting skills.'

There followed an enthusiastic round of applause from the audience.

'Weren't they great. Well next on we have got the Merton Marauders who are going to engage in hand-to-hand combat using real weapons, made in the way they would have been hundreds of years ago. Don't try this at home kids, this is the real stuff and highly dangerous if you aren't trained in old-fashioned combat. So let me introduce our fighters this afternoon. First we have Axel the axe man aka Steve Dent, come on out Axel!'

Axel appears wearing what looks like a sheepskin rug with arm holes cut in it and heavy woollen trousers bound together with leather straps. On his feet he has summer sandals, the type you could buy at any sports store. His chunky arms are heavily tattooed, which adds to his gravitas, and he holds a shield in one hand and a large axe in the other.

'Steve, or rather Axel has been re-enacting for ten years and has a pretty impressive kill rate. Give him a round of applause ladies and gentlemen!'

There follows a mild spattering of hand claps.

'Next out into the combat ring we have Torin Broadsword aka Roger Tombs. Roger, or should I say Torin, has been a mainstay of the Merton marauders for a number of years and carries the sword from which his name derives. Now his sword, I am told on good authority, is an accurate replica of an actual Crusaders broadsword, and, as you see, is so heavy it takes two hands to hold. Not a weapon to be messed with ladies and gentlemen.'

Torin Broadsword is dressed like a Crusader. Tabard, plastic chainmail, and a hand-painted shield strapped to his back.

'Give it up for Torin, ladies and gentlemen!' A polite round of applause follows.

'Number three is Garth the Gargantuan. Gargantuan by name, gargantuan by size. Here he comes. Garth, or Richard Forbes, as his wife knows him, weighs in at an impressive eighteen stone. Poor Mrs Forbes if you get my gist. Sorry Garth I shouldn't have said that especially as his weapon of choice is the Mace. This fierce weapon could shatter a man's skull with one stroke and Garth knows how to use it. Show Garth how impressed you are by his Mace.'

The crowd respond with slightly more enthusiasm.

'Finally ladies and gentlemen we have Max the Marauder, after whom the team were originally named. Max formed the group over ten years ago and as such is a seasoned combat artist. Max, otherwise known as Nigel Bradley, believes in authenticity and I am informed his costume has been hand-crafted, by Doreen, his wife, out of the finest Moroccan leather. Like Axel, Max's weapon of choice for today's combat is his axe, although I am told he occasionally likes to use his short sword as well. Lucky old Doreen. Let's give him a round of applause!'

A slow ripple of applause seeps across the combat ground. Nothing happens.

'And now we have Max the Marauder!'

Again nothing happens. Torin Broadsword looks at Garth the Gargantuan and frowns.

'Do we have Max anywhere in the tent please?'

No one appears. The crowd is getting restless.

Torin whispers to Garth. 'Where the fuck is Nigel?'

The crowd begins to slow clap.

'Come on Max, the crowds waiting! Perhaps he's having second thoughts, ladies and gentlemen, after all I would, seeing these guys and their weapons!'

More slow hand clapping. The compere is about to suggest the combat begins without Max the Marauder, when he notices the tent flap opening.

'Ah, here he comes ladies and gentlemen, Max the Marauder!!'

At that precise moment, through a break in the clouds, a shaft of light hits the tent like a spotlight, and out steps Moredeath the Bludgeoner, resplendent in his leather garb, which is straining from the pressure of the taught musculature beneath. Adorned by gleaming metal studs on his tabard, and with his shining broadsword strapped across his shoulders, he shimmers in the illuminating light. Even his leather pants are impressive looking, as though they have been sprayed onto his massive thighs. In his hands he grasps his Axe, known throughout the Bloodlands as 'The Swiper' for its ability to swiftly decapitate any enemy. The sun hits the blade and the beam sweeps the crowd like that of a lighthouse. It is a warning. There is danger here. The announcer, overjoyed at seeing someone emerge, shouts out 'here comes Max!'

Torin Thundersword shouts 'who the fuck is that?' but his question is lost like a child in a crowd, as applause rebounds across the arena. When the applause dies down Garth the Gargantuan shouts out, 'that's not Max!'

The crowd, thinking it is part of the show, shout out, 'oh yes it is!' Torin Thundersword shouts out, 'It's not Max!!' The crowd join in 'Oh yes it is!!' The announcer, always able to pick up on a vibe says 'Come on ladies and gentlemen, let's hear it for Max!' The crowd begin to chant 'Max!Max!Max!' as Moredeath moves towards his three opponents.

The first opponent he confronts is Garth the Gargantuan. Garth's eighteen stone of blubber is no match for Moredeath's twenty two stone of toned muscle. Moredeath is not out for a swift kill and turns his axe around and with the butt viscously jabs Garth in the belly. Garth looks confused for a moment before grasping his midriff and crumpling to the floor. The crowd roar. They love it.

'Oh that was a painful one,' says the commentator over the speakers, clearly enjoying the show. Moredeath turns to face Torin Thundersword who is enraged.

'You fucking idiot,' he shouts at Moredeath, 'you could have hurt him doing that!'

'He did,' gasped Garth from the floor.

'You see you did, you moron!' shouted Thundersword. He picks up his broadsword in two hands and swinging it wildly, aims it at Moredeath. The Bludgeoner steps back just enough to avoid any contact and as Torin Thundersword is pulled round by the motion of his own sword and begins a solitary dance. Moredeath swings The Swiper and with a single stroke takes off Torin Thundersword's head. The crowd gasps. Garth mutters, 'oh shit', and Axel the Axeman, who so far has been taking a back seat in the activities, soils his pants.

'Get him Steve!' shouts Garth to Axel the Axeman.

'Fuck that,' Shouts Axel the Axeman and turns to run but it is too late. Moredeath draws his sword and, with all the skill of a circus knife act, throws it towards the escaping Axeman where it embeds itself in his rib cage. Axel drops like a stone. Garth meanwhile has managed to raise himself off the ground. He sees no escape and so aims his Mace at the Bludgeoner's balls. The Mace strikes home. The Bludgeoner looks down at his groin before letting out a growl that could have come from a raging Gorilla. He looks up, and in one stroke, cuts Garth in two.

Whilst this is happening, the crowd are in full flight and the announcer is trying to bring them to their senses. 'Don't panic please, ladies and gentlemen, don't panic. We don't want anyone trampled!' It is hopeless. As Moredeath retrieves his sword with a decided squelch from the body of Axel the Axeman and rubs it dry on the dead man's body, the day is over. Mayhem rules, and the Bludgeoner, having smelt blood, is about to go on the rampage and would have done so were it not for tho oight of a figure in the distance. The Bludgeoner stops, sniffs the air and roars as he marches towards the Magician. The Magician waits for the angry beast of the Bludgeoner to get close before he says anything.

'You must listen to me Sire. I am not sure what has happened but if we don't stop and think about what we are going to do next I fear it could get worse.'

Moredeath grunts, aims his sword, and throws it with all of his might towards the Magician. The Magician holds the shard whispers and incantation and as the sword arrives at its intended destination i.e. his chest, it hurtles through him as though he were made of air.

The Bludgeoner howls with rage.

'Now I know you won't understand a word of this, but I have to tell you that I think something has happened with the What Will Be. Somehow..' The Magician utters another incantation as Moredeaths Axe spins its way towards his head. Swish! It passes through him leaving him unscathed.

'Somehow,' he repeats, 'we seem to have become tangled up in another world and we need to get back.' Swoosh a hand knife flies through him.

'You aren't listening.'

Moredeath charges the Magician, who quickly chants another spell and Moredeath freezes on the spot.

'Now look, this isn't going to get us anywhere. I need to get back to Naze. There are books I have to consult. I am going to have to trust the shard to find you a good hiding place meanwhile. Believe me I don't want this any more than you do. Now I am going to gather your things because we can't leave anything from our world just lying around. I have a feeling that somehow an imbalance has occurred. Things from this world, whatever and wherever it is, have found their way into ours, and vice versa. We need to rebalance it. You will have to remain here. We can't have any more disturbance until I am sure of what is happening.'

The Magician picks up the weapons, stows them in their leather sheaths on the frozen Moredeath, and casts a spell. At that moment he and Moredeath go their separate ways, the Magician back to Naze and Moredeath to a fine Art gallery in Kensington London.

Chapter Eleven

Kenny Catlin lay on his back in the cold mist, naked as the day he was born, but sporting a large erection. This was courtesy of the Viagra he had downed prior to entering the restaurant where he was going to meet Miss Debbie Lamb. He groaned and tried to roll over, unaware of his erection until it struck the ground.

'Holy shit,' he cried out, 'what the fuck?'

His head was spinning and he was disorientated. The last he could recall was standing in front of Debbie Lamb and her face as she saw his naked body. Then everything exploded and he became engulfed in a ball of intense light. He rolled onto his back again and ran a hand down to his groin.

'For fuck's sake,' he said to himself, 'when you want one you can't get one, and when you don't, the fucking thing is like a broom handle.' He managed to sit up, wrapping his arms around himself as he shivered with cold.

'Where the fuck am I?' His words dissolved into the mist.

From his seated position, he managed to roll himself on his side. Catlin was not the fittest man in Hollywood, in fact he probably ranked as one of the unfittest. His one exercise being sex and even then, he relied upon the enthusiasm of his partner or partners when he partied.

On his knees he felt his way along the wet ground.

'What the fuck am I doing outside? I'm going to fucking kill Bailey for allowing this to happen. That piece of shit is dead.'

His hand hit something. It felt like material of some sort. He explored it then found it was clothing and inside the clothing was a body.

'Fuck!' He withdrew his hand as fast as it would go. He tried to see through the mist to comprehend what it was he had just touched. What he saw made no sense. It was a body alright, but of a man dressed in mediaeval clothes and in his chest were a bunch of arrows.

'Oh no,' he called out, 'oh no, this is not happening. This is fucking not happening.' His first thoughts on the matter went along the lines, 'someone has given me some bad stuff. Someone has mixed hallucinogenics in with my Cocaine.' He was tripping. Yes that was it he was fucking tripping! If it was a trip, then wherever he was happened to be freezing. He shuffled about on his hands and knees until he came across yet another body.

'Oh, for fucks sake,' as all he could say.

Further on he managed to hit his head on something solid. It was a box of some sort, a chest with some insignia on it. It looked like a skull wearing a Hogs Head as a hat. There was a latch which had broken open, so he tried to lift the lid to see what was inside. It was no good, it was too heavy for him. He rummaged around on the ground and because the early morning light was getting stronger, he was now able to see what surrounded him. There were bodies everywhere. Arrows protruding from each and every one. It was carnage.

As the air thinned out under a weak sun, he began to breath the stench of death. He wanted to wretch but held it down. He needed to get something warm on before he got hypothermia. Before long he found a lance and took it back to the box where, after several attempts, Catlin managed to lever open the massive lid. He hit the jackpot. Inside there were layers of clothes, mediaeval clothes, but clothes nonetheless. He took out some pants. They were way too big for him, but what the hell he thought, I just need to be warm. He tied them around his waist with some pieces of leather he found, cursing his erection, which was uncomfortable when restricted by the clothing. Then he found a tabard on which was embroidered the same skull with the Boars head hat. It swamped him but was warm and that was good enough. Whoever owned it was a big man. Catlin's belly managed to fill parts of it. Maybe the wrong parts but what did that matter? The alternative would be to take something off the dead men and there was no way he was going to do that.

He sat on the open side of the box, confused and weary. Even the task of finding something to wear had worn him out. Whatever he had taken, it was bad shit, really bad. This was unlike any other sort of bad shit he had ever taken. Where were the colours, the feelings of euphoria, the sense of being detached? Everything you wanted from a trip, even a bad trip, was missing. This was far too fucking real. Whoever invented this stuff was a demon, a piece of shit that needed to be removed from the planet. He was thinking this to himself when out of the diminishing mist came two Knights on horseback.

'Oh fuck, that's just what I need, Ivanhoe and Sir Lancelot.'

'This is a rout' said Sir Bloatmore to Sir Sockamore, surveying the clearing. 'How could this be?' Sir Sockamore showed no signs of emotion.

'I blame the Magician.'

'The Magician? How so? These arrows have not left the quiver of the Magician.'

'He was supposed to guide the Bludgeoner into Naze. Look what has happened. Do you not think he is responsible? Is he a Magician or is he not? The man is a charlatan.' Sir Sockamore's voice had an unforgiving edge to it.

'Are they all dead' said Sir Bloatmore.

'Every man,' replied Sir Sockamore.

'I'm not, you fuckers.' Came a voice out of the mist.

'Who's there?' shouted Sir Bloatmore.

'Me,' replied Kenny Catlin managing to stand on his two feet proudly erect.

'Gadzooks!' exclaimed Sir Bloatmore. 'That is the insignia of Moredeath the Bludgeoner, no one else would dare to wear the Bludgeoner's mark.'

Sir Sockamore stared hard at Kenny Catlin. This was not the man he had seen riding at the head of the now-deceased warriors. But to say that it was not the Bludgeoner would lead Bloatmore to question how he knew. How could he admit that he had seen the Bludgeoner in the flesh not one day before? He was trapped. He tried to bluster his way through.

'I think you are mistaken Bloatmore, this man has nothing like the stature of the Bludgeoner. We have been told he was taller than any man in the land. Stronger than the strongest swordsman. That he was nothing short of a bear of a man. This....this is just a.....weasel.'

'What the fuck are you on about? Calling me a fucking weasel? Don't you know who I am? I'll fucking kill you, you piece of shit!' Sir Bloatmore turned to his companion and whispered.

'Perhaps this is some form of sorcery. Perhaps the Magician has transformed him into this form to disguise him from his enemies? We need to be careful. If it is him, any disrespect will end up with our demise.'

Sir Sockamore huffed knowing as he did that this wasn't the Bludgeoner his men had tried to kill, and he had no faith in Bloatmores assessment of the Magician's powers.

'Jesus, what sort of fucked up trip is this? Fucking Knights in armour and a field full of rotting bodies. It's like a scene from a fucking fantasy movie!'

And that is when it clicked. Yes that was it! He was having a bad trip and it was based on that fucking film script The Book of Words. He had only read an overview of the thing, but it was all about Knights and quests and all that fucking shit.

'You don't exist!' He shouted at the two Knights, 'you are a fucking figment of my imagination. All of this is just some illusion. So fuck off!!'

'It is clear he is suffering from some form of madness, perhaps due to the shock of the attack. We need to be cautious Sockamore. Whoever did this might still be about. The men need to search the woods and we need to get Moredeath to Naze. And where is the Magician in all this?'

'Where indeed,' replied Sockamore.

The last Sir Sockamore had seen of him was during the rout, when the whole place lit up with a ball of light, after which both the real Moredeath and the Magician had disappeared. Somehow that boar's arse of a man had performed some magic and the two of them were gone. He himself had left after that, and returned to Naze, in order to avoid being implicated in any way, and to report to the Lady Gosammer that the deed was done. His heart sank. The deed was not done. Moredeath was not dead, only disappeared and this imposter was standing in his place. How was he going to explain this to his beloved Lady? All of his plans to be her husband and eventually to be the King were going wrong. He hated that Magician more than ever and was determined to see the end of him. In his desperation he saw only one way forward. To fight fire with fire, or rather magic with magic. He turned to Sir Bloatmore.

'You take this....person to Naze if you will. I for one do not believe him to be Moredeath. I am going to put this whole thing right.'

'And how do you plan to do that Sockamore?'

'I shall visit the Bloodly Sisters.'

'The Bloodly Sisters! Are you mad? Those treacherous hags will devour you as soon as look at you. You can't do it!'

'I will put my life on the line for the Lady Gossamer and the future of Naze if needs be. Magic is the problem here and only magic can solve it. I will get that Magician if it is the last thing I do!' And with that Sir Sockamore rode away leaving Bloatmore to handle the irate Kenny Catlin.

Bloatmore's task was made easier when Catlin, overwhelmed by stress and the comedown from the drugs he had taken back in Hollywood stopped swearing at him and unexpectedly slumped into a deep sleep. The Knight ordered a cart from Moredeath's entourage to be brought forward and with some difficulty and much hilarity he was placed in it. Upon lifting him into the cart his clothing slipped and revealed an ongoing tumultuous erection.

'We shan't have any problem telling the time on the way to Naze,' quipped one of the men, 'who needs a sundial when you've got that.'

'Show some respect,' demanded Sir Bloatmore. 'Remember, Moredeath the Bludgeoner would take off your head as soon as look at you, were he not suffering battle fatigue. This man you are laughing at has taken more lives than you could imagine.'

In saying this, Sir Bloatmore felt a certain reticence in his own words. The man in the cart was nothing like the man he was supposed to be. This was not the man feared amongst the ten realms, or if it was, then something terrible had happened to him. The more he thought about it, the more convinced he became that it was indeed the Magicians doing. The man's magic had transformed a beast into this blob of a man sporting an untimely erection. The implications of the whole affair were enormous. Too great for a simple Knight to comprehend. He sighed. There was nothing he could do about it. His job, he told himself, was to get Moredeath safely to Naze castle, no more than that.

Chapter Twelve

The Greer swamp lay deep in the heart of the forest and the oddest thing about it was that it never appeared on any map. Its location changed, and at any one time to get there, you either wandered in by mistake, or on the rare occasion when anyone intended going there, it just appeared. So it was with Sir Sockamore. His determination to find the Bloodly Sisters meant the journey was shorter than he anticipated. He failed to notice the subtle changes in the forest that signified he was leaving the safety of the known and entering the unknown. The canopy of the forest for instance seemed strangely alive, though when he looked up to examine it in detail, he saw nothing unusual. No hint of the activity he intuitively felt going on above his head. Then there was the ground that after a short while became soft underfoot. His horse was almost reluctant to place its feet, lest they were sucked into the turf. The sense of unease that he, and his trusty steed, both felt, increased the further they went. Strange sounds fell to the ear, scratching and scutterings close by and distant whoopings and yells. Added to all of these disconcerting distractions was the fact he was certain when they approached the swamp the sun was out and the sky clear, but now, as they tentatively walked on, it was turning darker by the minute. Sir Sockamore's bravado was beginning to lose its edge.

'This place is not what I imagined,' he said to himself. 'Perhaps I was mistaken in coming here.'

A shadow of doubt crossed his mind as he weighed up the option of going back. Did he really love the Lady Gossamer enough to seek the help of the Bloodly Sisters? Did he really want to be King badly enough to risk entering further into the swamp? Did he really want to risk his own life in order to kill the Magician? He was about to answer these questions when he caught the scent of a flower, one he had never experienced before. Such was its fragrance that it intoxicated him. He wanted more. He breathed in the exquisite aroma as though downing a cup of fine wine and feeling its soothing effects upon the body. Even his horse, whose ears up until that moment had been flicking back and forth, and whose reluctant feet were objecting walking further, suddenly fell into a relaxed lollop.

The further they went, the more intoxicated they both became and the less Sir Sockamore found himself questioning the foolishness of his intentions. Everything was just fine. The strange noises were no longer annoying, the canopy full of darting creatures was no longer a distraction, and even the ground, which was getting decidedly boggy, seemed to be alright with his horse. No wine, no mead or strong ale had ever affected him this way. He wanted more. Nothing he had ever experienced felt as good as at that moment. Not winning the annual jousting competition, not seeing himself reflected in the burnished shield of a vanquished Knight, not even imagining spending a night with the Lady Gossamer came anywhere near this moment. Life could not be better in any way.

'Hello deary.'

It took a moment for Sir Sockamore to locate the speaker but when he did, he was unexpectedly taken aback. In his state of euphoria, he had forgotten about the hags. Somewhere deep inside, somewhere inaccessible, a large bell rang a stark warning, but it was so far away that it seemed utterly pointless.

'Good day old woman.' He replied courteously.

'Would you happen to be Sir Sockamore?' She asked.

'Why how observant you are.'

'Well deary, your fame is widespread, I am sure that anyone with a knowledge of the Knights of Naze would recognise your coat of arms immediately.'

Sir Sockamore smiled a knowing smile. An inner glow drifted through his heavily intoxicated body. Of course his fame would have spread to the Greer swamp, why would it not?'

'And to what do we owe the pleasure of your company?'

'Why madam it is to visit you and your sister.'

'Indeed. Well I am sure we would be pleased to entertain you in our humble home.'

'Then lead on madam,' said Sir Sockamore in a positively rousing way.

Sir Sockamore had never been in a cave before and despite his euphoric state of mind, the cold dank interior nevertheless brought his mood down a step or two. The walls were wet and covered in algae and there was a constant dripping sound in the background. The old woman shuffled ahead of him, like some forest creature out foraging in the night. She muttered to herself as she went. Sir Sockamore felt things crunch under his feet and now and again he slid on something slimy. All in all, the place was grim and grimy and not at all inviting. Then there was the smell, a mixture of old wet dog, leaf-mould, and smoke, the latter coming from a smouldering fire under a giant pot that steamed away, sending moisture into the air where it would cool and then slide back down the walls.

'Come in dearie,' the old woman said, beckoning the Knight forward. The distant bell continued to call caution, but the Knight was too far gone to bother with it.

'Sit down,' said the hag. Sir Sockamore sat as instructed but as he did so a fierce growl emanated from his right-hand side. He leapt up as a scrawny wolf the size of a man raised itself up and bared its teeth at him.

'Get down you beast!!' shouted the old woman with such a harsh tone of voice that Sir Sockamore's scrotum scrunched. The wolf sat back and stared at Sir Sockamore.

'Sorry about that dearie, I think you must have sat on his tail.'

He was reluctant to sit back down but the old hag insisted.

'Now,' she said, as she spat into the pot, 'tell me sir Knight what matter could be so urgent that you would want to visit our humble abode?'

The Knight was beginning to ask himself exactly the same question. Why on earth would he want to be there in that hovel of a cave with the hag when he could be back in Naze castle? His euphoria was wearing off.

'There is trickery afoot in Naze and Whattlewherrit the King's Magician is behind it.'

No sooner had he uttered the name Whattlewherrit than the whole cave broke into an ear-splitting cacophony. The wolf howled, the hag screamed, and her scream was accompanied by yet another. Somewhere in the shadows, out of sight, was the other Bloodly Sister, and, apparently, she was not happy either.

'Whattlewherrit,' shouted the sister, 'Who dares say that name in my cave!'

'Hush sister, it is alright' said the first hag who despite having screamed herself, seemed to have got her emotions under control.

'We have a guest'

'Who?' Spat the other hag.

'None other than Sir Sockamore, the handsomest Knight in Naze.'

'Who?'

'You know the one it was foretold would visit us.' She gave her sister a knowing nudge. Her sister looked blank for a moment before her face lightened up.

'Ooh,' she said, 'that one.'

'Yes, that one.'

'Do you mind me asking what exactly was foretold?' asked Sir Sockamore, who though still recovering from the shock of their reaction, was keen to hear of the future.

'Well, that would be telling,' said the hag.

'You can't leave me in suspense like that,' said Sir Sockamore, 'is it about the Lady Gossamer and I?'

'Well now you are an intuitive man aren't you? How did you guess that was part of the prediction?'

'And was it to do with me doing away with Moredeath the Bludgeoner?'

'Oh so true to the prediction I could swear you read the runes yourself.' Cried the old hag.

'And Whattlewherrit? Do I finally get to end his miserable life?' At this point the Wolf roared and jumped at the Knight and was about to rip open his throat when the hag spat out a spell and he whelped and ran to the corner of the cave.

'He gets excited when you use that name, best not repeat it when he's around,' said the hag.

His question about the runes was left unanswered but the Knight was too shaken to notice.

'Now from what you have been asking I am going to assume you would do anything to rid Naze of the Bludgeoner and the Magician, am I right?'

'Indeed, anything. If I could do that then nothing else would matter.'

'Nothing?'

'Nothing,' repeated Sir Sockamore earnestly. In his mind these two objectives could gain him everything he had ever wanted, the Lady Gossamer and thus to become heir to the throne.

'Well, I think we might be able to help you here,' said the hag. 'can't we,' she said, smiling at her sister.'

Sir Sockamore felt the thrill of ambition rush through him. With the help of the Bloodly Sisters he would become invincible. But he was still curious.

'So are you to summon up a shield of invincibility that will protect me in combat? Perhaps a sword that cannot miss it's mark. Or a lance that never breaks and always pierces my opponent's armour? Tell me, what is it that will enable me to achieve my goal?'

'Oh well now dearie that would be telling wouldn't it. Let us just say we are going to endow you with a power so overwhelming that no man will be able to resist it, and every woman will wish she were you.'

'So you are going to enhance my natural skills then?' The hag smiled.

'Something along those lines dearie. Now before we go any further you need to pledge that in return for our help you will commit to help us. Once you have pledged yourself, we can begin to help you.'

The tongue of the distant warning bell was wildly thrashing, somewhere in the depths of his soul, but he failed to heed its ominous call.

'Soup,' said the hag, 'we will share the soup of sisterhood and seal the bond.'

For a flickering moment Sir Sockamore found the sound of the soup of sisterhood uncomfortable, seeing as he was after all the manliest Knight in Naze, but the scent of the flowers still had hold of his mind. He was intoxicated enough for it not to matter.

The soup was disgusting, and it took all of his strength of mind not to spit it out but the thought of destroying his enemies and laying in his lady's bed enabled him to endure it.

'Right then,' said the hag, when they had eaten, 'tomorrow morning you will be a different person.'

Chapter Thirteen

The oarsman pulled them away from their mooring. It was night, and as they slipped away from the town, his passenger huddled himself in the bow of the boat, wrapped in a long black cloak, his face hidden from view. The oars slapped the water and the boat heaved forward against the tide. When they were far enough from the quay the boat man spoke.

'I never thought I would see you again Magician.'

'I was of a similar mind about Naze,' replied Whattlewherrit.

'There are proclamations all over the place with a reward for your capture. You must have done something really bad to upset the King.'

'It's all a mistake,' said the Magician, 'and I intend rectifying it. What I wonder is why you haven't sought the reward? After all, I have no doubt a man like you could use the money.'

The boatman nodded as though he agreed.

'Whose to say I haven't. How do you know I haven't alerted the King's men and they are waiting for you at the end of this journey?'

The Magician shook his head.

'Perhaps you have, but I don't think so. You have been taking me back and forth for years now.'

'Yes, and you have been decent to me. When my wife was poorly you gave me medicines and charged me nothing for it. And you have never uttered a disparaging word towards me. You are the only one who gives me the time-of-day Magician. Who never tries to cheat me or treats me like a piece of dirt. You know well how them lords and ladies behaves. A man gets sick and tired of the likes of Sir Sockamore and the Lady Gossamer with their fancy ways.'

'So tell me boatman, what is the news?'

'Well I only knows tavern gossip but it goes along the lines of you was supposed to protect the Bludgeoner and instead of which his entire retinue was wiped out. All but the Bludgeoner who is at this very minute not one day away from Naze.'

'The Bludgeoner. You must be mistaken.' The Magician shifted uneasily in his seat.

'Not as I have it, Magician. They tells me that Sir Bloatmore and Sir Sockamore was sent to find the Bludgeoner after news of a rout. When they gets there, every man jack of Moredeath's men has been slaughtered other than the Bludgeoner, who is alive, but is not his former self.'

'This is strange and worrying news indeed.'

'Not only that, but according to rumour Sir Sockamore has gone looking for you in the Greer swamp of all places.'

'The Greer swamp! Why would anyone go there?'

'As to that Magician I cannot say. The man must have been struck by the moon. No one goes there and comes out again.'

The boatman's news was deeply troubling to the Magician. How could Moredeath possibly have come back when he left him firmly in the What Will Be? And why would Sir Sockamore go to the Greer swamp unless it was to see the Bloodly Sisters? What heinous crime was he planning with the hags? There was trouble afoot. He needed to get back to the What Will Be and confirm Moredeath was still there and bring him back to balance the two worlds.

Mistress Munn was engaged in her monthly toilet when the Magician knocked on the huge oak door.

'Now who is that at this time of night,' she muttered as she traversed the winding staircase to the front door.

'It's you,' she cried, seeing the Magician. And then out of the blue, she embraced him.

'We thought you was gone for good. When they said you was missing we all thought...'

'Can I come in Mistress?' said the Magician who was struggling to get in the door and keen to get into the warmth.

'Oh yes of course. I am sorry Magician I was sorting out my twixt and in betweens when you knocked and it was such a shock to see you like this.'

The Magician tried hard not to think about what Mistress Munn had just said.

'I cannot stay long Mistress, I need to get back to the What Will Be.'

Mistress Munn looked shocked.

'You've been to the What Will Be? But your father......'

'I know, my father said never to interfere with the What Will Be. There is no need to remind me. The fact is, it was never my intention to go there. It just happened. Now everything is out of balance, especially as Moredeath is there at the moment.'

'The Bludgeoner is in the What Will Be? Are you certain? I heard tell that he is on his way to Naze, having been in some rout where all of his men was killed.'

The Magician explained what had happened and how he had tried to save the day by removing Moredeath from the storm of arrows.

'He and I were taken from the forest but we ended up in the What Will Be. It was nothing to do with my spell, which was simply to transport us elsewhere for a moment. Somehow something drastically wrong is happening and I have no control over it. It is why I am back. I need to consult my father's books. There must be a way to put this right.'

Mistress Munn let out a long and deep sigh.

'Oh Magician this does not bode well. I have a strange feeling in my loins.'

The Magician felt a dull cloud sweep over his thoughts. How many times had he heard Mistress Munn say exactly the same thing in the past. Of all the people he knew, Mistress Munn was one who always saw the worst in any situation and it always seemed to manifest in her twixt and in betweens. It was as if she had some kind of divining rod down there. He felt sure it was her propensity to always see the negative in life that had instilled in him his fear of so many things when a young boy. He wanted her to say everything was bound to be alright, to have some faith in him but of course she couldn't. That being so however, he was determined not to let her add to his deep sense of foreboding.

'I am sure it can be sorted Mistress,' he said. 'I just need to find the right spell.'

Mistress Munn grunted. 'You have heard about Sir Sockamore?'

The Magician nodded. 'I have.'

'There's someone we won't ever see again. The foolish man was so pumped up by his own self-importance that he thought he could tackle the hags. Men......they always thinks they are superior to us women folk, even the witches of the Greer swamp. I said to your father before he left that I had a stirring in my....'

'Please Mistress let's not go back over the past. There is too much to do now. I need your help. I need you to be my eyes and ears. I want you to go to the castle and then come back and tell me about the man they claim is Moredeath. I want to understand who he is and how he came to be in Naze. I also need any news of Sir Sockamore. You may be right, it may well be the last we shall see of him but I have a strange feeling it might not. The hags are cunning. If they can, they will use him. A man like Sir Sockamore is easily flattered and could be useful in any plan they might have.'

'When shall I go?' Asked Mistress Munn.

'Now Mistress. I have asked the boatman to wait for you.'

'But I haven't finished my monthly wash'

'I am sure such things can wait a day Mistress.'

Chapter Fourteen.

When Sir Sockamore awoke, his head felt as if it had been struck by a pikestaff. He tried to move, but it was as if he were down a deep well and someone had thrown a full suit of armour after him. The clatter and banging were so intense he cried out in his misery. Such was his pain that he could not think. He was sinking in a sea of agony and each stroke, intended to keep him from drowning, added to his burden.

'Gods arse!' He cried 'I am dying...I am not long for this world!'

What had happened to him? How had he come to this place? He tried opening his eyes and was barely able to lift the lids. When he did so the dim light burnt into his eyeballs

'Egads!' he squawked, 'what hellish place have I fallen into?'

Then with a fearful bolt of truth hitting him, he remembered. He was in the Greer swamp. The effects of the scent of the flowers had worn off and reality had kicked in. Why? Why oh why had he been such a fool? How could he even think of going there? Something had driven him beyond his understanding. His lust for power, his lust for the Lady Gossamer, his belief in his manly prowess. The latter of course was understandable, being the manliest man in Naze, the champion of the annual joust three years running, but the other two? Once again, he tried to move his head, but it rattled like a barrel full of stones. 'I must have drunk a gallon of mead last night to have ended up like this,' he said to himself.

He couldn't remember drinking anything other than that disgusting brew the hags had served up. 'Here's to the sisterhood of soup,' he seemed to remember them saying, as they served it up, and he blindly accepted their ridiculous toast. The sisterhood of soup my arse he thought, never would the manliest man in Naze toast to such a thing again!

He was determined to get out of the swamp as soon as he could move. He would tell them he would not require their assistance, thank them for their hospitality, and bid them farewell.

Summoning all his manly qualities. he lifted his head from the straw mattress and managed to sit up. As he did so he experienced an unusual discomfort in his chest, perhaps he had fallen over and bruised himself. At this point he could still not fully open his eyes but was able to peer into the gloom and see that he was in another part of the hag's cave. In this part, the dripping water had created strange formations that were like pillars of salt. Very unnerving to the hungover eye. Thank goodness he was in the peak of manliness, he told himself. There was no way he could have coped with the pain were it not for that.

Having sat for a moment, he used all of his strength to get up and stand. He put his hand out to steady himself. His head was spinning as he felt his way along the wall of the cave and out into the open air. Outside, the light was crippling, but he had to face it. He realised he desperately needed to piss. Not far from the cave he recalled there was a pond. He could have a piss near it and then get a drink, dunk his head in the cold water, and try to revive himself. Sir Sockamore made it to the trees by the pond but tripped at its edge and found himself on all fours staring into the water. For a moment he was taken aback. What he saw was the face of a beautiful young woman. He shook his head. It was a bad idea. The barrel full of stones returned. He clutched his head.

'Gods balls if this isn't the worst ever hangover,' he cried.

He looked back at the water. There she was again. Who was she and how was he seeing her reflection? He was considering this when another overwhelming urge to piss came over him. He managed to clamber up on his feet and reaching down tried to fetch his best friend out of his tabard. It was then he noticed he wasn't wearing his tabard. Instead, he was wearing a finely embroidered silk dress.

'What in the name of....'

His mind went into manly mode. Of course that was what must have happened! He had been out carousing and had deflowered some passing maiden and in their intoxicated state they had exchanged clothes. A night of debauchery often led to unexpected things. It was what being a Knight of Naze was all about, carousing. It didn't help him in his current desperate situation however, where his bladder was bursting, like a pig that couldn't fart.

He rummaged amongst the silk. 'How do you get into these damnable things,' he asked himself. He had never had to ask that question in the past because he had never worn a woman's garb. Eventually, he just hoisted up the dress and plunged his hands into his pants. His fingers urgently searched for 'sir trusty' his best friend. Sir Sockamore froze. He seized up as though he were made of stone when he realised, to his horror, 'sir trusty' was not to be found.

'Oh no!! Oh no!! Please tell me I am dreaming! Please Great Moyen let this be the worst nightmare ever from which I shall wake this very minute.....'

It was no good. As much as he rummaged back and forth 'sir trusty' was gone. Not only 'sir trusty' but also the two knaves! And he needed to piss or he would die. Against all of his instincts he lifted the dress further and squatted above the ground. A fulfilling hiss and a cloud of stream later and Sir Sockamore had had his first demoralising pee as a woman.

The cruel blow left him crumpled on the ground, unable to move. The witches had done this. They had taken his very manhood and turned him into his nemesis, a woman! Everything he had ever been, every action he had ever taken, every attribute he had ever had (and there were many) had been wiped out in one fell swoop. He had been castrated by swearing allegiance to the sisterhood of soup! In his misery he wretchedly remembered their words, 'tomorrow morning you will be a different person.'

How could he not have known? How could he not have foreseen their disgusting plan? What would become of him now. Now that he was no more than a woman? Little more than a beast of burden, a chattel, a thing to be played with, then forgotten. For the first time in his life, he felt helpless, and he cried. A hot lava of tears streamed down his face. He tried to wipe them away but the more he did this the more they came. How shameful, how humiliating, how....womanly!

It was an hour later when he summoned up the fortitude to move. He would go and see the Bloodly Sisters. He would demand they returned 'sir trusty and the knaves' to their rightful owner.

If they refused well he would.....What would he do? It wasn't as if he could chop off their heads, or pierce them with a well-aimed lance. He was powerless in such a situation. If he killed them both he would never get his friends back and how could he face life....as a woman? He needed to be careful not to aggravate them. He would charm them instead. Yes, that was it. Was he not known as the most charming man in Naze? Women fell for his amusing rhetoric every day of the week. The hags were after all just women, weren't they?

Entering the cave, his emotions were fluctuating between a brooding anger, and an equally strong fear of making things worse.

'Hello dearie.'

He turned to where the voice came from. He had expected the cruel rasp of one of the hags, but, instead, whoever said it had the silky slightly husky voice of a mature woman. Indeed the woman facing him was quite charming in appearance, if a little older than the maids he would usually admire.

'How are you this morning?'

'Madam...' he replied. He stopped momentarily. That wasn't his voice, it was the voice of a young woman.

'I'm sorry but I am very confused,' he continued. 'Last night I was a man and this morning...this morning I have been changed into the person you see here by those heinous hags the Bloodly Sisters.'

'Oh how shocking,' replied the woman, 'how on earth did that happen?'

'They tricked me. They told me they were going to help me defeat Moredeath the Bludgeoner and I thought they meant they were going to enhance my natural manly skills and instead look what they have done! I am ruined. They have turned me into......a woman!'

'Dear, dear, that is awful. How did they do that?'

'By great trickery. They got me to eat soup.'

'Soup? Soup doesn't normally do that to a man.'

'Indeed not. I have eaten soup many a time and nothing like this has ever happened. It was sorcery. They got me to pledge to the sisterhood by inviting me to eat and then saying I was joining the sisterhood of the soup. It was a spell don't you see!'

'How shocking. But didn't they do what they promised?'

'How so?'

'Well, am I not right in saying that you were promised you would have a power so overwhelming no man could resist it?'

'They said that but......' Sir Sockamore was suddenly aware of something very familiar in the woman he was talking to. He stared at her and tried to work out what it was.

'Sister!!' The voice came from the back of the cave, from where another good-looking woman appeared. 'You overdid it on the dead Crow in that soup last night,' she continued, and then she stopped in her tracks.

'Ohh, she turned out alright didn't she,' she said, looking at Sir Sockamore.

'Great Moyen!' exclaimed Sir Sockamore, 'you are the hags! You are the ones who tricked me! I demand my manhood back! At once!'

'Now, now dearie. I think you ought to be careful. You don't want to get too upset in your present, delicate state.'

82

'What delicate state?'

'Oh sister, you haven't told her about the phases of the moon yet?'

Just at that moment, Sir Sockamore clasped his belly. It felt as if someone had stuck a knife in his guts.

'What's happening!' He exclaimed.

'Congratulations,' said the first hag, 'you've just properly joined the sisterhood.'

Chapter Fifteen

Mistress Munn reached the castle minutes before midnight. She went straight to the kitchens where her best friend spent most of her time slaving over a hot fire pit cooking meals for the King and his household. She was as usual preparing breakfast, having only just finished clearing up after supper.

'Gladwell!' said Mistress Munn greeting her like a long lost sister.

'Why if it isn't Beth Munn! Oh, I haven't seen you since supper five moons ago. Where have you been?'

'If I told you all of the things that has been going on it, would make your curlies go straight it would.'

'Well, I shouldn't worry about that Beth, no one looks at them nowadays!'

They both laughed.

'Cover my face with bees if I tell a lie, but this has been the most troubling time I have knowed since the Magician's father disappeared.'

'Ohh, that sounds bad. Tell all.'

Mistress Munn gave her friend a run down of the news but omitted to say that Whattlewherrit had returned.

'So you see Gladwell things have been troubling.'

'You think you've got troubles Mistress. I have the Bishop of Nantes and his retinue coming this very week for the wedding celebrations and he can eat a whole table clean by himself, the gluttonous pig. I've only got one pair of hands and the other cooks relies on me to sort them out. Twenty five geese, six boars, ten stags, a hundred and twenty rabbits....I won't go on but you gets the picture. It's more like a pet cemetery than a kitchen in here when the Bishop comes to town. And then, on top of that, there's all the other guests, and that Moredeath...'

'Tell me about him,' interrupted Mistress Munn.'

'Well,' said Gladwell, 'I know this won't go any further than your ears Mistress but there has been no end of bother over the Bludgeoner.'

'Pray tell me more.'

'It seems....and hear I am only repeating the title tattle of the corridors; it seems he is not the man he was made out to be.'

'How so?'

'Well, for one thing, in stature, he is more like a greased hog than a stag. Round as a barrel, and dare I say it. a lot older than the King was given to understand. All this talk about men being affeared of him, they laugh at him in private and rightly so for...' and here Gladwell Jupp leaned into her friend to whisper, 'they say he has had a stiff pinklarry since the moment they found him in the woods five days ago.' She nodded her head and her eyes were widened knowingly.

'Five days!?' Said Mistress Munn.

'Five whole days. I tell you not a lie. As stiff as a well handle.'

'Surely that's not possible?'

'I tell you what, you can come and see for yourself.'

'Oh I don't think.....'

'I have to take him supper. He is usually asleep, so he won't know.'

Despite her immediate reaction, Mistress Munn was nonetheless intensely curious. She told herself it was nothing to do with the man's pinklarry but more to do with his overall looks. After all, hadn't the Magician asked her to find out as much as she could about Moredeath?

Within the hour they were entering Moredeath's bedchamber, and sure enough, as Gladwell Jupp had told her, he was asleep. They could hear him snoring soundly. By the candle Gladwell was holding, they rounded the corner of the room, and, to its flickering light, made their way to his bed.

'Hold this while I pull back the sheets,' whispered Gladwell.

'You mustn't do that,' whispered Mistress Munn.

'You've got to see it, or you won't believe me!' she said, and before her friend could object the sheet was removed. In the candlelight upon the wall an ominous shadow was cast. Mistress Munn stared at the thing blocking the light and gasped. Then she stared at the tattoo above his member, the one that read 'welcome to the club'. Last of all she stared into the sleeping face of Moredeath and her blood felt as if it had drained to her knees.

'We must go!' She whispered urgently.

'There's no hurry he isn't going to wake up.'

'No, we must go,' whispered Mistress Munn.

'What's the matter Beth?' Asked Gladwell.

'Nothing, but I need to get back.'

'I have a confession to make,' said Mistress Munn.

The Magician stared at her and then asked her what she was talking about.

'That day the King ordered you to the castle to tell you about Moredeath and the Lady Gosammer.'

'Yes.'

'Well, I followed you there and I hid behind the curtains at the back of the hall.'

The Magician frowned and then asked 'why?'

'I was curious. I am ashamed to say I wanted to see the What Will Be, and I knew he was going to ask you.'

'How. How did you know?'

'My friend Gladwell. She works in the kitchens and she overheard the King telling his men that he was going to tell you to look in the What Will Be to see what Moredeath was like.'

'So you saw what we saw?' asked the Magician.

'Indeed I did.'

'You saw the man and the woman?'

'Yes, and that's why I rushed back here tonight. The man in the What Will Be is the same one they are now calling Moredeath.'

'Are you sure?'

'Well, I saw him, and I saw his pinklarry, and I never forget a'

'Quite.'

'No, I means I never forgets a face, but more than that, did you notice the writing on his skin?'

The Magician thought for a moment.

'No, I didn't, I mean it was all so quick.'

'Well perhaps, because I wasn't worried as you was, I had a chance to see things different. He has writing on his body just above his pinklarry.'

'What does it say?'

'It says 'welcome to the club.'

'Welcome to the club? What could such a thing mean?'

'I don't know about that Magician but as sure as eggs aren't apples that is the same man.'

The Magician started to pace the room, as he often did when he was thinking hard.

'Could it be that Moredeath and the man we saw in the What Will Be somehow became entangled because we saw them both? That their fates became entwined? Perhaps in that moment the What Will Be was just trying to show me this was about to occur?'

'You means like a prophecy?'

'Well if you put it like that, yes.'

'Ohh I don't... I don't think you should interfere with a prophecy Magician.'

'Well, I can't leave the real Moredeath in the What Will Be can I? He would go on the rampage and kill everyone in sight. Think how unbalanced things would be then. And this stranger, he belongs back where he came from. What if Deathgrin finds out an imposter has taken his place? He would bring his armies to Naze and raze it to the ground. No, I must do what I can to put things right.

The Magician looked at Mistress Munn.

'I think you have another confession to make Mistress.'

She looked confused. 'Another?'

'Sir Godfrey of Merrelay.'

Mistress Munn blushed.

'Is there something you need to tell me about you and Sir Godfrey?'

'I don't think..'

'I know Mistress.'

'He told you?'

'Not directly no. Sir Godfrey would not do that. He would protect you from anything I believe.'

Mistress Munn's eyes began to water.

'It was all a long time ago Magician. Why bring it up now? What good will it do?'

'Because something is not right, and I believe what is happening in the What Will Be is connected to other things. Where did the Holy Wine come from? Where did the other relics come from?'

'Why the Great Moyen sent them. The book of words tells us about such things.'

'Have you read it?'

'Why, no one has read it. Except, of course, for the Bishop of Nantes, and them as is high up.'

'Exactly. So it could say anything and you wouldn't know whether the Bishop is telling the truth.'

'It is not allowed to question the relics, you know that Magician, on pain of death.'

'And immortality Mistress, what do you know of that?'

'You must not ask me any more Magician! I am afeared that the Bishop will find out and should he do so, can you imagine? If someone was immortal and I am not saying they are, but supposing they was, can you imagine what fearful tortures you could impose upon them, and they would never die? The thought of it might leave a person sleepless for years. Tired to their soul. Oh people thinks to themselves how wonderful it might be to live forever, but they never thinks how much of a curse it might be instead!'

The Magician pictured Sir Godfrey and began to understand how the man had aged as he had. Beset by the knowledge that no matter what terrible things might afflict him, he could never get away from them. Never find peace. He looked at Mistress Munn and felt a deep sorrow. Then he had an idea. It was just a germ of an idea, but it might work.

'I will say no more about it, Mistress. You are right, what good would it do to revive the past when the present has so much that has to be dealt with. Whilst you have been at the castle, I have had a chance to study my father's books and although they say little about the What Will Be I have at least armed myself with what magic there is in that respect. I must go back to the What Will Be and try to get Moredeath into his rightful place. I did not think I would ever be saying this, but he must marry the Lady Gossamer. If the imposter did so, then the world would never be right again.'

'When do you go Magician?' Asked Mistress Munn.

'Now,' said the Magician, and grasping the shard, he muttered an incantation. The room lit up with the brightest of lights and when she looked again, he was gone.

Chapter Sixteen

Back in the Greer swamp Sir Sockamore was still lamenting his decision to go there. The hags had turned him into a woman. A beautiful woman he had to admit, but a *woman* nonetheless. His attempts at charming them into reversing the results of eating the soup were to no avail and he put that down to the fact he was no longer a man. Were he still the charismatic Knight of Naze he had once been, then he was sure he could have turned their heads. Now, alas, he was but a beautiful maiden.

'How long does this phase of the moon last,' he moaned clutching his stomach, 'I am in agony!'

'Oh, just a few days dearie.'

'Oh, thank goodness, for I swear that I have not known such discomfort.'

'You'll get used to it.'

'What do you mean?' replied the incredulous Knight.

'Well, it's not just the once, silly boy. Do you know nothing about the nature of maidens?' The good-looking hag just chuckled.

'Believe me madam I have a pretty fair knowledge of maidens. As the handsomest Knight in Naze I..'

'Oh, hear we go,' said the other hag.

'What you knew about maidens was what you wanted to know for your own satisfaction sir Knight and not what they actually were. The stirring spoon does not know how the cooking pot feels, nor the mortar the pestle. You will learn pretty soon the difference between the two though, once we get to Naze.'

'Naze!? How so Naze,' shouted Sir Sockamore 'You are not able to loavo tho Groor swamp, you are tied to the spell that forbids you leaving unless in the company of a ....'

'Woman,' interrupted the second hag.

Sir Sockamore was speechless. So that was what it was all about! The hags had turned him into a woman so that they could leave the swamp. With him in his new body, they could travel wherever they wanted, and wreak havoc throughout the land.

'I will not go with you,' he shouted. 'If I don't go with you, then you cannot leave here.'

'Well sir Knight, that is your choice of course, but we thought you might like your manhood back, and the only way you are going to get that is by doing what we ask.'

'Are you saying you will undo this fearful spell and return my manhood if I go with you.'

'Oh yes dearie, of course. We just need you to do one or two things for us in Naze.'

At this moment the Wolf, who had been lurking in the back of the cave, howled, and pulled at the chain now holding him. Sir Sockamore felt a deep surge of uncertainty rush through him. It was as if the beast were trying to tell him something, to warn him, but then he shook his head and told himself he was imagining it.

'Alright, I will travel with you to the castle, but on one condition. Before the moon turns again, I want my manhood back.'

'That seems reasonable, doesn't it sister?' said one to the other.

'It does sister,' said the other.

'We shall pack to leave this morrow. You sir Knight shall be known as the Lady Sockamore, and we shall be your attendants. You shall be Sir Sockamore's sister, from Wendale.'

'But I don't have a sister in Wendale.'

'Of course you don't you, knucklebone!'

'He's not very bright is he sister?'

'He is still a man, sister, even though he is in a woman's body.'

The journey was not long for, as the sisters reminded the Lady Sockamore, where the Greer swamp happened to be depended upon one's desire to find it or avoid it. The hags wanted it to be close to Naze and so it was. The Lady Sockamore, never one for deep thought when she was Sir Sockamore, could not understand such things, no matter how hard the hags tried to explain it. In the end they gave up and accepted that he / she was as bright as a candle up a boar's arse. The Lady Sockamore rode ahead of the sisters as was befitting of a Lady. Her 'maids' sauntered behind, discussing their wicked plans.

The Lady Sockamore, meanwhile, was getting used to sitting side saddle. It had taken a great deal of argument with the hags before she would agree to such a demeaning thing. In the end they threatened to go back on their promise to turn her back into Sir Sockamore if she refused.

'What lady have you ever seen part her legs for a horse?' asked one of the hags.

'Well actually...'

The hag threw such a look at the Lady Sockamore that she felt herself shake. Now however, having spent an hour or two in the saddle, she was beginning to feel differently about the whole thing. In fact, much to her surprise she was starting to get used to a number of things. For a start the sensation of the silk dress and underwear she was wearing was not at all unpleasant. It was almost diaphanous and yet so clingy, in the nicest possible way. Not like the rough undergarments a Knight would normally wear beneath their tabards and hose. Then there were her hands. She found herself admiring her hands. They were so delicate and refined. She had often looked at the Lady Gossamer's hands and thought how wonderful they were but these, her own, were just as wondrous if not more.

In fact, the more the journey continued, the more things the Lady Sockamore found to like about herself. How strange, she thought, that something so utterly abhorrent as being a woman was beginning to feel familiar and, dare she say it, exciting.

She took the mirror which the hags had given her to tend to her hair out of its bag, and took a long look at herself. She had to say she was extraordinarily beautiful. So beautiful that, if it was possible to marry oneself, she might have proposed that very minute. She pursed her lips and fluttered her eye lashes delicately. Yes, there was no doubt her former self would have fallen hopelessly in love with the Lady Sockamore!

'What's she doing,' said one hag to the other.

'Looking in the mirror,' said the second.

'What for?' replied the first.

'Well I suppose to make sure she looks alright.'

'You don't think that vain popinjay Sir Sockamore is admiring himself do you?'

'No, he probably still can't believe he's a woman, that's all.'

'Well, I don't know sister. It looks to me as if he's paying too much attention to himself.'

'Herself sister! Don't forget we mustn't slip up when we get to Naze.'

'Well alright, herself, but I'm not happy with the way she is behaving. She isn't suffering enough for my liking. We don't want that ass of a man enjoying himself as a woman, do we?'

'She won't when she gets to Naze, and finds out what is in store for her, believe me.'

The two hags laughed so loud that the Lady Sockamore turned around to see what was happening.

'Alright dearie,' said one of the hags, 'just sharing a joke.'

The Lady Sockamore, somewhat confused, turned back. Were hags supposed to have a sense of humour? It was something she had never considered before.

Chapter Seventeen

On returning to the What Will Be, what hit the Magician first was the smell, as thick and pungent as a blacksmith's shop. The air both caught his breath and his imagination. What was it? What could produce such a tainted atmosphere? Then, as his eyes became accustomed to the strange lights all around him, he saw the boxes flying past him, and their strange noises, like beasts roaring in the forest. He backed himself against the nearest wall and stood bewildered as the Kensington night pursued its usual course. The Magician's return to the What Will Be was not at all similar to the first time he visited it. Then it was daylight and in the open countryside surrounding the country fair. An almost familiar scene for the Magician. This time though, it was night, and in the city. It shook the Magician to the core.

Unbeknownst to the Magician, the shard had taken him to the street in Kensington London in which the Stopes Fine Art Gallery was situated. For some reason beyond the Magician's comprehension, the shard had decided to send Moredeath here in order to protect him. His incantation on the combat field had asked the shard to protect the Bludgeoner, no more than that, and here he was, somewhere amongst brightly lit structures, the like of which he had never seen before, or could ever have imagined.

Confused as he was, he turned and tried walking into one, but found himself dazed as something hard smacked him in the face. A few seconds later, when he had recovered, he put out his hand and felt a cold sensation to his touch and something blocking its way, and yet there was nothing there! He could see everything in these strange places but to his amazement could touch none of it. Some remarkable spell had been put upon the place whereby you were only allowed to look but not touch. No wonder the shard had brought Moredeath here for protection. As he stood staring into the brightly lit and brightly coloured places, he noticed someone walking by and his blood ran cold when he saw that they were looking directly at the What Will Be by staring at a piece of slate in their hands. Magicians! They had Magicians in the What Will Be! He was going to follow the other Magician when the shard started tugging at his neck, pulling him on further down the street in the opposite direction.

It was not long before he found himself standing in front of Stopes Gallery and staring at the strange objects inside. From where he stood it was just a large space, all white, except for some peculiar pictures on the walls and odd plinths with shapes on them. Each painting and object had a light shining on it, as though several suns had been captured, and forced to shed their light in just one place. What magic. What brilliant magic. It was then the thought came to him, that perhaps the What Will Be was where Magicians went to live when they died. After all, as he watched the street, every person seemed to be looking into it, with their handheld shards. Perhaps he shouldn't be afraid after all.

He was thinking this when the shard around his neck throbbed and the door of the Gallery opened by itself. He walked in. Once inside, the door shut behind him and the noise of the street vanished. He was able to think clearly again. How did the Magicians in The What Will Be get anything done with so much distraction, so much chaos? It was a question he did not have time to answer because as he progressed into the back of the Gallery he noticed three large shapes. Standing beside one another were two of the most peculiar things he had ever seen, and alongside them, Moredeath the Bludgeoner!

He breathed a sigh of relief as he studied the Bludgeoner. Everything seemed to be in order. He was standing just as he was when he left him, frozen in time, his face fixed in a fierce gaze, as though he was looking at something in the distance. Taking the shard in hand he spoke an incantation out loud. There was a blinding flash of light and when he opened his eyes again, he found himself back in his study as if he had never been away. He looked around. Where was the Bludgeoner? To his horror, Moredeath was nowhere to be seen. The spell had not worked, and he did not know why.

'I can't understand it Mistress,' he said when, a short time later, he sat with Mistress Munn in front of a glowing fire.

'Well, I thinks you should have paid more attention to your studies Magician. Your father...'

'Please do not school me on what I should and should not have done. This is not my doing. I have used the right words in the right order, but something is getting in the way. There is a great deal more afoot than either of us may ever know.'

'I have prayed to the Great Moyen to help us. Lord, my knees are like an Inn keeper's daughters, I have been down on them so much.'

'Well, I don't think the Great Moyen has anything to do with this, or Inn Keepers daughters come to that. I don't know why you of all people still believe all of that claptrap. After all you have been our housekeeper here for many a year, in the house of Magicians. How can you be faithful to both?'

'I likes to keep my options open. You can never be too sure about such things, and magic is not as predictable as I likes things to be.'

Her words, though not aimed directly at him, nevertheless felt uncomfortable to the Magician. They touched his own misgivings about how things were currently going.

'What was it like?'

Her question suddenly broke into his train of thought.

'What was what like?'

'The What Will Be,' she replied.

For a second or two he wondered whether to answer. Should he talk about the What Will Be? Was that as bad as looking at it from a distance? Then he relented. He needed to talk about it. He explained about the invisible force that keeps you away from things. The boxes, that floated by like they were on water, when there was no water there. The lights, like a thousand suns brought down to earth, to light up so many things. The only thing he did not mention were the Magicians, each looking at the What Will Be.' Mistress Munn looked at him, wide-eyed, then her eyes narrowed.

'You wouldn't be pulling my leg, would you? '

'No, I wouldn't Mistress! I am telling you what it was like. You remember the room you saw with the naked man and the woman?'

'Yes.'

'You remember the colours, the light, a strange quality of everything?'

'I do, yes.'

'Well imagine that to be everywhere, but with noise and smells and people.'

'I don't want to Magician, such a thing scares me too much.'

The Magician did not want to admit it, but it scared him too.

'Now tell me Mistress, what has happened since I have been away.

Mistress Munn told the Magician all she knew about the comings and goings at the castle and the preparations for the wedding. Most of the news came from Gladwell Jupp, her friend in the kitchens, who, it seemed, had a network of informers feeding her the juiciest gossip. Amongst which happened to be the fact that the Lady Gossamer, when learning that the Bludgeoner looked nothing like his portrait, had slipped into his room one night to see for herself. She was so distraught she was refusing to come out of her room and demanding to know where Sir Sockamore was.

'Well, of course, no one has heard of him since he left Sir Bloatmore and the imposter in the woods.'

She went on to say that there were rumours that the rout on the Bludgeoners troops had been orchestrated by someone in the castle, but no one would say who it was. The King, according to Gladwell, was furious, both because of the rout and because the Bludgeoner was not the man he had been led to believe. He was heard to say that he believed it to be your fault Magician. That you had put a spell on the Bludgeoner and that it had gone wrong and somehow you turned the Bludgeoner into this shadow of the man he had once been.

'And did he not recognise the imposter from the vision in the What Will Be?'

'Oh no, he did not. By all accounts, the only thing the King remembered was the man's pinklarry doing what they all do when they sees a maiden, and as is so often said amongst my acquaintances, if you've seen one pinklarry you have seen them all.'

'Quite so Mistress,' replied the Magician, not wishing to argue the point.

'They are all out looking for you Magician. You needs to be careful.'

'I am doing my best Mistress believe me, but I have to focus on finding a way to get the Bludgeoner back to Naze. That is my priority. The spell I put upon him will not last forever and if it wears off, there is no telling what damage he might do in the What Will Be.'

Whattlewherrit looked down and stopped. 'Why have you got this Mistress?' asked the Magician, picking up a penis-shaped broach.

'Oh, that is to ward off the plague. Everyone is wearing them. I got one for you too just in case. They say that the plague is already in the North. It has yet to cross the borders of Naze but it will only be a matter of time. I have consulted with the Bees. They needs to know.'

'You know sometimes Mistress I am at a complete loss as to know what you believe in. The Great Moyen, pinklarry broaches, telling the bees. It is such a hodgepodge of superstition and falsehood I hardly know where you stand on anything.'

'Well, it's like I always tell young maidens about courting, if you aren't sure, then keep your legs closed and your options open.'

'But surely you have seen the lies and deception by those who profess to be followers of Moyen. Drinking and whoring, stealing from the poor? And these broaches, how do you imagine a pinklarry, cast in lead, will protect you from the plague? Whoever sold you these is a charlatan. There is no protection from such a disease.'

'Yes, but I don't know that, do I? It hasn't come my way yet, nor yours Magician, and nowadays if you isn't wearing one, then people backs away from you. You know there's them as would say what you do is not all it's supposed to be. I have heard them in the town saying its Hocus Pocus and the like. Especially since the rout took place. I always puts me best foot forward for you but it is hard to convince them as says magic has had its day and belongs to the old times. You know they calls you, 'him as lives across the water.' Like you don't belong in Naze at all.'

The Magician was aware of the fact but hardly put himself in the same category as a pinklarry charm, or a hive of bees, much less a follower of the Great Moyen.

'I need to go to the castle' said the Magician.

Mistress Munn drew breath.

'You can't go there Magician! By the Great Moyen what would give you that idea!'

'I need to see this Moredeath imposter for myself.'

'But it is too risky. If they should catch you, you would be flayed alive or burnt at the stake. The King is beside himself with anger and you know what he is like when he gets all wound up.'

'I realise this, but I have the shard to protect me.'

'A lot of good that is, if you ask me. It's nothing but trouble.'

'I didn't ask you, Mistress.'

Mistress Munn gave the Magician one of her earnest looks, the sort she gave him when he was just a boy, and he had done something wrong.

'This Gladwell Jupp you speak of. How reliable is she?'

'Oh I have known Gladwell since before you was born. When you was a baby and your wet nurse was too sore from your suckling, Gladwell lent her bosoms from time to time. You used to like a bit of......'

'Mistress please! How am I to meet with this woman now you have given me such news. I shall hardly be able to look her in the eye now you have told me this! Sometimes I wonder if you do it out of mischief.'

'There's nothing wrong with an honest bosom Magician. It's only you men what puts an implication on them. We was given them by the Great Moyen to suckle, not for any other purpose. All this jiggling and juggling stuff was invented by men, and you ought to remember that.'

'Can we get back to the subject Mistress? Gladwell Jupp. Would she be able to take me to his room as she did you?'

'I believe she would, but I should ask her first on your behalf. I don't want no harm coming to Gladwell.

'Thank you, Mistress.'

Chapter Eighteen

Kylie Knowles was scrolling through Instragram, looking at pictures of cats, when the glass doors of the Stopes Fine Art Gallery opened and in walked Rick Facile, lead singer of the Army of the Dead, with his manager, Dick Friendly. Facile was wearing his standard Army of the Dead clothing, bright red boots, ripped jeans with dyed blood at the edges making it look like he had been savaged by a bear and a skintight T-shirt with the words 'Money is Meaningless'. His retro Punk Mohican matched his boots and finished the look. The two men stopped by the first exhibit and stared at it as one would a dog dropping in the middle of a pavement.

'Nah,' said Facile, too small.

'Can I help you gentlemen,' asked Miss Knowles, who was not sure whether to press the panic button or not.

'Hello darling,' said Dick Friendly in his most patronising voice. Dick Friendly was wearing a suit and tie and looked like a city banker.

'Mr Facile here is looking to expand his portfolio...'

'I've never heard it called that before' said Facile laughing like a madman.

'He is entering the sculpture market, having already acquired enough paintings for his new house in the country. What can you show us other than your charming self?'

The young woman put down her phone. There was enough grease coming off this guy to keep a kebab shop going. She smiled.

'I will give Mr Stopes a call. Who shall I say is interested?'

'Tell him Rick Facile. I think he will be down pretty soon when he hears who it is.'

Sure enough it was only moments before Francis Stopes, owner of the gallery appeared.

'Gentlemen, how can I help you?'

Dick Friendly looked at the assistant and gave her a knowing wink. She cringed inside.

'Mr Facile here is into modern art. He has lots of pictures for his walls but wants something dramatic for the garden. A bit of sculpture. Not your Greek goddess stuff, he wants something modern. Something outlandish to go with his image.'

'Got to keep the image up mate,' Facile said to the gallery owner, giving him a nudge.

'I think I have the very thing,' said Stopes, the gallery owner, trying not to show his contempt of Rick Facile. 'Come with me.'

He took them around the screen that divided the gallery in two and introduced them to the latest works of Hilary Grant, the hyper-realist fantasy artist.

'Fuck me!' said Facile.

'My word!' said his manager.

'Impressive aren't they? This one here is called The Stinger and as you can see is a 50/1 scale representation of a desert scorpion complete with a fully functioning sting. There is enough venom in this tail to kill a small village in the Cotswolds.'

'Fuck me,' said Facile again, 'that's where my house is! It's fucking destiny.'

'Next to it is Medusa, and as you can see, she is larger than life and has fully functioning snakes in her hair.'

'How do you feed them?' asked Rick Facile.

'Ah, when I say fully functioning what I mean is that they are the latest robot technology. Come anywhere near her when she is set up and those snakes will writhe and they will seek out body heat. Their fangs have real snake venom in them and were you to touch them, you would not survive.'

'Shit!' Shouted Facile.

'Yes, Hilary Grant, the artist, wants the audience of his artwork to feel a sense of menace. His point is that art needs to connect with its audience and summon up deep primal feelings. Nowadays he says people just wander past sculpture without experiencing any connection. Having the possibility of dying a painful death should the Stinger strike you, or the Medusa's head attack you, evokes a visceral reaction to his artwork. You can't walk past a piece without wondering whether it will be the last thing you see.'

'What about this one?' Rick Facile was standing in front of Moredeath the Bludgeoner and was clearly impressed.

The gallery owner seemed momentarily flummoxed.

'Miss Knowles, can you come here a moment.' The young lady appeared.

'What do you know about this?' She looked at Moredeath and shook her head.

'I don't know anything Mr Stopes. I wasn't here yesterday. Mr Carson was looking after the gallery.'

'I see, well I can only assume that Hilary Grant has produced yet another in his series and had it delivered whilst I was away in Paris. Well, I have to say it is magnificent, isn't it? I mean it is so realistic, and dare I say it brutally sexual.' He touched Moredeath's bulging thigh and immediately jumped back.

'My word! He's even managed to replicate the heat of the human body!'

'Let's have a try,' Rick Facile grabbed a handful of thigh and laughed. 'Fucking hell what else is real about this.' Moredeath's eyes flickered and a deep growl came from somewhere within. The four onlookers stepped back.

'Well, before you go any further, I think we ought to confirm with the artist why this particular piece is deadly. I mean it obviously has an axe and a sword but what does it do with them and how?'

'I'll take them all,' said Facile.

'All of them?' Repeated the gallery owner, 'but we haven't discussed price yet and....'

'Mr Facile doesn't have a problem with money, and what he wants he gets.'

'I see, well then, we just need to deal with the paperwork.'

'Talk to him,' said Facile, pointing to his manager. 'I'm going to chat up the chick.'

'So I need these delivered to Hartford Hall. Mr Facile is having an engagement party.'

'Oh how nice.'

'He's getting engaged to Deloris Pops. Everyone will be there, Hollywood celebrities, all of your music royalty, YouTube people, TV Stars. It is going to be the party of the year. So I need these to be there.'

'You have my word. Mr Facile will not be disappointed.'

'Good.'

Meanwhile back in Naze, three elegant women approach the castle gates. The Lady Sockamore went to ride through the gates, forgetting that the guards would not recognise her.

'Halt!' Shouted one of the guards, 'where do you think you are going?' The Lady Sockamore was taken aback and scowled at the man.

'We are going to my....' She stopped herself just in time, remembering she was no longer Sir Sockamore, 'we are going to my brother's apartments' she said.

'And who might that be?' Asked the guard.

'Why Sir Sockamore of course.'

'Sir Sockamore eh? Have you got any documents that show who you are?'

'Of course not, you arrogant little pisspot. Since when does one need documents to enter the castle?'

'Since the Lady Gossamer is getting married and the Bishop of Nantes is in residence, that's when.'

The guard stared at the Lady Sockamore. He called over another guard.

'Do you see any resemblance to Sir Sockamore Ernie?' The other guard laughed.

'Well, I'm trying to imagine him riding sidesaddle Eric. Now let me think. Oh yes, I can see it now, his legs wrapped around the saddle, lance in hand.'

The Lady Sockamore, fired up by the insult, was just about to explode when one of the hags rode forward.

'Hello,' said the first guard, 'who have we here? A handsome woman indeed if I were bold enough to say so.'

'You just did,' said the second guard.

'Oh, so I did.' They both laughed.

'Don't tell me, you are Sir Bloatmore's second cousin, third time removed.' More laughter.

'I am one of the Lady's guardians, and her maid sir.'

'And a fine-looking maid you are indeed,' said the first guard sarcastically. 'I expect there's many a man who would find comfort in your soft bosom on a cold night.' He nudged his friend. The hag smiled but otherwise showed no emotion.

'And what gives you the idea that I wish to hear your opinion on the matter?'

'Oh, every maid wishes to know that she is a man's desire. That is a well-known fact. Just like the flower opens for the Bee, or the doe offers herself for the stag, it is a woman's place in this world to be wanted.'

'Indeed?' said the hag, 'and what in this process does the man provide?'

'Why he provides this!' said the cocky gatekeeper, grabbing his cod piece, but suddenly stopping when he realised all was not as it should be.

'What the Moyen!'

The Lady Sockamore looked on, and for once in her life, realised she knew exactly what the man was feeling.

'What's the matter?' asked his accomplice.

'It's gone! My pinklarry! It's disappeared.'

'Obviously a man doesn't provide that much then,' said the hag and pressed the horse's flanks and walked through the gates.

Out of earshot, but watching the entry of the two hags and Lady Sockamore, were Mistress Munn and another, whose identity was difficult to define, wrapped up as they were in a heavy cloak, with a hood, which covered their face.

'What's going on over there? Who are they Mistress?' whispered the Magician from beneath the hood.'

'I can't say as I knows Magician. Something is amiss. There is all sorts arriving from all over the land to attend the wedding. They looks important don't they? The shard buzzed beneath the Magician's cloak as if trying to forewarn him.

'We must keep an eye on them Mistress, something is not right about them.'

'I shall go and ask the gatekeepers what they knows.'

Mistress Munn strode across the courtyard and found the gatekeepers deep in conversation about something.

'What is the matter?' she asked. Mistress Munn was well known in the castle and the two men looked up at her respectfully.

'Eric here has had a turn Mistress. He thought his pinklarry had disappeared.' The man laughed heartily.

'It had I tell you! There was nothing in my cod piece.'

'There never has been,' smirked the other gatekeeper.'

'I'll say it again, when that woman looked at me, she did something.'

'I think you had what's called an aberration mate. You need to stop drinking so much.'

'Who were they?' asked Mistress Munn.

'Well Mistress, there's the thing. The young pretty one said she was Sir Sockamore's sister, and those with her were her guardians.'

'I see. And you have never seen any of them before?'

'Not a one Mistress.'

'And you are back to normal?'

'I am Mistress,' said the gatekeeper, clutching his loins.

'I see. Well as long as all is back to normal, I suppose that's all you can ask. Where was they going by the way?'

'To Sir Sockamores apartments, Mistress.'

At this Mistress Munn made her way back to the Magician and relayed the news.

'I didn't know Sir Sockamore had a sister?' said the Magician.

'He doesn't. Like you said, somethings not right.'

Mistress Munn and the Magician made their way to the castle kitchens where she knew Gladwell Jupp and her crew would be preparing the night's meal. As soon as they opened the small oak door that was the servant's entrance, they could feel the heat and smell the rich aroma of the cooking meats and the pastry pies. The kitchen was all hustle and bustle, with servants going here and there with steaming pans and arms full of vegetables ready to be cooked. There were geese being plucked in one corner and a pig roasting on a spit over the fire. Amid the apparent chaos, Gladwell Jupp stood commanding the other servants like a military commander might their troops.

'Come on with those pies, I needs to have them done so as they's ready before the geese! You over there move yourself and take them pans to the pantry! Lawks a mercy if this meal doesn't get done I shall have you all before the King his self for a flogging.'

'Mistress, I think perhaps we have come at the wrong time,' whispered the Magician.

'Don't worry Magician, it is always like this. Gladwell knows how to run her kitchens.'

The Magician was not at all sure interrupting the formidable Mistress Jupp was the right thing to do, but on the other hand, the sooner he got to see the imposter who was pretending to be Moredeath the better.

'Gladwell!' said Mistress Munn, beckoning her over to where they stood.

'Beth, what brings you here?'

'An urgent matter. I would not have come at such a time were it not so important.'

'What can be the matter, and who is this?' she replied looking at the still hooded Magician.

'Say nothing, nor show any sign of surprise, but it is none other than Whattlewherrit.'

Gladwell Jupp drew breath as though she had been plunged into icy water.

'Whattlewherrit? In my kitchen? What brings the fugitive Magician to the castle of all places! Don't you know how dangerous it is?'

'I know full well the danger of the situation but there is more at stake than you can ever imagine. If the marriage of the Lady Gossamer takes place, and is consummated, then the world as we know it will change forever.'

Mistress Jupp looked at the hooded Magician, then back at her friend.

'What is it you want of me?' she asked.

'We needs to see the Bludgeoner.'

'By the Great Moyen you are indeed travelling a dangerous path if you thinks it is safe to be around at this time. There is guards everywhere and the whole castle is a hustle and bustle with important people come for the ceremony. Indeed, the Bishop of Nantes and his retinue arrived last night. It is a veritable cooking pot of mixed vegetables all a boil. You needs to be careful you don't get scalded.'

Gladwell Jupp turned around and shouted some orders to the cooks and kettle boys.

'Give me time to sort this meal, and I will help you. Night is the best for visiting the Bludgeoner. Things calm down and with the going of the light we can walk among the shadows easier. You can hide in this pantry meanwhile. I am the only one as is allowed in there. She showed them into the tiny room where the two of them settled, as best they could, for the wait.

Chapter Nineteen

Night came, with a restless sky blocking the Moon and threatening rain. There was unease in the air as three shapes dodged in and out of the shadows in the corridors of Naze castle. Down in the main hall the King and Lady Gossamer, together with a hundred guests, were finishing their meals. On the first floor, tar torches belched out their greasy light and gave what little substance they could to the night.

Since his arrival at the castle, Kenny Catlin had been confined to bed, unable to move. His continuing nightmare had traumatised him so much he could barely stand, unlike his penis which remained ever alert and was giving him a hard time.

It had been three days since he had been found in the forest amongst the corpses of Moredeath's men, but to Kenny Catlin it felt like an eternity. The 'trip', which he was convinced he was on, seemed neverending, and was full of strange people coming and going, looking at him, and talking about things he did not understand. He should have read the full script. The film script 'The Book of Words', may well have given him the answer to this nightmare. Everything that was happening had to do with that shit fantasy film score and what he had read before he went to Klines that afternoon. As usual he was lazy and just scanned the thing. There were Knights, and dragons, and quests, and all the usual bullshit fantasy stuff, and somehow, because of what he had sniffed up his nose before this all happened, it had fucked with his brain. But what was worse was that his body had given up. No matter how he tried he had no energy to do anything. He was captive, in a state of shock.

It was how, when he awoke that very morning, and found the man putting the leeches on his dick, all he could do was to tell him to 'fuck off!' He didn't fuck off. Instead, he continued.

'Ignore him,' said the King, 'carry on.'

'I think this will help, your Majesty,' said the man as the slimy worms stuck their teeth into Catlin's favourite organ.

'I hope so apothecary, we must get his fever down, and this,' he said pointing to Catlin's penis.

'He can't show up at the wedding ceremony with his pinklarry protruding. It's not etiquette.'

'Quite, your Majesty.'

'If I could get my hands on that Magician, I would have him burnt at the stake for this! This lard of a man is not going to be able to protect the Kingdom. And what of my daughter? What is she going to say when she sees him? This is not the Bludgeoner to whom she was betrothed. He has been shrunk and emptied of his vitality; all his muscle has been turned to flab. Look at him, would you be afraid of that?'

'I would not Sire,' muttered the apothecary, hoping he was saying the right thing.

'You need to get him standing. He needs to be able to attend the ceremony tomorrow whatever happens. I can't have the Bishop of Nantes and all the other guests thinking they have been brought here for nothing.'

'I will do my best Sire.'

'Do it man, or you will lose your head.'

The apothecary nodded sadly.

If the apothecary was not enough, then came a tailor and his assistant to measure him for his wedding garb.

'If we are to adjust his tabard and hose by tomorrow morning it is going to take all day. I mean just look at this.'

The tailor held up the tabard that Kenny Catlin had arrived at the castle in.

'How does this bear any relationship to that?' He asked pointing to Catlin.

'I mean it's like asking the Lady Gosammer to walk around in a tent. The girth of the man may be sufficient to fill it, but in all the wrong places. I can feel the pain in my fingers from the needle already. To alter this in order to get it to the right size will wear me out; and this fabric, I swear it is made from recycled sailcloth it is so rough. I am not used to such course material.'

'What are we going to do about his hose with...with?' Asked the assistant pointing at Catlin.

'Ohh don't even ask. The King assures me that the apothecary is dealing with it. They say it has been like that for three days now. Heaven help the Lady Gossamer if she is expected to down his expectation.'

There had been maids and cooks and cleaners coming and going all day whilst he lay immobile, shouting abuse as best he could, and now night had fallen and he was worn out. Despite his best attempts at staying awake, his eyes closed and he fell into a dream. His dreams made more sense than the reality in which he found himself. It was in this state that the door opened and three shadowy figures entered the room.

'He's over there,' whispered Mistress Jupp. They crept over and lighting the lamp Mistress Munn had brought, shone it upon his face.

'Do you not recognise him Magician?' she said.

'I cannot say Mistress.'

'Then what about this,' she pulled back the sheet. The Magician backed off.

'It looks vaguely familiar,' he replied. It wasn't anything he saw that made him uncomfortable, however. It was the shard. Every time he moved forward towards Catlin he felt the same feeling he had felt at Merrelay castle. A vague humming and the prickle of young nettles on his skin.

'I think I have seen enough,' he said, but in his mind he was thinking more of the shard and it's reaction. There was definitely something about the man that was not of his world. It was just as he was considering this that the door began to creak open. Mistress Munn grabbed his arm and that of Mistress Jupp and pushed them towards the curtain that separated the room. They watched as the dark shape of someone entered the room. The shape crossed the room to the bed and took a small vial from beneath their cloak. They pulled the stopper and gently turning Catlins head poured some substance into the ear of the sleeping Catlin.

'There my dear, let that be an end to you. I should have known never to trust Sir Sockamore to rid me of your presence. But he at least has got his comeuppance. The Bloodly Sisters will have seen to him and now I am free once more from this putrid alliance.'

The shadowy figure left the room and once the door was closed, they came out from behind the curtain.

'That were the Lady Gosammer's voice!' said Gladwell Jupp.

'Indeed it was,' replied Mistress Munn.

'She has poisoned him!'

'I believe you are right. We need to leave at once or else we will be judged the villains of the crime!'

They left the room and made their way out of the sleeping quarters of the castle, and back down to the relative safety of the kitchens.

'I need to go back into the What Will Be Mistress'.

'You be careful Magician.'

'I shall. I need you to keep an eye on the comings and goings at the castle whilst I am away. If, as we fear, the Lady Gosammer has poisoned the imposter, there will be all hell to pay. No one will suspect the real culprit. The King will be looking for someone to blame.'

'And it will be you Magician, mark my words. He will say it is to do with your magic, you can be sure of that.'

'Maybe Mistress, maybe, but if I can get Moredeath himself back here in time, then the balance will be restored. Now I want you to pay particular attention to Lady Sockamore and her maids. There is something about them I fear. The shard was not happy when they appeared.'

'I shall do that Magician. But how and where shall we meet again?'

'I will let you know as soon as I am able. In the meantime be careful.'

Chapter Twenty

On his third visit to the What Will Be the Magician found his way straight to the art gallery where he had left Moredeath. As before, the shard opened the door and in he walked. The What Will Be still smelled strange but he was getting used to lights and the sounds. He crept through the room, making his way to the wall that divided it, and rounded the corner to where the Bludgeoner was. His blood sank to his shoes when, turning the corner, he found himself confronted by an empty space. Where there had been two strange artefacts and the Bludgeoner, now there was nothing.

He looked around every space and even opened the doors at the far end of the room but there was no sign of the Bludgeoner. His worst fear had come to pass. The spell must have worn off and the Bludgeoner was loose on the streets of the What Will Be, carving his way through anyone unfortunate to come close by. His heart sank. He had failed, and now the rift between his world and the What Will Be would never be mended.

Straightaway his father came to mind. As if standing behind him, he heard his voice telling him to keep away from the What Will Be and only to use the shard in the direst emergency. Why hadn't he listened? Why had he been so stubborn and so sure of himself? He could have just let Moredeath die in the hail of arrows, but no, he had to show he was clever and had power, to prove he was greater than the Bludgeoner. How wrong he had been. If Moredeath had died, who would have cared other than the King? Certainly not the Lady Gossammer. It was pride that had undone him. He wanted to let the Bludgeoner know how powerful he was, and now look, here he was, lost in the What Will Be, whilst back in Naze what he had done had so many repercussions, he dare not think.

He left the gallery and stepped out into the rain. The boats without a river now actually had a river of sorts and were slushing by, sending small waves onto the walkway. People were running and carrying personal tents on sticks under which they sheltered from the rain. So many new things to marvel at, and yet nothing felt marvellous when he knew he had failed.

As he passed by the strange buildings with their protective screens, a thought came to his mind. What if he didn't go back? What if he stayed in the What Will Be? What difference would it really make? Apparently, he was a useless Magician and one with a price on his head. As Mistress Munn had told him only recently, he was defined as 'him who lives over the water' by the people of Naze, as if he were some sort of oddity. Perhaps that was the truth of it. He was an oddity. It hadn't struck home whilst Cornelius was alive, for there were the two of them, but once Cornelius disappeared, his own isolation became more apparent, and he began to question his very reason for being. Strange questions came to mind, like what is a Magician's place in the world? Should a Magician change things, or should he try to keep the world as it is? Does magic have its own purpose? Or is it simply at the command of those who know how to summon it? And if so, isn't it a most dangerous thing that should be discouraged? Sometimes he would talk to Mistress Munn about these thoughts, but she was no help.

'You can give a poor cook the same ingredients as a good one and they will both make a pie but only the good cooks works out right,' she once said. What a wretched pie he had managed to cook!

He walked late into the night, over bridges that spanned a dark and ominous river flowing beneath the arches, as though it was itself alive. Everywhere he went, people were looking into the What Will Be. How could it ever be stable with so many curious minds poking and prodding at it? And the thought then came to him, if he was in the What Will Be, then which What Will Be were they looking at? Were there endless worlds he was unaware of? His mind refused to even think of it. Tired and disconsolate he ended up on a park bench and lay his head down to rest.

It was morning when he awoke and felt his tired bones and muscles rubbed sore by the solid slats of the bench. He eased himself up, just as two women went running by, plugged into the What Will Be by strings coming out of their ears. Not only that but they were talking to the What Will Be and it was talking back! The sense of despair that had washed over him the night before returned once again. What kind of Magician was he if he could not talk to the What Will Be? Where did they get their power and how was it that everyone knew magic? He was hungry and looked eagerly at the ducks and geese on the lake in front of him. He was not a cook by any means but he had seen a goose plucked and gutted and knew that over an open fire they could be roasted. For a moment he seriously considered the implications of capturing a goose, plucking it, gutting it, starting a fire and then waiting for it to cook, and then his mind overrode his ambition with a dose of realism. Who did he think he was fooling? He could not even cook an honest egg.

Taking to his feet again, he wandered out of the park to where the crowds were beginning to mill about, and it was not long before he noticed a man sitting in front of one of the buildings. He was not smartly dressed like everyone else. In fact he looked as dishevelled as himself and as he sat there people were throwing money into a box at his side. Perhaps, thought the Magician, that was what you did to get money in the What Will Be? You sat on the ground and that was a sign you needed money. If he had money, he could buy some food. So as soon as he found a place far enough away from the other man he sat on the floor and looked hopeful. Nothing happened. Then he realised he needed a box. On the street corner there was a pile of old rubbish waiting for collection and he took a spare box and sat back down with it. To his amazement moments later someone threw a coin into it, and then another one. He did not know how much money he had or what it was worth but after a while he scooped it up and began walking the streets again. It wasn't long before he saw some people leaving a building holding food in their hands and eating it. He decided it was time to test his worth. He walked into the shop and, standing in line, waited, whilst looking at the pictures of all sorts of foods.

When his time came, he pointed to a Double Big Whopper Max, and held out his handful of money. The assistant looked disgusted. It was as if they had never seen money before. They took it under protest and handed over the bun. The Magician took it out on the street and bit into it. It was foul! There was no taste to it, and not only that, as soon as you started to eat it, it just vanished into thin air. Perhaps living in the What Will Be was not going to be that easy.

He was passing a shop when he noticed What Will Be screens, dozens of them all showing the What Will Be. He wandered in and to his amazement not only were they showing the What Will Be but the What Will Be was speaking to him.

'Now to showbiz news,' said the What Will Be, 'The engagement party of the year is taking place tonight at Rick Facile's sprawling Cotswold home. Rick is getting engaged to Deloris Pops and the stage is set for a fantastic night in more than one way. The themed party is based on Ye Merry Olde England. Rick is out to make a splash and to show off the latest acquisitions in his extensive art collection with a stunning set of sculptures by none other than Hilary Grant the hyper realist fantasy artist.' The screen shot scanned the The Stinger, The

Medusa, and to the Magicians amazement, Moredeath, at which point the Magician dropped his Double Big Whopper Max and, walking forward to examine the screen, trod it into the carpet.

'Excuse me sir but we don't allow food in the shop,' said a voice. The Magician did not hear it. He was transfixed. How did Moredeath get into the What Will Be and how could he reach him now?

'Sir I am afraid I shall have to ask you to leave....'

'Where is that?' Asked the Magician and how do I get there?'

'That is Rick Facile's home. Everyone knows Rick Facile. He is world famous.'

'World famous?' repeated the Magician.

'Look I really must insist...'

'How did he get in there?' Asked the Magician.

'In where?'

'In the What Will Be.'

The Magician pointed to the screen.

'I think I need to call the police. You obviously have a problem.' The man walked away, pulled out his mobile, and dialled the police. The Magician meanwhile pulled out the shard, pointed it at the screen, and once again he whispered an incantation, hoping this time it would work.

Chapter Twenty One

The Lady Gossamer sat at her sewing in the early morning light . Her embroidery was of the heraldic shields of all of the eligible Knights of Naze, all bar that of Sir Sockamore whom she loathed and who would never appear in her work.

'That is a pretty task and well done my dear,' said her father, who was standing behind her, admiring her work. 'All the young Knights of Naze. All bar one I think?'

'You are correct father.'

'I shouldn't start on him too soon,' said the King. 'There has been no news from the Greer swamp so there may not be any need. What encouraged you to undertake such a task my dear?'

The Lady Gosammer found herself shifting in her seat. What would be the outcome should she tell her father the truth? The honest truth that every Knight on the screen she was embroidering marked a night spent with the owner of the shield. All twenty-one of them had fallen for her charms and Sir Gladmore whose shield she was currently sewing had lain beside her in her bed only last week.

'Well father, I thought it would be a good wedding gift for Moredeath. It could hang on our bedroom wall and remind him of the dynasty of which he has become a part.'

'What a splendid idea daughter. And I take it from your offer of such a gift you are now resolved to approach the impending nuptials with a positive attitude? I know he would not have been your first choice for a husband, but the needs of the Kingdom always must come first.'

'So I was taught from childhood father.'

'Quite so. And had I had a son....but let me not dwell on might have beens.'

'Perhaps if you had not had my mother's head, removed she would have been better able to produce a male heir. It is difficult to produce progeny without a head.' The bitterness in the Lady Gossamer's voice cut the air cold.

'There there, daughter we have been through all of this before. Your mother was a difficult person and her close acquaintance with some of the Knights of Naze brought disrepute upon the crown.'

The Lady Gossamer bit her lip, but in her mind she thought her father's hypocritical defence of his actions despicable. Had he not Sired numerous offspring out of wedlock? Too many to mention but then he was a man. It was different for men, especially when they were kings.

'Let us move on from this subject, it is like a thornbush catching the clothes of our otherwise close relationship. Tomorrow all will be put right when the bedsheets will reveal the union between Naze and the Bloodlands and we shall become invincible.'

The Lady Gossamer said nothing, but only thought of the poison she had poured into the Bludgeoner's ear the previous night and how in a matter of hours her father would find his plans ruined. Not only that but she had other plans of her own. Having bedded all bar one of the Knights of Naze she had now chosen who would be her long-term bed mate and she would force her father into agreeing a marriage with him on the basis that the Bludgeoner was now dead. If the Kingdom was to have a strong heir, then that man was going to be her choice, and not her father's.

'Have you spoken with the Bludgeoner this morning father?' She asked coyly.

Her father grunted. The question clearly disturbed him.

'I have not but the apothecary is to see him first thing.'

'And how is that going?' she asked, 'has he managed to rid him of the ill humour from which he has been suffering?'

'He is doing his best and knows that his head is on the block if he does not find a way of restoring the Bludgeoner to full health. I have every faith in his skill.' Despite the King's positive words his voice failed to match their intent.

'And what if he cannot?' asked the Lady Gossamer.

The King breathed deeply and strode towards the window.

'You cannot marry a man who is unable to stand excepting his pinklarry. A Kingdom cannot be held together by a bedridden sluggard with a hard-on. Whatever that Magician did to the man, it will take a great deal of undoing. But Kings need to look further than the limits of an ordinary man's scope and point of view. The Bludgeoner has a father, and Deathgrin will surely revenge his son's diminished state if the marriage does not happen, and we refuse to abide by the marriage contract. Think on it daughter, Naze at war with the Bloodlands. We would be crushed and put to the stake, all of us, if you do not marry the Bludgeoner.'

The Lady Gossamer found it difficult to swallow the lump that had developed in her throat. In her haste to rid herself of an unwanted suitor she had not bothered to look beyond her own needs.

'Surely the Knights of Naze would be able to....'

'My dear daughter, being but a woman you have never seen a pack of hounds put upon a stag. I can assure you it is not for want of the beast trying to fight back that's it is overwhelmed. Deathgrin and his men would take us apart just as the hounds do the stag. It is bad enough that the rout took place. Somehow I need to place the blame for that upon one of Deathgrin's enemies. Word needs to find his ear that they tried to stop the marriage because our allegiance would have been too strong for their liking. Such things can be done, there are ways for that to be secured. But his diminished state that is another matter.'

The Lady Gossamer put down her needle and thread. What had she done! She had condemned them all to all-out war with the fiercest of enemies. She must own up. The sooner her father knew the better. She was about to confess when there was a knock on the door.

'Who is that?' shouted the Lady Gossamer.

'Tis me your Ladyship, Appleyard the Apothecary.'

'Go away!'

'I am sorry your Ladyship but I need to see the King. I have important news that cannot wait.'

'Come in Appleyard!' shouted the King. In walked Appleyard, a lithe man whose hose betrayed a want of thigh. The Lady Gossamer felt herself feel faint, for surely he had come to give news of Moredeath's death.

'I am sorry to bother your Majesty's, but I felt you had to know.'

'Know what?'

'Well your Majesty, the Bludgeoner, he has made a remarkable recovery.'

The Lady Gossamer gasped and began to choke. The King looked at her, slapped her back soundly, and told the apothecary to continue.

'Last night I paid the Bludgeoner a visit, and bled him, and I have to say I had no hopes of ridding him of his malaise. I was certain he would die in the night. Then this morning I visited him and could not believe my eyes. He was up and about and his....pardon my mentioning this in your company my Lady, his

116

pinklarry was no longer reaching for an imaginary blossom. Indeed, he was cursing and flailing around the room saying things no one could understand but as hail and hearty as if someone had prescribed him a tonic in the night.'

'And you take no credit for this apothecary? How so?'

'I would do so were it my doing Sire but if I was to say so then it would be a lie. Whatever happened came not from my hands.'

'Well you are a remarkably honest man, apothecary and remarkably stupid for being so. I would have rewarded you handsomely for your success but now you maintain no part in it, you deserve nothing. Be gone.'

The Lady Gossamer was feeling giddy and confused. She had administered the strongest of poisons and instead of killing the man it had revived him! How so? Was this man, as they had all said, like a horse in his constitution? Her head was in turmoil. On the one hand she was glad that Naze would no longer be razed to the ground by Moredeath's father Deathgrin, but on the other now she would have to marry the man. Was there no pity in circumstance? Were the scales of life always balancing one evil against another?

'Well my daughter, it looks like the nuptial bed will be heated with passion after all.' The King laughed. 'Mind you, you have to hope that the Bludgeoner's pinklarry makes a showing on the night, now that he has temporarily lowered the flag so to speak.'

The Lady Gossamer's heart shrank at the thought of that bloated carcass thrashing away at her. After all, she had seen full well what was on offer whilst administering the poison to his ear. There must be something she could do to save the day.

'I am off to see the Bishop of Nantes my dear. Keep sewing, you only have twenty-four hours if you are to give this to your intended as a wedding gift.' The Lady Gossamer picked up her needle and stuck it in the back of her hand hoping the pain would temporarily stop her mind from imploding.

Chapter Twenty Two

The two hags and the Lady Sockamore were ensconced in the quarters of Sir Sockamore. Having already had an altercation at the Castle gates, the hags had decided it was best for them to keep a low profile until the next day, the day of the wedding. It was then that they would unleash their dastardly plan, of which they had yet to inform the Lady Sockamore. They had decided to leave it to the last moment to inform her that she was there to seduce the Bludgeoner and ruin the wedding plans. All in all, they both thought it a great plan. Not only would it put the land of Naze in turmoil but it would also mean Sir Sockamore, in his new guise, would at last know what it felt like to be a woman at the hands of a man. There was nothing more the hags would enjoy than to know that the Bludgeoner was beating the dust from my Lady's bedstraw with her underneath. Beyond this wicked plot, they had a more important task to undertake, namely finding the little turd of a Magician, Whattlewherrit. It was to this end that they planned to pay his home a visit to see if that was where he was. They would do so the very same evening.

'You, my Lady, will attend the feast,' said one of the hags. 'You will help to set the stage for tomorrow's activities.'

The Lady Sockamore was confused.

'How so?'

'Oh, you have a very important part to play.'

'Indeed, and what might that be?'

'You are skilled in the art of seduction are you not?'

'Indeed,' replied the arrogant Lady, 'when I was myself and not in this guise, I was said to be irresistible to the ladies.'

'Only if you paid them,' muttered the second hag.

'Shush sister, let us be grateful that our sister here knows of the art of seduction.'

'And why is that, pray tell,' asked the Lady Sockamore.

'We have a little task for you this night sister. We need you to seduce Moredeath he Bludgeoner.'

'I will do no such thing!' protested the Lady Sockamore. 'What on earth makes you think I would go anywhere near a man for that sort of thing let alone the Bludgeoner! He is said to be a beast in men's clothing.

'That is the bargain you signed up to when you became a sister of the soup. You wanted to stop the Lady Gossamer marrying the Bludgeoner ,am I not right?'

The Lady Sockamore said 'yes but.....'

'You wanted power over all men, was that not true?'

'Yes perhaps I did but...'

'You wanted to become King is that not right?'

'It is but...'

'Then you shall have all of these things, but perhaps not in the way you imagined you might achieve them. Our desires seldom allow room for reflection on the path we need to take, to attain our goals. We see the things we want but in looking up to reach them, miss our footing and fall into the midden of our craving. That, or else we have to tread upon the carcasses of others who have fallen because they got in the way. Nevertheless, if we are to succeed, we go on undaunted.'

'There is a big difference between falling into a midden or putting your foot on a rotting carcass, and lying abed with a man, especially a beast like Moredeath.'

'There you are sister. I told you it wouldn't be long before our sister came to see the terrible plight a maiden faces.'

'You aren't taking me seriously!' The Lady Sockamore stamped her feet. 'How on earth do you think I should bed down with a man when I am one!'

'I think you had better take a look in your undergarments and refresh your memory dearie.'

'You may have turned me into a woman, but I still have the feelings of a man. Can't you understand the nature of a man is not something that changes just because he looks like a woman! Inside this beautiful and utterly attractive creature you have made me beats the heart of a Knight. Once the handsomest man in Naze!'

The first hag turns to the second.

'Did you remember to put the toad's bane in the soup sister? I told you about that at least three times.'

'I don't know if I did sister.'

'Well, that would explain things if you didn't.'

'Stop! You are toying with me. You know full well what you have done. You want me, the handsomest man in Naze, to feel detestable. You want me to know what it is like to be ravaged by some brute. Well I just won't do it. I will not let his hands or his pinklarry anywhere near me, and that is an end to it.'

The sisters looked at her, and the second hag just said, 'we'll see.'

When night drew its curtain upon the day and the river ran silver with the light of the nearly full moon, two figures made their way to the quayside. There, they hired a boatman to take them across the water. It was a cold night and the boatman shivered as they went on their way. Somewhere in the distance they heard the cry of a wolf and an answering call. Apart from the slap of oar on water, and the coughing of the boatman as his lungs became accustomed to the chill of the night, there was little to be heard until the boatman spoke halfway across the channel.

'There ain't no one there.' He said. There was no response. 'The Magician, well he's long gorn and his servant Mistress Munn she's back at the castle. Everyone's there tonight for the feast. What would you fine ladies be doing crossing the water on a night like this, to visit no one?'

The two hags looked at one another.

'Tell me boatman how long have you been at your trade?' Said the first hag.

'Oh I suppose nigh on forty year give or take a year. I ain't much on figures.'

'So you have seen a lot of things in your time on the water.'

'Oh I'll say. Mostly pisspots going about their thieving businesses. Taking tutherun's money. But I have also dragged many a corpse from this very straight. But, and here's the rub, never have I taken two pretty and elegant ladies across the water to see someone what ain't there and that makes me wonder..'

'You should spend less time wondering and more at your oars my man.' The second hag intervened.

'Sister we are being less than honest with this man. He deserves some answer.' The first hag scowled but said nothing.

'We have come to the wedding of the Lady Gossamer to Moredeath the Bludgeoner as servants to Sir Sockamore's sister.'

'Oh, that pisspot,' said the boatman instinctively.

'If you are referring to Sir Sockamore then I am inclined to agree with you my man. However, we serve her Ladyship and cannot be heard to express such a point of view for fear of the consequences. As to our journey tonight, our purpose is not to visit but rather leave something for when the Magician returns. Without revealing the nature of our Lady's business, which I am sure you will understand is not for the likes of anyone else to know, we just need to visit the Island and then return before the tide turns.'

'He ain't coming back' said the boatman dismissively. 'If he does the King will have him hung drawn and quartered.'

'Well, that is as it might be, but who knows the future?'

Back in Naze, a mile across the water, Mistress Munn was making her way across the cobbled courtyard by the castle keep. She had been tasked by Whattlewherrit to keep her eyes and ears open and was doing just that. In her wicker basket she had provisions from the kitchen and was taking them to the guards on watch around the castle. If there was one way of keeping abreast of the news, apart from her good friend Gladwell Jupp, then it was through the guards who gossiped more than the fishwives on the docks. 'Feed a man food and compliments, empty his loins, and laugh at his jokes, he will be putty in your hands,' Gladwell used to say and she was right. Not that Mistress Munn had any intentions of going anywhere near any man's plums at her time of life. But food was a different matter. Give a man a good pie on a cold night and he will soon tell you whatever you need to know about goings on at the castle.

It was as she approached a low part of the battlements that she chanced to look over to the Magician's island, and stopped in her tracks. Though it was hard to see much by the light of the moon, she could make out the shape of the Magician's tower and at the foot of it, a small twinkling star moved. At first, she thought she was imagining it, but she blinked and sure enough it was still there. Someone was walking with a lantern. She was sure of it now. Someone had travelled the water and landed on the Magician's island! She stared in horror to think that anyone would be so bold as to do such a thing. No one would do that unless it was on the business of the King, or else by invitation of Whattlewherrit. She needed to find out who it was and what their business must be.

Taking her provisions, she made her rounds, knowing it would be at least an hour before the boatman could row his way back. There was time to finish her chores before making her way down to the quay to find out who was returning.

Chapter Twenty Three

Her night-time rounds had proved fruitful. The information she had secured enabled her to piece together the goings on at the castle. At the cost of twenty pies, she had learned enough to know that the Bishop of Nantes had planted his spies throughout Naze weeks before his arrival and they had been gathering information for the Bishop that he might use against individuals to bend them to his will.

The Bishop was all about coercion and control and his fearful commissions dealt swift and awful punishments to those seen as opposing him in any way. Many a man and woman had died in cruel torture or at the stake for opposing the Bishop. Mistress Munn shuddered when she thought of such things.

As for the Bishop himself, he was a vindictive pompous hypocrite who, rumour had it, had a preference for things better not spoken about. He was a dangerous man and Mistress Munn was well aware of his hatred of the Magician and all he stood for.

Then there was the astonishing news about the pretender. The man thought to be the Bludgeoner had somehow made a miraculous recovery and, according to various guards around the castle, was causing mayhem. Ranting and raving and talking about all sorts of things no one could understand, and demanding to be taken back to his own world.

Mistress Munn knew his secret but dare not speak of it. Who would believe her if she were to say he had arrived from the What Will Be? If any of the Bishop's spies caught wind of such a thing she would be in chains within hours and tortured until she confessed she was a witch. The Bishop would have no talk of the What Will Be. It was forbidden to entertain such a thing, even though he knew, in private the King had made use of the Magician's powers to see it.

Finally, she had caught up on the fact that his sister and her maids had settled into Sir Sockamore's apartments but had not been seen since. It was as if they did not want to draw any attention to themselves and that in itself was unusual, given that one of the court's main attractions was to parade oneself in one's finery and, if possible, gain favour with the King. Whattlewherrit was right when he pointed them out and said something was wrong with them. She needed to find out exactly what that was.

At the turning of the hour, she made her way down to the quay and, in the shadows, waited for the boatman and his passenger to arrive. It was to her surprise that when the boat moored, not one but two individuals disembarked. Even by moonlight she could see by their clothing they were women. Ducking in and out of the shadows she followed them as they drifted through the streets leading up to the castle, and with her keen sense of hearing, homed in on their whispered conversation.

'What if the Magician does not come back sister,' said the first.

'Then we shall have to find him. Someone must know where he is. I suspect that dried-up woman, his maid, would know.'

Mistress Munn's hackles rose at their description of her.

'They say she is as close to him as anyone. A gossipy woman by all accounts and a bit simple to boot.'

At this point Mistress Munn had to grip her fists tight together to prevent herself confronting the woman and giving her a piece of her 'simple' mind.

'Some say she knows everything that goes on sister. It would be good to find her and use a little persuasion. Squeeze some information from her dull head. Sir Sockamore hates her almost as much as he does the Magician. He would not be averse to doing some squeezing in his new role.'

The woman chuckled and for a moment there was something old and wheezy about it, almost a cackle. It sent a shudder down Mistress Munn's spine. What did she mean when she spoke of Sir Sockamore's 'new role?'

'She has other things to do first sister. Let us not divert her from our original plan. Tonight, we must visit the castle kitchens and set in motion the seduction of Moredeath. Then we shall deal with Whattlewherrit, if of course he does not come back and find our little note.'

The two sisters both started laughing and once again it was a deep rattling cackle, not at all befitting the voice of refined ladies in waiting. Mistress Munn's soul turned cold at the sound, which was more animal than human. Much was amiss with these two, she thought.

Gladwell Jupp was up to her arms in smoke and steam. Stirring pots and basting meat. Her once-white apron was smothered in swipes from her greasy hands. Everything was in full swing for the evening's activities and there was more sweat fallen into the evenings meals than she would like to admit. 'Everything adds to the flavour,' she would say, 'except a sneeze. I don't tolerate those in my cooking even if it is for the Bishop of Nantes.' It was a surprise to her when she looked up and found her old friend, Mistress Munn, standing by her side.

'Gladwell, I must speak to you,' she said urgently.

'Oh Mistress, now's not the time I'm afraid, as you can see I am up to my armpits in victuals.'

'This cannot wait,' said Mistress Munn.

'Well you can talk and I will listen but there is no time for me to stop.'

She turned her head away from Mistress Munn and shouted across the kitchen, 'get them pastries out of the oven before they scorches and turns black as a Moorhens arse!' All around was clatter and confusion and the smell of roast Boar turning slowly on the spit filled the air with a rich meat-heavy cloud.

Turning back to Mistress Munn she said, 'I am sorry I can't be away from here or lord knows what might happen to the meal. Tell me what you needs to say.'

'There is mischief afoot and it involves your kitchen.'

'What! My kitchen? How so?'

'Those ladies in waiting what came with the Lady Sockamore are plotting something as will happen tonight and I heard them mention your kitchen.'

'Lawks a mercy and what could that be? I runs a tight ship here, no one has said nothing to me about schemes and plots. Are you sure you heard right Mistress?'

Mistress Munn turned to look over her shoulder, making sure no one was close.

'I fear there may be a plan to put something in Moredeath's food, something that will turn his head.'

'As far as I hears, his head is already turned! My understanding of it is that he is as mad as a March hare on mushrooms.'

'Well, that's as maybe but all I ask is that you keeps an eye out for goings on. Something is afoot and needs to be quashed before damage is done that can't be undone.'

'I thank you for your advice. I shall keep a keen eye on me, now that I am forewarned. We can't have my kitchens used for trickery. Indeed we can't.'

Chapter Twenty Four

The Magician found himself in a strangely familiar setting. Having moments before been staring at a TV screen, which he believed to be the What Will Be, he now found himself in the topiary gardens of Rick Facile's home in the small village of Upskirting in the Cotswolds. The shard had somehow located Moredeath, who had been shipped by Rick Facile's team, together with The Stinger and The Medusa, and taken the Magician there. The setting was strangely familiar to him. It reminded him of a similar garden he had looked down upon, at Merrelay castle, when visiting the old Knight who had found the Holy Wine, the Knight whom he now knew was once Mistress Munn's lover, and with whom he had shared some of the Holy Wine.

Whattlewherrit found a small recess in the hedge in which there was a bench, and decided to sit, whilst he considered his next move. He realised, to his chagrin, he had made too many rash decisions recently and needed to adopt a new approach if he was to avoid getting himself enmeshed in further difficulties. What was becoming quite clear to him was the fact that what he had set in motion by trying to save the Bludgeoner could not be undone. It was not simply a matter of wishing Moredeath back to Naze and the pretender back to the What Will Be. So many other things had shifted as a result of what had happened. It would be impossible to put them right. All he could do was try his best not to disturb things any more than necessary and if possible, return the Bludgeoner to his rightful place.

No matter what had happened or was to happen next, he knew his view on life had profoundly changed. At the time he was sent by the King to meet Moredeath he was, he had to admit, a touch arrogant, having never really been challenged. Naze had fallen into a slumber in the later years of Cornelius' tenure as King's Magician and when growing up, he had taken for granted the respect Cornelius had earned. Before he was born, Whattlewherrit knew, life was hard, and wars were fought on a regular basis. In those days the court Magician was something of great importance, whereas nowadays the role was little more than keeper of the shard.

He reached for his neck to check the shard was still in place and it struck him that were it not for the shard he would be no more than the apothecary with his potions and pills and leeches. This he felt, more than anything, was what he had to learn. He had to learn humility. It was going to be a hard lesson but one he knew he could not avoid. Part of the lesson would be to admit he had failed when it came to the disappearance of Cornelius. He had not tried hard enough to discover what had happened. He should have entered the Greer swamp. He should have confronted the Bloodly Sisters and had he been unsuccessful, then at least he would have died trying.

In a moment of decisiveness, he promised himself, when he had sorted out the business with the Bludgeoner, he would go looking for answers to the mystery. He was mulling this over when heard footsteps on the gravel path and voices. He ducked into the undergrowth to listen.

'So, these statues need to be placed around the garden and lit up.' There were two men, both of whom wore bright orange tabards, the likes of which the Magician had not seen before.

'It's a bit late to tell us this now, isn't it? I mean how do we get the electrics in place in time?'

'I don't know mate. This whole thing is a fucking nightmare. It took me three quarters of an hour to get through the security checks this morning. But you know what these celebrities are like, they snap their fingers and expect everything to be done at the drop of a hat.'

The Magician listened intently but could not understand a word they were saying. People in the What Will Be seemed to speak a different language, one where he could only catch a word or maybe two before it became too difficult to understand their meaning.

'I think if we get that giant scorpion thing in place somewhere round here, we can pick up the wires from the orangery over there. Then the woman with the bad hairdo, she can be placed somewhere near the swimming pool. There's electricity to run the pumps and the lights in the pool house. Then all we have is Conan the Barbarian who weighs a fucking ton. The others seem to be made of fibreglass but Conan is something else. Have you touched him?'

'No. Why? Should I?'

'He feels warm, just like a human.'

'What?'

'I tell you, it's spooky. He is soft and warm. But the gallery guy warned us that each one of the sculptures is potentially lethal and not to mess around with them.'

'What do they do?'

'Well the scorpion stings, the Medusa bites or at least her hair does, and the big guy, I don't know. No one seems to know what he does but he has huge fucking axe and a sword and both look as though they have dried blood on them.'

'Well, in that case I hope you are going to pay me danger money for this.'

126

The other man laughed. 'You are getting to see the entertainment world's great and good. That's your bonus. Just think, you can live on this story for years to come.

'Tight bastard,' laughed the other man.

The Magician would wait. He told himself that night would eventually fall and when it did, he would find the Bludgeoner and take him back to Naze. Meanwhile, he would watch from his sanctuary and take note of everything he could about the What Will Be. Something told him it might not be his last visit, even though he hoped it was.

With all good intentions but having had no sleep for several days, Whattlewherrit fell into a deep slumber in the hedge. He dreamt he was flying, just like a bird, and was looking down on the land below. He saw Naze as an eagle would. The dense forest where, not many days ago, he had visited Merrelay castle, and then further on the clearing where he had come across Moredeath and his men. Despite the horror of almost being obliterated by the falling castle walls at Merrelay and the hail of arrows raining down on Moredeath, flying as he was above the earth it all seemed so far away, so detached. There was a peculiar separation between the visceral nature of the world he had recently experienced and the place in which his mind was now floating.

The silence above Naze gave him a sense of peace he rarely experienced whilst on the ground. Here, nothing mattered. Here in the sky above the green canopy, following the snaking silver river that ran through the land, where the boats and the comings and goings of everyday life were taking place, Whattlowhorrit was free. Oh that his mind could experience life that way always. To be apart from, and yet a part of, all that existed. To know that whatever was happening, be it castles tumbling, arrows raining, Bishops condemning, children crying, none of it really mattered. Above it all was peace, total peace.

It was as this thought came to mind that he looked down and to his surprise saw a part of the forest that appeared to be covered in mist. A dense dark mist. The Greer swamp! He was moving towards it at speed and despite his attempts at flying away, it drew him down towards it. As he fell, he heard the sound of a wolf crying out, a fearful soulful howl that echoed in his very bones.

He was falling faster now and in fear of his life went to clutch the shard but to his horror it was not there!

He shouted out in his despair and woke himself up with a start. He was shaking, sweat running down his body. His breath was short and rapid, and his eyes darted swiftly about, trying to focus on something familiar with which to ground himself.

It was dark, pitch black where he lay and it took him a few moments to realise where he was. He sat up and peered through the leaves of the hedge to see that the grounds were lit up. Rows of lights strung everywhere along the walkways, all through the garden. The house itself was illuminated with coloured lights and there was noise, a terrible regular booming, like cannons being fired relentlessly. Above the sound of the cannons, all sorts of terrible unfamiliar musical sounds were being thrown, here, there, and everywhere. Even where he sat in the hedge, some distance away, it was almost too much to take.

What horrendous part of the What Will Be had he come too? The sooner he found the Bludgeoner the sooner he could make his way back to Naze. He told himself he must focus his mind. There was much to be done.

Chapter Twenty Five

Sir Godfrey of Merrelay had barely had chance to get over the Magician's visit when it was time to pack his bags and set off for Naze. Despite his considerable misgivings, he knew he had to face the inevitable reckoning. The one he had been avoiding for years. The Great Moyen was not going to let him get away with drinking the Holy Wine after all. Despite his prayers and his monk-like solitude, he had obviously not been forgiven. He would have to face his fellow Knights and confess. More than that, he would have to do so in front of the Bishop of Nantes, who would, no doubt, demand he was burnt at the stake. The problem being that he would have to be burnt forever because having drunk the wine, he was now immortal. What unimaginable pain was he going to have to endure for the sake of saving his own pitiful life?

He should have died of thirst instead and been honourable, but even the strongest of Knights would have found it irresistible when on their knees with thirst. More shameful however was that when returning to Naze, his love for the Mistress Munn blinded him to the fact that their joint immortality could only be a curse and not a blessing. He looked down at Mortimer, his pet rat.

'Well Mortimer, old friend, what can we do but to obey the Great Moyen and face the consequences? I shall of course remain silent about Mistress Munn's having supped the wine. She did not know what I was doing to her. Why should she suffer for the sake of my love?' The rat nosed around the Knights clothing, finding somewhere safe and warm to burrow into. Despite its lack of conversation, the old Knight nevertheless found it a comfort to express his feelings to his furry friend.

If the Knight's rusty armour and worn tabard were not sad enough, his horse, once the pride of Naze, had long since dipped in the back, narrowed in the shoulder, and sloped in the neck. Its gait was ungainly, and every so often its back feet clipped its front.

Sir Godfrey sadly gave the appearance of riding a pantomime horse as he made his way towards the castle. Once the talk of the land, the proud and brave Knight had become a mockery of himself, but he had lost the heart to worry about such things. As soon as the guilt, of what he had done, had hit him, all those years ago, his self-respect died. He had become nothing but an empty shell.

Were it not for Mortimer he would have found it difficult to have any feelings at all. But then there was Mistress Munn, always at the back of his mind. He dared not think of her openly, the pain would be too great. So he had kept her memory locked away as if it were a precious jewel, knowing it was there, but never opening the box, for fear of the consequences.

He had been on the road a day when he came across a young man on foot, heading in the same direction. Seeing he was unarmed and heavily laden, he decided he would approach him and ask him his business on the road. The young man exhibited all the traits the Knight remembered from his own youth. A certain loose swagger, a strength of thigh, and a lightness of countenance from skin the sun had yet to parch.

'Good day young man,' said Sir Godfrey, 'and where are you heading this fine morning?'

'Me sir?' replied the young man, 'why I am heading to Naze with my wares.'

'I see. And what might your wares be may I ask'

'Why sir, I am a seller of badges, pinklarry badges.'

The old Knight responded to the young man by giving him a perplexed look.

'Pinklarry badges,' he repeated once again.

The old Knight still looked confused. 'I am well aware of what a pinklarry looks like but why would anyone deign to wear such a thing?'

'Why sir, because of the plague.'

'The plague? How so the plague. There is no plague in Naze,' responded the Knight.

'Exactly,' replied the young man, 'and that is why. These authentic pinklarry badges modelled on a real pinklarry, cast from a man who had the plague and then recovered, are a dead certainty, guaranteed to stop you getting it.'

The old Knight, brought up in an era of chivalric rhetoric tried to hold his tongue lest he was too offensive, but he could just not accept the proposition that a cast from someone's pinklarry was able to stop the plague.'

'Forgive me young man if I seem old fashioned,' he said, 'but this is a remedy I have not heard of before. How many of these have you sold?'

'Hundreds Sire, perhaps more than hundreds. Actually, I can't count so I don't rightly know.'

'And of the people who have not bought them, how many have died for want of a badge?'

'Now there is a question I cannot answer.'

'I see. And you have walked through lands where there is plague in order to sell these?'

'Lord no Sire! I wouldn't do that.'

'Why not?'

'Well you see sir these badges are for places where there isn't any plague. Why would I do such a foolish thing?'

'Why, to prevent those who haven't already got the disease from catching it.'

'Oh no sir. These badges are only for plague free places.'

The old Knight shook his head. All the years he had been away from others hadn't helped him to understand them any better.

'I must move on,' he said, 'I have to get to Naze castle.'

'Do you want to buy one of my badges before you go, Sire?'

The old Knight looked forlornly at the young man. He did not explain but only said, 'I have no need of such things,' and then rode on.

As he rode towards Naze, Sir Godfrey found his mind wandering. He had always been a spiritual man, and even as a boy his ambition was to serve the King and the Great Moyen, but there had been doubts along the way. The Book of Words foretold the quest for the last item of the Holy Quartet but it didn't actually foretell it would be the wine. It only described the terrain the valiant Knight would have to travel through, in order to get to the end of his quest. Mountains and lakes, frozen tundra and deserts, all of which the valiant Sir Godfrey had traversed in his pursuit of the last missing piece of the puzzle. The artefact that would finally prove the book of words to be true. Hidden as it was in a cave in the outlands of Yar, it fulfilled the prophecy. The same prophecy that the, 'four things cast to the wind shall be gathered together and peace will reign,' led the young Sir Godfrey to seek out the fourth artefact, wishing all to be finally in harmony. But it hadn't happened.

In his mind he had come to believe that the reason for this was his sin. Drinking most of the wine to stay alive in the cruel heat of the desert on the return journey, he had broken the prophecy. Sharing what remained with Mistress Munn had sealed its fate. Reluctantly he also had to admit, refilling the bottle with his horse's piss hadn't helped. Why hadn't he just refilled it with wine? Oh, so many questions burdened him as an old man. He tried to think himself back into the mind of his youth. Why did he do so many of the things he had got wrong? Why did he think that he, Sir Godfrey of Merrelay was so important when he was young? Surely, he knew his own vulnerability?

It was as these questions beset him, he found himself in a strange part of the forest. One he could not recall. A mist hung over the trees and strange scratchings and squeakings came from the canopy and the forest floor. His horse's feet began to press deeper into the turf as if it were wet and thick, and his steed showed a reluctance to move on, as if it were wary. He sniffed the air. There was a pleasant, sweet odour that suddenly came upon his senses. He took a deeper breath. Sure enough it was as though he were smelling the richest scent of any flower he had ever known. He began to feel different. What was this place? He should have felt intimidated, not recognising it but for some unknown reason he felt the opposite. In fact, he hadn't felt this good in years. His aching limbs stopped hurting, his eyes saw better than they had seen for a long time, and he heard sounds he surely could not have heard, even in his youth. Nothing seemed a burden in his current state of mind. Something was calling him on into the misty interior of this peculiar place. He had no choice but to follow.

It might have been an hour, it might have been a day. He could not tell. But eventually he came across a cave hewn out of the sheer rock face of an escarpment. Somewhere in the back of his mind, he felt a nervous tremor, but it passed before he could catch hold of it and question it's meaning.

The old Knight, reinvigorated, walked into the dark recess and felt his way along the walls. They were wet and slimy. What did that matter? Nothing seemed to make him uncomfortable in his present state of mind. He smelt the acrid aroma of old smoke. Someone had lit a fire here maybe days ago, maybe weeks. However long ago it was, it still tainted the air.

His curiosity tweaked, and he determined to go on. He took out his flint box with its small pocket of dusty shavings, and struck it. The shavings caught fire and for a moment or two, he could see at least a few feet ahead. To his surprise and immense satisfaction, on the wall not an arm's length away, was a tar and reed candle. He held the spluttering shavings to it and it slowly ignited. On he went deeper into the cave until he came across a large cooking pot.

Clearly the reason for the fire. He looked in to see some very unappetising cold soup or gruel. Someone had been living in the cave, but who?

It was then he heard the whimpering. At first, he mistook it for the sound of the wind but then there would be no wind so deep in a cave. As it happened once again he followed the sound, holding his candle high, searching amongst the shifting shadows on the walls for anything that might be making such a sound. And then he found it. Chained to the wall and lying on the floor was the most pitiful beast. A once proud wolf lay like a dusty carpet, its eyes barely able to open.

'What have we here Mortimer?' He whispered. The beast moaned softly.

'Someone has chained this poor beast to the wall and left it with no sustenance, not even a bowl of water to keep it alive.' The beast rasped a sound he could not make out.

'We shall have to give it something to quench its thirst, although I am not at all sure it will have any effect. The poor beast looks as if it is already dead.' Mortimer squeaked as though in agreement.

'Well said Mortimer,' said Sir Godfrey, 'some of this gruel would be better than nothing.' He found a wooden bowl on a rough bench nearby and dipped it into the soup and took it to the wolf. The beast raised it's eyes slowly and sniffed at the gross mixture. Sir Godfrey thought it would reject the gruel but it was so obviously starving and in need of water it began to lick the contents of the bowl. Slowly, tongue full by tongue full, it managed to swallow a small amount of the liquid.

'If we could undo these chains Mortimer then we might be able to get it outside and find it something of substance to eat.'

'No time,' said a gruff voice, 'no time.'

Sir Godfrey, though still under the influence of the exotic flowers, stood bolt upright and felt the hairs on his moustache stand straight.

'Who is there!?' he said.

'It is me Godfrey, your old friend Cornelius,' croaked the voice.

'But where?' replied the Knight.

'Before you. In the shape of a wolf.'

Sir Godfrey felt a freezing numbness envelop him. Cornelius? His old friend. Could it be?

'The Bloodly Sisters overcame me and turned me into this beast and now I am undone. There is no time to talk.' The beast drew a heavy breath.

'You must get to Whattlewherrit and the shard before the Sisters do. They have taken the form of younger women to hide their hideous shapes. The Lady Sockamore is not what she appears, she is..........'

The wolf's eyes closed and Sir Godfrey heard a hideous gasp as all life left his old friend. Sir Godfrey shook his friend. 'Cornelius! Cornelius!' He cried, but it was too late. Before his very eyes, the pitiful beast changed shape and the chains holding him disappeared. He saw his old friend, the Magician, Cornelius, lying on the floor, such as he had never seen him before.

'My dear friend, whatever happened here, I will do my best to avenge you,' said Sir Godfrey, tears coming to his eyes. 'The Bloodly sisters shall not get away with this.'

Chapter Twenty Six

Whattlewherrit felt a strange pang of emptiness surge through him, as though something had been taken away from him. It was momentary but nevertheless there. Something had happened, somewhere far away. He wasn't sure what.

He did not, however, have the time or the inclination to work out why he felt the way he did. There was too much to be done in the What Will Be and the distractions were such that they took all of his concentration.

Rick Facile's party was in full swing by the time he crept out of the hedge where he had been sheltering. It was night and the whole garden was ablaze with brilliant strings of lights and exotic people parading in their costumes. Although Rick Facile had called it a themed party, his guests, who had little knowledge of history, had come in all types of costume, but it didn't seem to matter. There was laughter and shouting and general mayhem, accompanied by the awful thud thud thud of the noise he found so difficult to ignore and to understand. Nevertheless, he knew he had to overcome his aversion and find Moredeath.

As he walked towards the house in the direction the shard wanted him to go, he came across the first of the statues that had accompanied Moredeath in the art gallery where he had originally left him. The Stinger, the giant representation of a desert scorpion stood in all its glory, lit up by the lights the workmen had installed. People stood around marvelling at it and discussing how real it looked, and how deadly. The Magician, who knew nothing about art or scorpions, stared at it, believing it to be a real creature and wondering who had managed to capture and kill it. Some brave Knight no doubt had risked his life to bring it to this garden. Whoever owned the property was indeed an important person to possess such a thing.

He walked on, jostled by the inebriated throng who saw nothing strange in his attire, who joked and laughed, and seemed totally oblivious to the fact he came from another world and should not have been there. This was encouraging to the Magician who did not want to explain his appearance.

Now and again people would stop him and ask who he was supposed to be. To which he answered simply, 'I am the Magician from Naze.' They seemed satisfied with this answer which surprised him but then he thought, this was, after all, the What Will Be, where everything was known. As to their attire, Whattlewherrit had come to the conclusion that, in the What Will Be, it did not matter. Whatever he anticipated, something stranger came along that shocked and surprised him.

He was heading in the direction of the house when the thumping noise stopped, and a really loud voice spoke out, saying that it was time to head for the house, where Rick and Deloris would pledge their vows. Gradually Whattlewherrit found himself in a stream of people heading in the same direction. They were all talking incessantly, and clearly very drunk.

When they reached the house, the Magician had to pinch himself to make sure what he was seeing was real. What was this place that held on to the daylight whilst it was night outside? How could it be that the chill air of the garden was replaced by a balmy warmth, when there was no sign of even a single fire burning? Everything was soft and bright and even the ground under his feet was covered in some kind of tapestry. No stone floors in this palace. The more he looked, the more he believed this to be the richest castle he had ever been in. Above the heads of the crowds, he could see a platform upon which stood two gold thrones, the seats and backs of which were covered in thick red velvet. The all-enveloping voice then announced the arrival of Rick and Deloris, to which there was rapturous applause. People whistled and cheered and threw their arms in the air as if they were at the finest tournament, pledging their allegiance to the King and Queen.

Two people came and sat on the thrones, both dressed in the most elaborate costumes. The King had a sword at his side as befits a King and the Queen wore a crown. It was as he suspected. He was in the royal palace and some major event was taking place.

'Ladies and gentlemen,' said a man dressed as a courtier, speaking into a talking stick, 'we are all here tonight to celebrate the engagement of Rick to Deloris.' A loud cheer went up. 'As you know Rick and Deloris have been together for five months now and have had plenty of time to get to know one another and to realise they want to make a public statement.' Another cheer went up. 'The King and Queen of pop are going to make it official.'

'Get on with it, Blade,' shouted Rick Facile, 'I want some supper and a shag!' The crowd laughed. The man called Blade turned to face the couple and began the ceremony.

'Well let's make it quick then,' he said. 'Do you Rick Facile take Deloris Pops to be your long-term partner to love and to shag so long as you both feel up to it?'

'I do,' replied Rick Facile.

'Do you Deloris Pops take Rick Facile to be your long-term partner to love and to shag as long as you both shall live?'

'I do,' replied Deloris Pops.'

'Well, that's it then,' said the man called Blade. At which Rick Facile and Deloris Pops stood up, and fondling each other's bums at the same time, snogged each other heartily, much to the amusement of the gathered crowd. The music blasted out, the crowd cheered and waiters carrying trays with glasses of champagne suddenly appeared, offering them to the happy crowd. Not wishing to appear different, the Magician followed everyone else in taking one. He downed the glass, and gradually stiffened up as the strange drink bubbled its way down his throat, and then seemed to be bubbling its way everywhere else. This was not good. Someone had poisoned him, he was sure of it. Within moments everything seemed to be different. He was thinking, but his thoughts did not seem to go anywhere. It was as though he had a great fever. He touched his head. He was hot. He clutched the shard. Something was not right. He could feel its solid shape, but it felt distant, not as it usually was. At the same time, the room seemed to be swaying in an unpleasant and disorientating way. He needed to....

Deloris Pops and Rick Facile were well into the celebrations when they parted company. Rick, rather than paying Deloris attention, as she had hoped and expected on their engagement night, decided to give a guided tour of his art to several celebrity friends and seemed to have forgotten all about her and their promise to 'shag so long as you both feel up to it.' This and the effects of alcohol and non-prescription substances meant she was not in a forgiving frame of mind. She staggered off, determined to pay him back for his lack of interest, and found herself in a quiet spot in the garden down by the duck pond. As fate would have it, this was where the workmen had placed Moredeath, but had been unable to secure the lighting in time for the party. For the very same reason, this was why Deloris Pops inadvertently bumped into Moredeath, letting out a loud 'fuck me' as she rebounded off the all-too-solid body of the Bludgeoner. She got up from the wet grass and looked at him. Although she knew Rick had purchased some ultra-realistic statues, she had not seen any of them. Her interest in art was about the same as that of golf, and of most other things Rick was interested in.

She turned on the light of her mobile phone and examined the Bludgeoner. 'Fucking hell. Why on earth did Rick buy this,' she thought to herself, it looks like a fucking Viking or something. Nevertheless, as she lit up Moredeath's face, she couldn't help but think he was not ugly, just solid. That was the word 'solid.' A thick jaw, heavy eyebrows, a brutal scar down one cheek. Not really her type but on a bad night.....She touched his muscle-bound arms and pulled her hand away immediately she felt the warmth. Fuck, she thought, I didn't expect that! In the gloom she did not see the slight twitch of Moredeath's eyelids or the tensing of his mouth. It took her a few moments to compose herself. Part of her wanted to walk away, go back to the house, but part of her was immensely curious. How could the sculpture feel so lifelike? What was it about the thing that drew her to it in such a magnetic way?

She touched its thigh and felt the warmth through the leather. The strong muscles beneath were relaxed but they were nevertheless there. She had to admit that he was a magnificent specimen. She thought of it in the same way that she might look at a stallion. Admiring its strength. She told herself not to be stupid. It was a statue and a crazy thing to spend so much money on. Rick had told her what he had paid for it. 'House money,' she replied. Rick had laughed and said, 'House money if you are fucking poor Deloris, but we aren't.' He then told her about the nature of the sculptures and how they were 'deadly' and why the artist made them that way, so that they would engage the viewer. That all went over her head. Art was for rich people, posh people who could tell you where the grapes in a glass of wine were grown and who went to Wimbledon, and Henley and places like that.

Without thinking, she ran her hand up Moredeath's thigh and over his prominent codpiece. It was a wicked thing to do but wouldn't everyone be curious? There were laces holding it in place. What she wanted to know was just how accurate this piece of sculpture was. She fumbled with the laces but being pretty much out of her head, only achieved her goal with great difficulty. The codpiece slipped away to reveal the truth. The sculpture was totally accurate. She gasped and then said, fucking hell, again. Immediately though, it dawned on her that she needed to put the codpiece back into place before anyone found it like that. Rick would go mental if he thought she had interfered with his artwork. She was like a child, trying to cover up some misdemeanour before her parents came home. She lifted the moulded leather and tried to get it over the sculptures voluminous replicas. For some reason it didn't fit anymore and the more she tried to make it, the less it did so. Something was happening, something she could not explain. Until it hit her. 'Oh shit,' she said out loud, 'oh holy shit, this thing is totally accurate.' The more she tried to handle the statues accurate parts into the codpiece the larger they grew. And they grew large. Deloris felt a twinge of excitement coupled with an equally disturbing feeling of doing something she was going to regret.

'What the fuck am I going to do? How do I get this back down...?' There were several ways known to the drunken Deloris who had, under other circumstances, had to deal with very similar situations during her adult years. The question was, which one? She did not have time to decide. All of a sudden, the statue began to move. Not only did it move, but it grunted in a most disturbing manner. That of an enraged beast.

Moredeath had slowly been coming to life again. The spell the Magician had put on him was wearing off and he was mad. People looking at him and touching him. Leaving him in the dark, lifting him up and putting him in a box, then manhandling him again and offloading him into a strange place with crowds of strange people walking by. And he unable to lift a finger to kill them. Then as if this was not enough, some strange woman touching him and undoing his codpiece when he hadn't seen a woman in days, it was all too much. He picked her up.

Instead of being scared or disturbed, Deloris felt a sudden surge of desire, an urgency. There was something about this man, if indeed he was a man, that was deeply attractive to her. Moredeath however had no such feelings. He just did what any self-respecting barbarian would do under the circumstances, and having done that, moved on to find someone to kill.

Chapter Twenty Seven

Back in Naze, it was the evening before the wedding. Garlands made from evergreen shrubs, and the few late season flowers from the forest, had been hung in the great hall. Festive fires were lit and torches blazed. Either side of the great hall, tables were laid with bowls of food, wine and mead. At the end of these stood the table at which the King, the bride-to-be, and the groom, together with the bishop and other dignitaries, were to sit. This table was raised to be higher than the others on a small platform. Down the middle of the long tables, serving maids came and went, bringing in more food and wine for the guests as they arrived, and lighting candles, so that the once austere hall took on a radiance normally only seen at the winter festival.

As far as the King was concerned the day had been arduous. He had been plagued by a stream of visitors who appeared to want to deliberately disrupt him, when he was deep in thought about how to deal with the issue of Moredeath. The truth was, since the Bludgeoner's arrival at the castle, he had been trying to come to terms with the fact the Magician had shrunk or rather diminished the bridegroom. Moredeath was now a mere blob of a person compared to his former self. Where once he could demand respect by nothing more than his physique, now no one would look on him with anything other than pity, or contempt. Even his clothes were being re-sewn to fit his unenviable shape. His daughter, the Lady Gossamer, had wept when she heard of his state.

'I would rather marry Sir Sockamore than the man now laying in that bedchamber,' she cried.

To hear her say such a thing appalled the worried King.

'But daughter, you must understand the nature of politics. To refuse the Bludgeoner's hand now would set him and his father Deathgrin upon us. Though I hate to bring such thoughts to mind, your position, should they decide to retaliate, would be worse than I could bear to imagine.'

His daughter had sobbed wildly at the position she was in. She had done the same when he had told her that a miracle had occurred, and overnight the Bludgeoner had recovered from his stupor and was fully engaged with the world.

'Think on this daughter. Suppose the Magician is found, and I do not immediately burn him at the stake. It may well be he could return the Bludgeoner to his former self. Would not that be a better outcome?'

His daughter wept once more. Quite clearly there was nothing to be done to console her.

'Why don't you go back to your sewing my dear? Finish that tapestry you were making as a gift to Moredeath. Show him what you have accomplished over the past year.'

She left in tears. The King felt sure, given time, his daughter would understand that to offer up her maidenhead for the sake of the realm would be the best solution for everyone.

The next to arrive was Sir Bloatmore, a harmless but somewhat bumbling Knight whose allegiance to the King was boringly unquestionable. Bloatmore was the Knight who had been sent to find the Bludgeoner with Sir Sockamore, after the rout had taken place, and was now petitioning the King on behalf of his companion, the missing Knight.

'Sire, I really think we need to find what happened to Sir Sockamore. His sister has arrived at the castle and no doubt she will be wondering why no one has searched for him.'

'A fine-looking woman Bloatmore. I caught sight of her yesterday with those two saucy maidservants, who I have to say are not in themselves unattractive.'

'Yes Sire, but Sir Sockamore...'

'I am not given much to thoughts of marriage these days, but I can tell you that the lady would serve me well enough in my bedchamber. As long as I didn't have to think of her brother, of course.'

'But her brother your Majesty...'

'Would it be too much for a King to want to engage in a bit of mutually enjoyable bed-play with the sister of one of his Knights? I think not Bloatmore. Indeed, I have allocated the lady the seat next to mine at the feast tonight. I think, after a glass or two of wine, she may well accede to my request to rearrange the bedstraw this very night.'

'Sire..'

'Enough Bloatmore. We shall talk of rescuing her brother after the meal. If the lady proves to be compliant then of course I shall be far more inclined to send out a party or two to find her brother. If not....well we would have to see.'

'But isn't that...'

'What Bloatmore?'

141

'Nothing Sire.'

If it was not enough for the King's patience to be tested thus far, no sooner had Sir Bloatmore left, than the Bishop of Nantes arrived. The King had been avoiding him since his arrival at the castle. The man was a vexation to the spirit, with his feigned obedience to the Great Moyen. The King knew of his debauchery, and lust for power and possessions. The bishop entered the room dressed in his scarlet silk robes. His gaunt thin face, with its grey translucent skin, was hung below by jowls that wobbled when he moved. Some disease or other had wasted the once rotund cleric. It had left his flesh empty, like a punctured bladder. The King thought he looked remarkably similar to a tall, withered turkey. All except for his dull watery eyes, which were closer to those of an old blind dog. He was not an attractive man

'Bishop, what can I do for you?' The King's voice was courteous, and yet had an edge that hinted at his annoyance.

'Your Majesty. I understand that the King's Magician has disappeared?'

'You are correct Bishop.'

'And that he has caused much mischief in so far as the bridegroom is concerned?'

'How well informed you are Bishop.'

'I like to think so your Majesty. It pays, if one is to keep ahead of others, don't you agree?'

'As long as you do not imagine it is good to keep ahead of your King.'

'Quite so your Majesty, the thought had never occurred.'

'So Bishop, what is it you wanted to see me about?'

'The Magician's island.'

'How so?'

'If he ever returns, I assume he is to be punished for his trickery? Death itself would seem too small a punishment for such a wicked crime. Perhaps the wheel or to be hung, drawn and quartered would be appropriate...' The old Bishops eyes opened wide, and his mouth hardened, as though he were imagining the Magician's pain.

'I shall be the arbiter of that Bishop. I am well aware you are always in favour of painful retribution.'

'It cleanses the soul, your Majesty.'

'Quite. But what is this about? Surely not what kind of death I am to impose upon the Magician?'

'No indeed your Majesty. It is about the Magician's home.'

'His island?'

'Yes, his island.' The Bishop's jowls wobbled and he coughed. Taking a handkerchief from his sleeve, he spat into it, and briefly glanced at the contents before putting it away again.

'I was thinking, the church could do much with the island as a sanctuary. Perhaps a monastery? Somewhere I might be able to reside when visiting the castle.'

'Are you implying your accommodation is in some way lacking?'

'Why of course not, your Majesty.'

'Well then?'

'I have been praying to the Great Moyen lately, about how the church might make its presence felt once the marriage has taken place. As you are aware, the bridegroom is not, how shall I say it, an avid follower of the Great Moyen. If the presence of the church is distant, then the people may well begin to doubt their faith. But suppose there was a great monastery built on the island. One which bestowed sanctuary to the needy, food to the poor? Economic benefit and of course above all spiritual sustenance to the people of Naze. Surely this would encourage Moredeath to see the strength of the church.'

'And would this monastery have a choir, Bishop?'

'Indeed it would, your Majesty.'

'And would the choir have choir boys?'

'Absolutely, your Majesty.'

The King exhaled loudly. 'I thought it would.'

'Boys taken from the streets and given warmth and succour,' said the bishop, a salacious smile creeping across his thin lips.

'Yes well, I don't need to know more Bishop. Let me say that I will give your proposal deep thought, and will pray to the Great Moyen for guidance.'

'Your Majesty is so kind.'

'While you are here, I need to tell you that your place, and that of the arch deacons, at the top table, has had to be reconsidered. The Lady Sockamore and her maidservants will be at my side. Diplomacy you understand. Given that her brother Sir Sockamore has gone missing, I thought it only right to show how much we valued his service to the crown.'

143

The Bishop's face took on the look of a man who has mistakenly eaten a raw jalapeño chilli and swallowed it whole. His watery eyes narrowed in contempt and the veins on his face reddened with angry blood. The King had him cornered. He could not afford to complain, given that his request for the island remained in the balance, but the humiliation was as intense as a man could suffer. The King would be made to pay for this insult, he would see to that.

Chapter Twenty Eight

The Lady Sockamore had not left the rooms in the castle that belonged to her former self, Sir Sockamore, since her arrival with the Bloodly Sisters, who were now posing as her maids. She did not want to be seen too often, for fear that someone would recognise her resemblance to the handsome Knight she had once been. This, despite the fact the Bloodly Sisters had made such a fine spell that even the Lady Sockamore could not find any similarity. Other than how the Lady, whose body she now inhabited, was as beautiful as her former self had been handsome. Just half an hour spent in front of the mirror was enough to confirm such. She had had to amuse herself because the Bloodly Sisters were here, there, and everywhere, or so it seemed. Keen to plot and plan the demise of Whattlewherrit and the removal of Moredeath the Bludgeoner. That very evening, they had crept into the moonlit night, and as far as she could tell from their conversation, had ventured to the Magician's island, leaving some sort of trickery for him to find. A spell that would catch him unaware. She wanted to be there when it took effect. To see the Magician suffer the consequences of some terrible curse would give her great pleasure. Her mind drifted for a while as she considered the possibilities. It was not long however before the sisters called to her attention the fact that she had to get ready for that evening's activity, the pre-wedding feast where the great and good of Naze would be gathered to toast Moredeath and the Lady Gossamer.

'So my dear,' said one of the hags, 'you once said you would like to be admired by every man in Naze.'

'Did I?' Replied the Lady Sockamore.

'Yes you did, before you ate the soup with us.'

'Ah well, that was because I was intoxicated by those damned plants that grow in the Greer Swamp. Indeed, I blame all of this on them. The moment I rode into the swamp I began to think in a strange way and to be quite honest, had it not been for that intoxication, I would never have travelled into the interior. Whatever was in that perfume dulled my senses and now look what has happened!' The Lady Sockamore scanned her body.

'You have become a beautiful woman.'

'Exactly. But I should be a dashing Knight, attending the ceremony tonight in full dress, and sporting a manly persona. And here I am, nothing more than a woman.'

'I thought you were beginning to like being a woman?'

'How so?'

'Those long hours spent in front of the mirror, admiring yourself.'

The Lady Sockamore felt trapped. It was true she did spend an inordinate amount of time preening herself but then, and here was the rub, she did the same thing when she was a man. There was no way she was going to agree with the hag.

'I just can't get used to who I am at the moment, that's all. I have a need to check I have not changed back.'

'Oh, you have no reason to be concerned in that matter, my dear. Only when you have fulfilled your task will we reverse the spell.'

'What is the task? You keep mentioning it but never say exactly what you want me to do?'

'I am sure we told you, didn't we sister?' The hag looked at her sibling.

'Your task is to seduce Moredeath the Bludgeoner.'

'I've already told you, I refuse to do that. You cannot expect me to go anywhere near that man! What if he wants to hold me? Or heaven forbid kiss me? You can't expect me to do things with another man.'

The hags laughed.

'The Bludgeoner is not renowned for his prowess in kissing my dear. Such a man has no thought of the tender side of love. His approach to desire is the same as his approach to combat. He does not hold back, his weapon goes straight in and out, no fancy footwork or swordplay. A repulsive thought is it not, sir Knight? Perhaps that is how your many conquests have felt.'

'Nonsense! Why would any woman think such a thing when engaging with the handsomest Knight in Naze? Why I am skilled in the art of courtly seduction. My sword stays sheathed until all appropriate formalities are fully accomplished. What you are now suggesting is preposterous. Comparing me with Moredeath is like comparing a fine-bred stallion with a serf's pig.'

'Supposing then, by magic, we turned Moredeath into the image of your former self. Do you not think you would feel differently?'

The Lady Sockamore huffed and stamped her feet. 'You just don't understand, do you? You have only done half a job here. You have changed my body but not my temperament. I am still a man inside. I do not know what women think any more than you would know how a Knight of Naze thinks. All you have done is to trap me in a woman's body.'

'So you want us to finish the job?'

'Indeed I do not! I want you to give me back my proper body. I want hair on my arms and on my legs, I want my strong manly muscles back, and most of all I want sir trusty and the two knaves returned to their proper place. I want to stand like a man when I piss. To be Sir Sockamore again!

The hags gave each other a knowing look.

'Let us explain what will happen tonight,' said one of the hags. 'We will put a potion in the Bludgeoner's food that will enchant him. He will have eyes for no-one but you. Having fallen desperately in love with you, he will refuse to marry the Lady Gossamer. His refusal will cause the King to have to find another suitor for his daughter and...'

'It would be me, wouldn't it?' said the Lady Sockamore hopefully. 'You will turn me back into my former self and I will ride into Naze, welcomed as a long lost hero, and sweep her off her feet.'

'How insightful of you to envision such an outcome,' said one of the sisters.

'But wait a moment, is there not a flaw in this plan? If the Bludgeoner is madly in love with me, I mean of course the Lady Sockamore, then won't he be slightly upset when I disappear?'

The hags looked at one another and nodded.

'Oh, he will be greatly enraged of course but we shall make sure he thinks the Lady has gone back to her own home and, given some appropriate misdirections, the Bludgeoner will wander into the Greer Swamp, never to be heard of again.'

The Lady Sockamore clapped her hands in jubilation and said it was a splendid plan and, given the outcome was all she had wanted, agreed that for one more night she would play the part.

'There will be no one-to-one combat, however. The moment there is any sign of him unsheathing his broadsword I am away! You must make sure I am not left alone with him.'

'Of course, my dear. We can't have that brute of a man deflowering our protégé can we?'

'Indeed,' was all she could reply.

Chapter Twenty Nine

The Bishop of Nantes was enraged. Being turned off the top table and having to eat below the salt was the greatest humiliation he could imagine. Not only was it an insult to him but to the church too. He would be a fool not to recognise what it meant, politically. The King, thinking he would be unassailable with Moredeath as his son-in-law, was finally making a play against the church. The Bishop knew the King had always paid lip service to the church. Never once had he willingly gone to the chapel in Naze Castle. Official occasions he marked, under protest, but of his personal obedience to the Great Moyen there was no sign. With Moredeath in place, there would be little incentive to change his point of view. Indeed, the Bishop knew things could only get worse. He needed to re-establish the church's role in Naze, and his plan for the Magician's island was key to this happening. Give the common people plenty to do, and as a result enough to buy food and drink, and they would be more inclined to support the church. Give them a concrete symbol of the Great Moyen, such as the intended magnificent monastery, and they would be in awe of his power. There was no time to lose. He would go there, with his archdeacons, that very evening and sprinkle the site with holy water, thereby claiming it in the name of the Great Moyen.

When the three clerics finally fussed themselves into the boat, the boatman coughed, spat into the water, and then said, 'where to', in his most disinterested voice.

'To the Magician's island my man,' replied the Bishop.

The boatman said nothing but only grunted. That fucking island was going to be the death of him. How many more times was he to cross the channel with a boatload of arseholes? Knights, fine ladies, and now clerics. The fucking Magician was not even there. Why did they want to go if he wasn't about? It was none of his business, of course, and he needed the money, but something peculiar was going on.

'How long will it take my man?' said the Bishop.

'Oh here we go,' muttered the boatman. 'They can't help it, can they? I'll bet they wouldn't like it if they was with a whore, and she said the same thing to them, 'how long will it take my man?' They wouldn't put up with that would they?' He drew breath before answering.

'About half of one hour each way.'

'Can't you do it quicker than that?'

The boatman's face contorted as though he was struggling to release an uncomfortable fart. His mind went back to the image he had conjoured up, of the cleric and the whore. 'Can't you do it quicker than that?' She was asking him.

'There is a current running in the wrong direction. A quicker journey would be made when the tide changes direction. If you was to delay your journey some two hours....'

'That is not possible, we have to be back in time for the festivities this very evening. Are you not aware of such?

The boatman grimaced again.

'Strange to say I was not invited,' he replied. 'It is not in my social calendar.'

The Bishop sneered at him but it had little effect. Lowly in status though a boatman might be, he knew they depended upon him for their lives. The channel between Naze and the island was notorious and very few ventured across it unless their journey was essential. The boatman knew full well why the dynasty of Magicians had chosen to live where they did.

It was a long haul but eventually the pod of clerics see-sawed their way from the boat and precariously gained a foothold on the land. The boatman cursed under his breath, then called out to them.

'How long shall I wait?'

The Bishop replied they would be only a short time as they needed to return to Naze for the meal that evening. The boatman brought his oars onboard and, having tethered the boat, decided to take a short nap.

The Bishop and his deacons made their way toward the Magician's tower. As they walked, the Bishop envisioned his grand monastery positioned, as it would be, in direct opposition to the castle. It would have to be at least as tall and would have the finest masonry work and stained glass windows. He would make sure it was the greatest building in the land, outshining all others. There would be sufficient room for a hundred monks, a choir that would out sing any other, gardens where produce would be grown and a warren and carp pond for meat and fish. A brewery for ale would brew the mellowest ale and there would be apiaries with the best bees to provide honey to eat and for mead. Such a glorious vision he had of the enterprise that in the imagination of his mind it was almost built. He would go down in history as the man who had created it all. Bishop Righteous the Third, of Nantes. His heart swelled at the thought of his name being remembered forever. The monastery would be his palace and his retirement home, where he would eventually be buried in the grandest crypt ever built. He would show the King who had the most power. The King might have Knights and physical power but the one who ruled the minds of the people was truly the one who ruled the land.

It was not long before they reached the door of the tower and the Bishop noticed a rolled-up note pinned to it. He edged closer and saw that it had written upon it, 'Do not open unless you are the owner of this island.'

Clearly the Bishop was curious. Not only was he curious, but in his own mind he needed a justification for looking at the note and soon found it. The Magician was a wanted man and thereby no longer considered a free man. This being the case, and only free men could hold property, the island no longer belonged to him. Furthermore, the Bishop had made his claim to the island by petitioning the King, who would doubtless agree to his request in the morning. Therefore, the Bishop told himself, he was effectively the person to whom the note belonged. Having made this logical deduction, he had no hesitation in unpinning the note and reading it, as it's rightful owner. He drew a slow inward breath as he read the message.

'To whoever reads this. From this day forth you will be free from the burden of the past and all things will come to you as if to a newborn. Nothing you do will ever concern you long enough to warrant your discomfort.'

The Bishop stared at the note. What a peculiar thing for it to say. What did it mean? Was it some sort of sign from the Great Moyen that his past sins would be absolved? That the future would be as that of a newborn child, nurtured and suckled, wrapped in warmth and comfort, without having a care in the world anymore? He stopped for a moment and then saw it all. The Great Moyen had sent it as a sign. It was a gift, a reward for his dedication and service and of course for planning to build the greatest monument to Moyen there had ever been! What joy he felt in his heart to think that this miracle had occurred. He turned to the arch deacons.

'We must sprinkle the land with Holy water,' he proclaimed. He pulled out his pinklarry and pissed heartily, much to the apparent discomfort of the deacons. He needed a piss, he told them, and the Great Moyen had ordained him holy, so everything that came from him must also be holy.

On the boat on the way back to Naze, the Bishop sat wondering what it was going to be like, receiving the reward the Great Moyen had sent him. Perhaps the most satisfying thing was that he was finally to be forgiven for drinking some of the holy wine. A fact he had hidden for years. Not one soul knew that some years ago he had found temptation creeping into his mind to taste the wine. So much so that by the early hours of one fateful morning, he was overwhelmed by desire as he had never been before. In such a state he had approached the holy relic, uncorked the bottle and had taken a swig, only to find, to his disgust, it tasted like horse piss. It was as much as he could do to put the bottle back together, so that it looked untouched. The result of his crime however was uninspiring.

Whatever qualities the holy wine had once possessed, these had diminished over the years. He felt not a single change to himself other than the massive disappointment that had plagued him ever since. Surely no one else in the land could have felt as wretched as he did, having committed such a crime and found no benefit. Now, however, thanks to the note from the Great Moyen, he knew he had been absolved. That was clearly what it was telling him. The gambling, the wrongful burnings at the stake, the envy and bitterness, the choirboys......he was free from that and all other sins. A light-heartedness came over him and he smiled peacefully.

'Are you alright Bishop?' asked one of the arch deacons.

'Why do you ask?' replied the Bishop.

'Oh, nothing, your Eminence. Just the turbulence of the waters can be distressing.

The deacon did not want to tell the Bishop he had never seen him smile before.

Chapter Thirty

Kenny Catlin was confused. For the past few days, he had been in a trance. His world had been blown apart. One moment he was in Klines restaurant, in LA, about to carry out his intended seduction of the delightful Miss Lamb, the next he had landed in some place where Knights in armour still existed and draughty castles with itchy bedstraw and gruel were the only comfort against the night air. He remembered little of the past days, other than that he had come across a slaughtered army, he had a stiff cock that you could have hung a bath towel over, and then the comings and goings in the night in the room in which he still lay. Then there was the apothecary with his bloated leeches sucking on his bleach white body, the tailor complaining about getting his clothing to fit, and finally, the whispered voices of women in the night talking about him as though he were someone else.

Finally, there was the moment when, despite being deeply asleep, he felt something trickle into his ear, and a warmth course through his body, so that when he awoke that morning, he felt more present and alive than he had done for days. The old Kenny Catlin had returned, and he was determined to find out what had happened. Laying as he was, staring at the ceiling, he watched a spider climb a strand of web, then drop back down, but then try again. He was reminded of the story of Robert the Bruce and the spider, and how it taught Bruce about resilience, and never to give up. Catlin got out of bed and, with his shoe, squashed the spider. He didn't like insects, especially when they were trying to teach him a lesson.

Having got out of bed, he felt the chill air of the room. He looked around for his clothes and then remembered. The only clothes he was wearing when his life exploded in a flash of light, were his monogrammed shorts which happened to be around his ankles at the time. Where they had ended up, God only knew? This was why, he recalled, he found himself in some mediaeval outfit that swamped him but was nevertheless cover against the dank atmosphere of the forest clearing. He searched the room and to his disappointment found the self-same clothes and decided they would have to do until he found something better.

Since the last time he had worn them, the tailor and his seamstresses had been and gone, so that when he put them on this time, they actually fitted his somewhat neglected frame. He looked at the emblem on the tabard before putting it on. A fearsome hog's head eyed him up, as though daring him to wear the tunic. He put it on. No fucking pig was going to intimidate Kenny Catlin, the King of Hollywood! Whatever this was, wherever he was, Kenny was back and he was mad. Really mad.

There was a table and a chair in the room, and he sat down to think through the options. If it had been some crazy drug-induced trip he had been on, then why was it ongoing? Admittedly everything had seemed that way to begin with, but now he was fully alert, and aware, there was no way he was stoned. He knew the feeling too well to know this was something different, something real, in its own perverted way. Having discarded that option, he considered the terrifying possibility that he had had some sort of brainstorm. He remembered reading a book once by some psychiatrist guy who used to see a patient who thought his wife was a fucking hat. If people could think things like, that then maybe that was what was happening to him. Perhaps he was imagining it all? It felt so real though. But wasn't that exactly what the guy with the Fedora for a wife thought?

There had to be an answer to it all and that answer lay outside this film set of a world!

No sooner had the words entered his head than it all fell into place. That was the answer. This world was real enough but it was make-believe. Someone was setting him up. It was The Truman Show all over again. Everybody except him knew it was a setup. They had drugged him and dropped him into an elaborate con where he was the sucker. He racked his brains to think who would do such a thing and quickly decided there were too many to count. His anger turned to rage at the thought that he was being manipulated and humiliated by someone unknown. Whoever it was, they were going to get sued so hard they would be eating out of dumpsters. The question was, what should he do next? He could rant and rave at the next person he saw, he could demand to know who was behind it all, but was that the way to get them? His natural cunning told him that the unexpected was what caught people off guard. Let them film him, let them play him. But if he knew what was going on and played them instead, their plan would fall apart, and they would have to show their hand. In the meantime, he would keep an eye out for hidden cameras and clues as to who was doing this to him.

He searched the room and came across the huge casket he had stumbled across in the forest in which he had originally found some clothes to wear. He lifted the heavy lid and rummaged inside. There were more clothes, a dagger in a leather sheath, an elaborate helmet in the shape of a boar's head which, when he tried to lift it, was so heavy he had to let it go. These things were like no theatre prop he had seen before. They certainly seemed real. There were oddments like leather belts, and drinking vessels, and then underneath it all, a bunch of letters tied with a cord. He undid the cord and unrolled the letters. They were written on vellum and in an elaborate hand he could only just read. The first read :-

Dear Plumpy,

I know you are unhappy with the current situation and your father's decision to have you marry the Lady Gossamer but you are a big boy now and you have to be grown up. Spending your days carousing and decapitating people here, there, and everywhere is all very well but now it is time to settle down. Your father is very upset that you killed his court jester and doesn't believe it was an accident. Now you be a good boy and behave yourself and marry the Lady Gossamer and I will try to calm your father down.

I have put some warm socks in your trunk as I know you get cold feet. Don't forget to put them on and to have them washed at least once a month.

Yours

Mummy

Catlin stared at the letter. 'What the fuck' he thought. He opened another.

Dear Plumpy,

Your father has asked me to write to you, to tell you, you are not to attack any of our neighbours' castles anymore. He is very upset at this constant looting and pillaging. You don't seem to understand that just because you feel angry all the time, you can't just wage war on everyone and run off with their women. It isn't helpful. The people are getting restless and that just doesn't do. Now I know how hard it is for you to 'behave normally' with your temper and your father and I hold ourselves partly responsible for this but you have to take some responsibility yourself too. You are still my little 'Plumpy', as always, but you must try to be a good boy. Though I hesitate to mention this, when your father gets angry with you, he tends to thrash the bedstraw somewhat and at my age it is very tiring. So please consider your dear mother and try to calm down.

Yours

Mummy

It was as he was considering what he had read, and was about to read another, when there was a knock upon the door. He called out to tell them to come in.

Mistress Munn entered the room sheepishly. She was not at all sure what she was doing was the right thing, but in the Magician's absence and knowing mischief was afoot, felt obliged to try to interfere. She was surprised to see the Bludgeoner up and dressed. The last time she had seen him was the previous night when the Lady Gossamer had poured poison into his ear.

'Forgive my intrusion, sire,' she said, 'but I really need to speak to you.'

Catlin looked at her and wondered how much she was getting paid to pretend to be a medieval serving maid.

'Who are you?' asked Catlin, caustically.

'Why I am Mistress Munn, the Magician's maidservant.'

'Of course you are,' said Catlin. 'I thought there would have to be a Magician in all of this.' He felt like laughing but decided to hold back on his true feeling of contempt for whoever had written such a pathetic script.

'I am here to tell you that I know the truth about you and that you are not who they say you are.'

'Is that right? Well, who exactly do they say I am?'

'Well,' said Mistress Munn, 'they say you are Moredeath the Bludgeoner come to marry the Lady Gossamer, but we both know you are not.'

'Do we?'

'Yes we do. I knows it, and you knows it too. I recognised you from another place in the What Will Be where you was standing naked, with your stiff pinklarry, and a young girl.'

Catlin was trying to play along with the game, but this was getting far too close for comfort. Had they filmed him with Miss Lamb? Got a record of the whole thing? How else would this bizarre old woman know what had happened in Klines?

'One minute you was there and the next you had changed places with the Bludgeoner.'

'Stop!' shouted Catlin, who was getting a really bad vibe. His mind was trying to work out what devious plan was being played out in this obscene mediaeval version of the Truman Show.

'Who's paying you?' he asked

'Why the Magician pays me,' answered Mistress Munn innocently.

'No, who is really paying you to do this? To pretend to be a stupid old woman. Who auditioned you? Who sent you for a screen test? Who is behind all of this?'

Mistress Munn looked blankly at Catlin and began to wonder whether what they had all been saying was true, that this imposter was indeed a madman who shouted and raved about things no one else could understand.

'I don't know what you are saying, but I came here to tell you that your life is in danger. There has already been one attempt upon it, and I have no doubt there are others on the way. You needs to know that you don't belong here and I am the only person that can help you. If anything happens to you, then the real Moredeath will never return and the What Will Be will be disrupted forever. Given the choice, I would let it happen, seeing as you are not a good soul and takes advantage of young maidens, but there is only one way of putting things back together again.'

Catlin sat with a menacing grimace on his face. Despite his initial plan to play along with everything, this old woman was pressing every button and it was working. He told himself to be calm, and that he couldn't win if he didn't play along with the charade.

'Alright,' he said, 'where am I?'

'Why, you are in Naze.'

'Naze? Where is Naze?'

'Well Naze is situated between the Southlands to the South and the Northlands to the North.'

'Fuck that's original,' said Catlin, 'and what year would this be?'

'It is the year 1207, by the grace of the Great Moyen.'

'1207,' repeated Catlin, whose knowledge of history was about as good as his knowledge of astrophysics. She might as well have said any number between nought and two thousand and he would have been none the wiser.

'So let me get this straight,' he continued, 'you say I was brought here by some chance occurrence, and there is someone called Moredeath the Bludgeoner who has taken my place?'

For some inexplicable reason Catlin's mind jumped wildly to thinking of some medieval brute sitting in his jacuzzi back home, plastering himself in his expensive cologne.

'That's right. The Magician, bless his soul, was trying to save the Bludgeoner and, in doing so, got tangled up with the What Will Be.'

'The What Will Be? What is that?'

'Why it is what it says it is - What Will Be.'

'You mean the future?'

'Oh no, the future is uncertain, the What Will Be is what will be.'

For a moment Catlin's mind slipped out of gear as he tried to come to terms with what she had just said. His meagre intuition told him her words sounded quite profound, and yet he couldn't grasp exactly what it was.

'Supposing I was to believe all this bullshit,' he said, 'what can an old woman like you do to put it right?'

'That I am not sure of, at the moment, but all I can tell you is that there may come a moment when you will have to trust me and when that comes you must do what I say.'

Catlin stared at her. He did not trust anyone ever. It had been his trademark and it had served him well. He thought about The Truman Show and how Truman Burbank had been betrayed by all of the actors in the show for years. This old woman was an actress.

'Sure thing, whatever you say.'

Mistress Munn did not know what a 'sure thing' was but took the rest of the sentence to mean he would comply, at which point she left the room.

Catlin sat thinking. It was going to take all of his cynicism and his cunning to come out of this without getting shafted. Whoever had set this up knew about the delightful Miss Lamb and no doubt how he had drugged her. They were playing him and enjoying every moment. He looked around the room again for hidden cameras or microphones, moving the sparse furniture, lifting the tapestry on the wall and even the bedding, but he could see nothing. His paranoia was ramping up. He told himself to hold on, it would be alright, but he didn't feel it.

Mistress Munn left the imposter and made her way down the corridor, occasionally looking into the courtyard below, and beyond it, to the castle gates. Due to the impending wedding the courtyard was unusually busy but with her eagle eye she noticed a slight commotion taking place. A small crowd had gathered around someone who had recently arrived. She stopped and stared and then upon recognising who it was, gasped.

Chapter Thirty One

The arrival of Sir Godfrey was being treated as a great thing. After all, he had been a recluse for so many years but was still remembered for his gallant quest and the recovery of the holy wine. Despite his derelict state, he still managed to attract many admirers, who clustered around his aged horse. The old Knight was bemused and frightened by so many people taking an interest in him, and tried unsuccessfully to steer his way to the stables where he needed to feed and water his horse. Were it not for Mistress Munn, who had dashed from the upstairs window from where she had spotted him, he might never have reached safety.

'Back away! Back away! Can't you see Sir Godfrey has had a long journey and is exhausted. Make way! Make way!'

The old Knight looked down and saw who it was. His old eyes watered and his heart beat faster.

'Is that you Beth'

Mistress Munn looked up at the old Knight and smiled.

'It is indeed'

'Then my journey has been worthwhile.'

Mistress Munn blushed. Despite his rusty armour, threadbare clothing and his oh so old face, she saw only the man she had loved all those years ago, and who had vanished like a ghost from her life. ''Make way, make way,' shouted Mistress Munn to the crowd as she hustled past them, leading Sir Godfrey's horse. She walked to the stable and once they were inside closed the door on the outside world. Sir Godfrey dismounted with an aged groan and a rusty creak of armour.

'My apologies Beth. Time, that wicked thief, has robbed me of my ability to present a better man to you. For all that, I would want to kneel before you and tell you how much I have waited for this moment, to apologise for my long absence, but I fear I would never get up again.'

'There is no need for any of that. I know you never meant ill of anyone in your life. It is just good to see you again. Particularly at such times as these.'

'Indeed,' replied the old Knight. 'I have not known such goings on. It is as if the world has gone mad. Why, on my way here, I was accosted by a man selling pinklarry broaches of all things.' Sir Godfrey glanced at Mistress Munn's cloak and saw she was wearing one. She noticed his look of surprise.

'I know Arthur, but before you says anything, 'tis better to be safe than sorry and, as I said to Whattlewherrit, if you doesn't want to stick out in the crowd, then what harm does it do? I don't want to be labelled a witch for not wearing one.'

'Whattlewherrit.' muttered Sir Godfrey sadly. He touched Mistress Munn on the shoulder in an affectionate way before continuing.

'Beth, I have some bad news.'

'Has something happened to Whattlewherrit?' Her face darkened.

'No, not to him, but to his father.'

'You have news of Cornelius?'

'Alas, yes, but it is not good news.'

Mistress Munn drew breath.

'Whilst on my journey here, I happened upon the Greer Swamp. Not knowing where I was, and befuddled by the atmosphere, I came upon a cave.'

'The Bloodly Sisters!' exclaimed Mistress Munn.

'Exactly Beth.'

'You met the Bloodly Sisters?'

'Indeed not, or I should not be here. I did however find Cornelius.' Sir Godfrey stopped for a moment. He could not tell his beloved the circumstances under which their old friend, Cornelius, had passed away. He left the details for his memory alone.

'He was about to die when I found him. The sisters had held him captive and left him in their cave.'

Mistress Munn's eyes welled up and her lip quivered.

'I did what little I could, but it was too late. However, before he died, he whispered a few words of warning to me. The Lady Sockamore and her servants are not what they appear to be. The Bloodly Sisters are behind it.'

'I knew it!' cried Mistress Munn. 'I knew there was something untoward about them the moment I saw them and so did Whattlewherrit. More than that, since their arrival they have visited the island. Something wicked is afoot.'

'You must be careful Beth. Those who underestimate the sisters do so at their peril.'

'I have no fear of them two hags Arthur, not now I knows what they have done to Cornelius. My well-being is of no consequence, especially if they intends harm to Whattlewherrit. As my dear old mother used to say, 'Hell hath no fury like a woman's corns.'

160

Sir Godfrey wasn't quite sure what ill-fitting footwear had to do with things but had long-ago accepted Beth's tendency to throw such expressions into otherwise intelligible conversation.

'Valiant talk my Beth, but remember the curse we are both under. We may not fear death but there is worse than that, living in perpetual pain or misery. And should the sisters find this out about either of us, they would not hesitate to use it against us.'

Mistress Munn huffed, and then said, 'We shall see.'

Chapter Thirty Two

Whilst the great and good of the land prepared themselves for the evening in their rooms, in the kitchens of the castle, all was hustle and bustle. Gladwell Jupp was her usual fraught self, shouting directions and whopping the serving boys with her wooden spoon when she found them misbehaving. She was deep in her arms in pastry, one of her favourite tasks. 'You can't beat delving into the soft fleshiness of a good pastry,' she used to say, 'always reminds me of nights with my dear departed husband. He liked a good belly rub if you knows what I mean? And the benefits of pastry to the hands is not to be underestimated. They always comes out cleaner than they goes in.' She was giving the pastry a deep massage when her friend Mistress Munn arrived.

'Gladwell I needs to speak to you.'

'Go on Beth. Don't mind me getting on with my pastry.'

'Arthur is here.' Gladwell gave the pastry a good thump.

'Sir Godfrey is in the castle?' She asked

'He is.'

'Why that good for nothing philanderer. He fair broke your heart.' She thumped the pastry again with a clenched fist as though it was someone's face.

'He is a good man,' said Mistress Munn.

'A good man indeed.' Thump, Thump. 'A good man doesn't leave a good woman without a word, and disappear for years on end.'

'There are reasons Gladwell.'

Thump, thump, thump.

'Oh yes, there are always reasons. Men are full of reasons. They are born with them Beth. If I could count the number of reasons men have given me over the years, they would be greater than the weevils in a sailing ship's biscuit barrel.'

'He is not like that.'

'Oh, so you say, but believe me they are all the same when their cod piece comes to the fore. That and their stomachs of course.'

Mistress Munn noticed that her friend Gladwell had formed a slab of pastry into the shape of a pinklarry and was slowly strangling it.

'Trust me Gladwell, Arthur has his reasons, and he has apologised.'

'Apologised has he? Well so he should. I remember how your heart was broke, and I won't forget it.'

162

'You are a good friend Gladwell, and I know you are saying these things because you intend well, but there is no time to doubt Arthur now. Things are afoot. I have come to warn you to look out for the Lady Sockamore and her maid servants. All is not well with them.'

'How so'

'Let us just say they have bad intentions, and they may well start in this very kitchen.'

'Not whilst I'm in charge!' Said Gladwell authoritatively, finally putting an end to her pastry pinklarry by pulling its head off.

Back at Kenny Catlin's rooms, he had his second visitor of the day in the shape of the King.

'You seem to be better today Moredeath,' said the King, somewhat tentatively. He did not want to do anything to provoke his future son-in-law and certainly did not want to raise the issue of the Magician and what had happened. Catlin stared at the King, trying to see if he could spot makeup on his face. The King coughed during the embarrassing silence that followed.

'I realise that your entry into Naze was not that which we had planned but I can assure you the wedding will have no such problems. Tonight we will feast in prenuptial celebration and you will see that Naze is in fact the most welcoming of lands.'

Catlin continued to stare. It was a technique he had used often when driving down the prices of contracts for his TV shows. Silence spoke a thousand words in his book.

'Well, I can see the tailors have made a splendid job of adjusting your costume. It looks....well it looks..snug.'

Catlin spoke at last. 'Who is paying you?'

'I beg your pardon?'

'Who is paying you to do this?'

The King looked confused.

'I do not understand what you are saying Moredeath. How could anyone pay a King to do anything? The notion is preposterous. Kings are not boatmen or hostlers for hire. If you mean someone from the Northlands, then why would I have you marry my daughter in order to protect Naze and then take payment for it?'

'I was told that someone was out to kill me, that I am in danger.'

163

'Who said as much? I will have them hung in the square for such treachery.'

'I will find out,' said Catlin, 'believe me, I will find out who is behind all of this and when I do, they are dead meat.'

The King shuddered. A threat from anyone else he could dismiss, but even from a diminished Moredeath, he dare not.

'There is no need to fear anything whilst you are Naze. I will make sure of that. I have guards posted everywhere and the Knights will be at hand to ensure your personal protection.'

'You aren't going to give up acting this out, are you? Even though you know I have seen through this charade. Well, you tell whoever is behind all of this, that I intend seeing them rot in hell for what they have done.'

The King was shaken. There was only one thing to which Moredeath could be referring and that was his transformation from a muscle-bound bear of a man to the pathetic flabby older man the King saw before him. There could be no mistake Moredeath knew it was the Magician who had done this, and he was telling the King in no uncertain terms he was going to pay for what had happened. There could be no other interpretation.

'I can assure you that once we find the person who has done this, they will be punished,' said the King. 'But for the moment there is a wedding ceremony to be performed and a feast this very night. I ask you to delay your revenge for one night and one day, that is all. My daughter's bedstraw awaits your pleasure. A maiden, without compare in all the land I can assure you. If she is anything like her mother, your sweetmeats will certainly need replenishing by the end of the wedding eve.'

Catlin smirked. This two-bit actor wasn't getting anywhere with him. 'Ok old man, this is the last time you act out being a King or anything else for that matter. You might as well rip up your equity card. I will go along with this game for a while longer but you, and all those involved in it, are going to pay for messing with me.'

The King felt his blood go cold. He took his leave.

Having left Catlin the King made his way to his daughter's apartments. He knocked on the door but did not await a reply and walked straight in. The Lady Gossamer was sewing the final threads of her tapestry and looked up, startled by her father's appearance.

'What is the matter father?' She asked, 'you look concerned.'

The King took a seat beside his daughter.

'Oh my child, what have I done?'

'What have you done?' she asked.

'I have brought a madman into our lives. The Bludgeoner is threatening to kill us all. His words are strange and convoluted but there is no doubt he means to wreak revenge upon us for what has occurred. He thinks someone paid me to attack his entourage and turn him into a shadow of his former self.'

'But why?'

'Who can tell? We still don't know who attacked him, or why. And then there's the Magician of course.'

'I have a confession father.' The Lady Gossamer looked down towards her needle and thread ashamed to look her father in the eye.

'What is it my child?'

'This last night I took myself to Moredeath's room and there did administer poison in his ear.'

The King gasped.

'But how so? And if this be true, why is he not dead?'

'That I cannot say. I gave him enough to kill ten men and this very morning he is up and well. I fear that what they say about him is true. He may not look as strong in stature as he did but there is no doubt he is indeed the Bludgeoner.'

The King's face drained of blood.

'What are we to do?' he asked.

'We find someone to blame of course,' she replied, 'then we hunt them down and execute them.'

'But who?' The King looked perplexed. The Lady Gossamer smiled softly, then whispered.

'Sir Sockamore.'

'Sir Sockamore?' exclaimed the King, 'but he is an honest Knight of the realm. I mean I can't stand the man but nevertheless....'

'Think about it father, we may not even need to find him. If, as they say he wandered into the Greer Swamp, we can safely assume he will not return. What matter if he is accused of the crime? He will not suffer as a result.'

The King shook his head.

'But my child, his reputation will be forever sullied. Think on it, death for a Knight would be a better thing than dishonour.'

The Lady Gossamer leaned into her father and put her hand upon his shoulder.

'He has no offspring, no wife, what does it matter?'

The King did not want to mention the fact that he had every intention of bedding the Lady Sockamore as soon as he could. His mind had already envisioned their coupling, in fact, about every five minutes since he had first seen her. He knew she would not be the type of woman to offer her gifts without a promise of marriage. How could he besmirch the name of her family and yet still make her queen.

'Oh, I think we need to consider this further my child,' he replied, much to the Lady Gossamers annoyance.

'Then take time to do so father, but think on what the Bludgeoner said, and weigh it in the scales against the name of Sockamore. I believe you will come round, if only your good sense prevails.

The King grunted and said, 'perhaps.' He gave his apologies, said he had things to see to, and then left. The Lady Gossamer looked at her needlework and then began stabbing it viciously in the space where the crest of Sir Sockamore would otherwise have been.

Chapter Thirty Three

The party at Rick Facile's Cotswold home in the small village of Upskirting was in full swing. Rick and Deloris Pops had pledged their vows, and then fallen out. Rick insisted on showing off his art collection, much to the chagrin of Deloris. Deloris had stomped off into the garden and found the 'statue' of Moredeath and, to her utter amazement and confusion, had been literally swept off her feet and fucked by a mediaeval porn star. She lay watching the night sky in a field at the edge of the garden, wondering what drug she had inadvertently taken that had created this crazy situation, and when it was going to wear off. She didn't feel doped up. The ground was hard beneath her, the grass already damp in the night air, her back was definitely aching and there were parts of her that felt as though she had been straddling a bull long enough to win the top prize in a Texas rodeo. She reached out, to turn to move, and found her head swimming. Her mind was desperately trying to grasp whether she was under the influence of drink and drugs or whether something unimaginable had happened. The act of sitting up, having worn her out, she collapsed back down in tears.

In another part of the garden, two of the guests were loitering by the statue called 'The Stinger'. To the background music of the Army of the Dead playing out in the house, they were engaged in a serious conversation. One was Rick Facile's manager, Dick Friendly and the other Facile's solicitor, Max Moran. Moran took a deep draw on his cigar and, leaning his head back, blew it into the night sky.

'We've got to do something, Dick,' he said, his smoke-tainted words blowing across his compatriot's face. Dick Friendly waved away the smoke but took on board the words. Moran didn't seem to notice, or else care.

'What do you suggest?'

Moran drew another lungful of smoke.

'I am not sure. We need to get enough money together to cover the losses, before Rick finds out.'

'He's just spent a fortune on these fucking statues,' replied Rick's manager, looking at 'The Stinger.'

'I know. Well, you were with him when he bought them, so you can take responsibility for that.'

Dick Friendly scowled at Moran.

'I had no choice. What did you expect me to say? 'You can't afford these Rick, because Max and I have been siphoning off your money and using it to speculate in dodgy film deals.'

'For Christ's sake Dick, don't tell me you couldn't divert him in some way? Tell him there were better investments. It wouldn't take much. Ricks a moron, he wouldn't have known any better.'

'Rick thinks he's got enough money to buy whatever he wants and if it wasn't for us, he would have. We've built a house of cards that's about to collapse if we don't get an urgent injection of funds. I've got to pretend that everything is alright, otherwise Rick will find out what we've done. He might be uneducated, but he's not an idiot, he is street savvy. I blame Catlin. If he hadn't gone missing, and the film had gone ahead, we would be rolling in it instead of looking at a jail sentence.'

'Let's not go there, Dick. Calm down, we just need to put something together that's all. Catlin disappearing like that couldn't have been predicted. We were just unlucky that's all.'

'Do you think he did murder that girl?'

'What the Lamb woman?'

'Yes.'

'I don't know. Kenny Catlin was always a mean and unforgiving man, but I never heard of him being violent at all. Who knows though? People's personal habits, especially when it comes to sex, are often bizarre. Maybe he was into rough sex and it went wrong. At the end of the day, it doesn't matter. I can't see him coming back, not with an International Arrest Warrant out on him. It's too late for us anyway, the film isn't going to be made, the money has gone, we aren't going to see that again.'

Moran dropped the remains of his cigar on the brick paving and ground it into the cracks with his expensive shoe.

'One thing is for sure, we've got to find a way forward before it gets any worse.' And with that he walked away.

Whattlewherrit was confused when he woke up again after his glass of champagne. He was certain that Moredeath, along with the strange statues of The Stinger, and The Medusa, had all been placed in the garden not far from one another. Indeed, he had even watched workmen prepare the ground for them and discuss what needed to be done. But try as he might, he could only find the two weird statues and not Moredeath. He had been walking for quite some time, and had wandered off to the very edges of the garden, when he stumbled across a young woman sitting on the grass. She was crying and was obviously distressed. Unsure of what to do, he thought of Mistress Munn's words to him about how he could be detached and aloof, and needed to take more care of ordinary people. It was not something that came naturally and always made him feel awkward. Nevertheless, in a moment of unusual empathy, he crossed the grass to talk to her.

'Are you alright?' he asked. It sounded rather stupid to ask such a question, given the circumstances, but it was the best he could think of.

'No, I'm not,' said the young woman.

'Well, is there anything I can do?' Asked Whattlewherrit mustering up his best intentions but already feeling out of his depth.

'You can tell me this is all a fucking nightmare,' replied the woman.

'It is all a fucking nightmare,' repeated Whattlewherrit dutifully.

'Are you taking the piss?' She looked up at Whattlewherrit, examining him with her tearful eyes.

'I don't think so,' replied the Magician.

'Well, it sounds like it,' she replied.

'I am looking for Moredeath,' he said, 'the Bludgeoner.'

Deloris Pops scanned the Magician.

'I wondered if you had seen him?'

Deloris Pops wiped her nose on the sleeve of her jacket and sniffed deeply.

'What does he look like?' she asked.

'Oh, about six-foot-six, broad as an ox, a scar down one cheek and an axe.....'

'Stop!' she screamed.

'Why have I said something wrong?'

'You know him?' she hissed.

'Unfortunately, I do,' replied Whattlewherrit, 'he has been a great problem to me for several days now. I just want to find him and get him back where he belongs.'

'He's just a beast,' she said, 'he behaves like a fucking animal.'

'Yes, that's him,' said Whattlewherrit, 'have you seen him'

Deloris didn't want to tell the Magician about her encounter with Rick's 'statue' but she did want to find out what was happening to her.

'Who are you?' she asked, 'and what have you got to do with that thing, whatever it is?'

'My name is Whattlewherrit and I am the Magician of Naze. There has been an unfortunate accident and Moredeath should not be here in the What Will Be.'

'What the fuck are you on? You aren't helping me here; you are making it worse. I need you to tell me I am not going mad!'

'You are not going mad,' said Whattlewherrit. 'It is all quite simple. I looked into the What Will Be at the King's behest. I should have refused but in a moment of weakness I succumbed. In that moment two things seem to have become entangled. A strange naked man with a stiff pinklarry, and Moredeath riding through the forest. I have deduced this from a great deal of thinking. This is why, when I tried to save Moredeath later on, the two of them swapped places and now I am trying to get them back where they belong.'

Deloris Pops stared at Whattlewherrit and just shouted very loudly, 'piss off!'

Chapter Thirty Four

Bishop Righteous the third of Nantes stared into the mirror. He had his holy vestments on and was wearing the eternal underpants over his elaborate silken hose. The monogrammed shorts were only worn on very special occasions and apart from the odd evening when, in his rooms, he would parade around with them on, they stayed firmly in the wooden box with the Geekie. The large KC on them was clear, and the Bishop put forward a leg to show off the two letters. Much debate had taken place over the years about the meaning of them and after several synods, the church had finally decreed the letters stood for 'Knight of Compassion'. This was how he pictured himself, a warrior in a similar fashion to the Knights of Naze except his battleground happened to be the minds and souls of the people. He picked up the Book of Words, that cryptic text written by the hand of the Great Moyen himself, telling of the Great Moyen's intentions. The Bishop, as all students of the seminary he had attended, had studied it with intense interest for many years, looking for clues, hidden meanings, and teachings that could lead to the church fulfilling its true purpose. Only divine intervention could lead to an understanding of the book and the Bishop regretfully had not received such. He went with what previous Bishops had deduced and added only what he felt would enhance his status as a 'Righteous' man. So it was that the Bishop had interpreted one passage to say that, once a year, followers of the Great Moyen should gather together and listen to a long speech he would make, and then pay a tithe directly to himself. This had worked very well. His second addition to the accepted wisdom of the book was that the bishop must, despite his obvious reluctance to do so, visit local whore houses, where he would bless the fallen women and accept whatever gift they might be able to offer. Taxing though it was, the Bishop made sure he did his duty at least once a month, usually on a Sunday after church service.

As well as the book of words, the Bishop had in his room the Holy Wine, which, since visiting the Magician's island, was giving him less concern than it had. It seemed obvious the Great Moyen had forgiven him for drinking from the bottle and he looked forward to the promises made in the note he had found on the Magician's front door. Finally, there was the Geekie, the Great Moyen's mouthpiece.

The Geekie was simpler to understand than the Book of Words because the Great Moyen had, in his infinite wisdom, included a set of instructions on how to use his mouthpiece. In the box ,in which it arrived in Naze, there was a small pamphlet on how to throw your voice, and how to operate the Geekies head so the Great Moyen's words, spoken via the Bishop, could be heard by the congregation. The Bishop picked up the ventriloquist's dummy, and spoke into the mirror.

'Nie Nords, Nadies, and Gentelnen. We are gaddered togeder to narry Nordeath the Gludgener and de Nady Gossaner.'

The Bishop had run through the speech numerous times over the past weeks but wanted to be word-perfect on the day. With all of the great and good of the land in attendance it would be the ideal opportunity to bring a serious note to the occasion. The Bishop raised an authoritative eyebrow to himself, whilst practising his facial expressions.

The great mystery to the Bishop, as it was to everyone, was how the Holy Relics came to be, and how it was that the Great Moyen had seen fit to distribute them throughout the land, at different times, in the history of Naze. Had it not been for the angel Debbie, who called herself, 'The Lamb', they might never have been found. She foretold their existence when she appeared in person one night to the Sisters of Irreverence, and then, having given the great news, disappeared as mysteriously as she had appeared. From that day forward, the search was on and once the Book of Words and the Eternal Underpants were found, only the Geekie and wine remained. The wine was the last to be discovered.

The Bishop looked at the bottle and thought about Sir Godfrey of Merrelay. The church had wanted to make him an honorary archdeacon, but he would have none of it. He disappeared into his castle, having delivered the bottle, and was not seen again. Rumour had it that the King had summoned him to the wedding, and so it was not beyond imagining that the bishop might actually meet the man he admired so much. A man of selfless dedication and such profound honesty as it would be hard to find another to touch him in all the land.

There was a knock at the door. The bishop told the visitor to come. He was surprised to see the Lady Gossamer enter.

'My Lady,' he said, bowing slowly.

The Lady Gossamer eyed up the bishop, and tried to keep a serious face. The Eternal Underpants were not in her view at all flattering and the Geekie just added to the overall look.

'To what do I owe the pleasure?'

'Bishop, I see you are prepared for the night's festivities, and no doubt tomorrows.'

'Indeed, my lady. What an honour to be presiding over your matrimonial celebrations.'

The Lady Gossamer smiled, though in her heart she was furious at being used by her father as a way of cementing the Bloodlands and Naze, especially as Moredeath had turned into a barrel of a man with less hair than you would find in a monk's comb.

'That, Bishop, is why I am here.'

'Of course.'

'I gather that you were enquiring about the Magician's island?'

The Bishop looked wary, as though he wasn't sure whether he ought to admit he had. The Lady Gossamer sensed his concern.

'The King told me of your conversation, so you don't have to worry,' she said.

'I see,' said the Bishop, 'and what might your interest be in it, my lady?'

'I thought I might offer you support in your plans to build a monastery there.'

'That is most kind.'

'The King is in two minds about it but with a little persuasion I am sure he can be brought to your way of thinking.'

'That is...well it is, positive, is it not?'

'It could well be, if it were mutually beneficial.'

'How so?'

'I give you support and help the King make his mind up in your favour, you give me support in return.'

The Bishop looked confused.

'In what way may I be of assistance my lady? Just speak the words and I am your servant.'

'Good. Well, what I want you to do is to find a way to annul the marriage before it has been consummated.'

The mouth of the Bishop's Geekie dropped wide open.

'My lady? I...I...think I must have misheard.'

'I think not Bishop. Before the Bludgeoner is able to thrash the bedstraw with me upon it, I want you to find a reason why he cannot, in the eyes of the church, marry me. It's all very simple.'

The Bishop looked aghast.

'But my lady....'was all he could say, before the Lady Gossamer turned away and was gone.

Chapter Thirty Five

In the grand hall the lights were lit, the fires stoked, the tables laid, and the tapestries hung awaiting the grandest night of the decade. Within the hour, the Knights of Naze, their ladies, the Bishop and the arch deacons, the King and the Lady Gossamer would take their places alongside dignitaries from throughout the land. Serving wenches filled jugs of beer and mead, and on the top-table, fine wine was poured in preparation for the royal party to arrive.

Down in the kitchens, Gladwell Jupp felt as if she had lost a stone in weight, and mopped her brow, as the heat from the roasting meat blasted out from the great fireplace. The hustle and bustle was deafening, as orders were shouted and pots and pans clashed together. The day had been long, oh so long and her head was spinning with recipes, timings, soups and spoons, spillages, and the general mayhem of an overworked kitchen. It was no wonder then, that by the time one of Lady Sockamore's maidservants slipped into the chaos, she failed to notice the intruder. Furthermore, she had her back to her when, unnoticed by anyone, the maidservant slipped a potion into the soup. Having done the deed, she slipped back to the room where her sister, and the Lady Sockamore, were waiting.

'Did you do it?' asked her sister.

'I did.'

'What did you do?' asked the Lady Sockamore, who was on edge because she knew wicked deeds were afoot. The hag looked at her.

'Tell her sister,' said the other one, 'she will find out soon enough.'

'Well dearie, I just happened to put a little something extra in the soup.' she replied.

At the word 'soup', the Lady Sockamore felt a chill run over her. She would never again be able to eat a bowl of anything that looked or behaved like soup.

'What exactly did you put in it?' asked the Lady Sockamore.

'A love potion, dearie.'

'A love potion?'

'Indeed. But a very unusual one, one that will see an end to Naze.' The hag cackled a raspy wet cackle which the Lady Sockamore found repulsive.

'Why would a love potion do such a thing?' she asked.

'Ah dearie, that is the wonderful thing about love, it is as toxic as the strongest Hemlock, and as poisonous as the Mandrake root if taken in too large a dose.'

'But who is to be the object of this love potion?'

'Ah well, there you have the nub of it dearie. Every man at the feast tonight,' replied the hag.

'Every man? To what end would you make every man fall in love? And with whom would they fall in love?'

The hag laughed a wicked laugh and just said, 'you will see my dear, you will see.'

The Lady Sockamore felt a deep sense of foreboding creep through her. It was then that the other hag handed her a dress the colour of a deep red rose.

'Here, put this on.' she said brusquely.

The Lady Sockamore looked at the dress with disbelief. There was nothing of it. It seemed to be made of material that was as fine as a spider's web. Not only that, but when she held it up to put it against her ample breasts, she discovered that there was practically no material to cover her cleavage. Similarly, the back of the dress scooped down so low, most of her back would be on show.

'I can't wear this!' she protested, 'it is unfinished. Were I to wear it, it would show half of my body! No maiden protecting her modesty would ever wear such a thing.'

'It is the latest fashion in the Bloodlands my dear, and as you well know, your task is to seduce the Bludgeoner. You need to entice him with your feminine charm.' replied the hag.

'But to wear this would be no more than to throw a tempting morsel to a hungry dog, and you know full well what happens then. I will not be consumed like a juicy ham.'

'Try it on dearie,' said the hag, in tone of voice that denied objection.

The Lady Sockamore did as she was commanded. Having put the dress on, she realised it clung to her voluptuous torso, and was as though she was all but naked, and yet somehow, due to the subtle hues within the material, the eye could see nothing. Only the possibility of what lay beneath was bequeathed to anyone looking. Below the tightly formed waist, the material of the dress fanned out as though it were liquid. Any movement she made caused it to flow around her feet with the shimmering colours and slow movement of a dazzling Salmon caught by the rays of the early morning sun. It was almost too beautiful to look at for any length of time. As the Lady Sockamore herself found, if one did so, one became entranced.

'What is this made of?' she said as she swayed in the dress, making it shimmer.

'Why nothing special, my dear. It's just something we threw together.' The hags laughed.

The Lady Sockamore inadvertently stroked her body sensuously. The hags watched, but said nothing.

'I suppose for one night I could wear such a dress, but then you must keep your promise. You must change me back to my former self.'

The hags smiled and nodded as one. It was at that moment that the sound of trumpets in the distance announced the party was to begin.

'We must go,' said the Lady Sockamore.

'Not yet dearie. We shall wait a short while. We need to make an entrance. We don't want to shuffle in with the hoi polloi.'

In the hall below the room where the Bloodly Sisters and the Lady Sockamore stood, a great surge of people flooded through the huge oak doors. Knights and their wives, officials of state, dignitaries of all manner went to take their places, hustling and bustling to secure a seat as close to the top table as they might. The room was all chatter and anticipation, for it was that very night that they would see Moredeath the Bludgeoner for the first time. Only Sir Bloatmore amongst the Knights had actually seen the Bludgeoner, and he had been sworn to secrecy by the King as to what had happened. Amongst the other Knights, Moredeath's fame went before him, and everybody knew what a beast of a man he was, but none could truly imagine what this towering hulk would be like in the flesh. Moredeath was undoubtedly the main attraction, but for the ladies of the realm in particular there was great interest in Sir Sockamore's sister the Lady Sockamore. Rumour had taken hold. It was whispered in the corridors and bed chambers of the castle that the Lady Sockamore was a great beauty, and her maid servants, although clearly no longer maids themselves, were none the less very attractive. The mystery that surrounded them led to even greater speculation and anticipation. Why was it Sir Sockamore had never mentioned his sister? How was it she had appeared, as if by magic, to attend the wedding ceremony, whilst her brother had disappeared? There was nothing the ladies of the realm liked more than a mystery about which they could tittle tattle.

It took a good half an hour before the room settled, and even then, there was a boisterous buzz about the place. The master of ceremonies made three attempts at hushing the room before he could announce the arrival of the King and his daughter, the Lady Gossamer.

The room stood in silence as the King and his daughter walked slowly down the aisle between the two huge tables that stretched the length of the room. When they had reached the top table, they took their seats on the highly ornate thrones carved with the King's coat of arms. The King gestured to the assembled guests to sit.

There was a soft thud as one hundred guests returned to their seats, followed by a murmuring as the crowd discussed the King and his daughter. No sooner than the King had sat, than the master of ceremonies announced the arrival of Moredeath. The room fell into a deafening hush as the great doors opened, and in walked Kenny Catlin, wearing his cut-down version of Moredeath's tabard and hose. At first, it was as though the whole room had been plunged into the icy waters of a lake. The shock of seeing him overwhelmed all other sensations, and took the breath away. Those near the door stared in disbelief as Catlin strolled down the aisle, a look of dismissive contempt on his face. Those further up craned their heads to catch a glimpse of the man they had been waiting to see. The underwhelming appearance of Catlin was such a disappointment, people found it difficult to comprehend. Where was the giant ox of a man that was to marry the King's daughter and protect the Kingdom? Who had spread the stories about his stature and his overwhelming presence, his menacing façade, his brutal attraction for certain types of maiden? The King reached his hand over to his daughters and squeezed it tight. He knew what the room was thinking, and it concerned him more than he could possibly express. The man walking towards him was supposed to boost his position as ruler of Naze but instead was making a mockery of the crown.

As Catlin walked towards the top table, he was thinking of vengeance. Whoever had set him up in this mediaeval Truman show had money, pots of money. This wasn't a cheap production, no two bit 'B' film. He knew how much it cost to hire actors, film sets, crew members, designers. For Christ's sake, the wardrobe costs on this sham show would have cost a mint. There was only one man who could have done this. Lenny Lane, billionaire entrepreneur, who had been his nemesis ever since he had shafted Lenny's wife at a party, under the influence of too much drink and a heavy helping of drugs. It wasn't as if his wife was even slightly of starlet quality. It was just a stupid mistake. This was Lenny's revenge. So be it. He would play it out because he had no other choice, but it had to end sometime, and when it did, he would find a way to pay him back.

The road to the top table seemed to take forever as he watched the stunned faces of the assembled party. In his mind he knew they were deliberately goading him with their dismissive staring. He scowled and occasionaly snarled and grunted at the tables on either side, at which they backed off, as if he were some sort of caged animal that had escaped the zoo.

By the time he reached the top table and was seated next to the Lady Gossamer, soft mutterings had turned into audible expressions of dismay. Words such as short, overweight, balding, disappointing, punctuated the air as Catlin was pulled apart by the assembled guests. The King did his best to override them with impromptu conversation about the wine but was in no doubt

Moredeath had heard the disparaging remarks. Fortunately the master of ceremonies struck his ceremonial stick on the door and called out 'Bishop Righteous of Nantes!' The bishop entered, with the arch deacons in tow. He was wearing the Eternal Underpants and holding the Geekie, whilst his arch deacons held the Book of Words and the Holy wine. The guests fell silent in respect. All apart from Kenny Catlin who, on seeing the Eternal Underpants, began to seethe, and could not hold back anymore. He stood up and shouted out, 'Those are my fucking shorts!'

The assembled crowd gasped. No one understood the meaning of what he said but it was an affront to the Bishop, a total lack of respect to the holy relics. He was about to launch into another tirade when he saw the Geekie and with all the self-control he could muster, slowly sat back down, realising he was playing right into the hands of his protagonists. It was an elaborate charade, designed to trap him into admitting what he had done that day in Klines. By parading these things, they were showing him they knew he had drugged Debbie Lamb, they knew he had his shorts down to his ankles and a stiff cock and was ready to....His thoughts were interrupted by the master of ceremonies once more.

'Sir Godfrey of Merrelay!' He shouted.

All heads turned away from the bishop and the arch deacons, towards the door where the aged shape of Sir Godfrey appeared. Rusty and worn, like an old cottage gate, he creaked into the hall. His long eyebrows almost covering his sad watery eyes with his similarly unkempt moustache.

His diminished frame seemed barely able to carry the weight of his clothing and was stooped so that he had to crane his head up in order to not to be looking at the ground. There was hardly a shred left of the man who left Merrelay all those years ago in search of the Holy Wine. It was as if life had sucked him dry and left but a husk. But for all of his wanting, as he slowly made his way to the top table where the King had awarded him a place of honour, he found himself the subject of rapturous applause.

The assembled hall treated him like a returning hero. His eyes watered more. His heart was moved but was at the same time weighed down by the heavy knowledge that he was a fraud. He had to pass by the Holy Wine on his way to the top table. Only he and his beloved Beth knew it was filled with horse piss and not the pressing of the fruits of heaven. It seemed an eternity before he reached the top table where he went to lower himself into his seat. Unfortunately, due to the age and condition of his armour, his knee guards locked into place before his arse hit the seat and he was strangely suspended in mid-movement, confined by his inability to lift himself up again.

'Punish me some more Great Moyen, I deserve it,' he thought to himself. He had no option but to maintain the uncomfortable posture or ask for assistance. The latter would be too humiliating.

The last guests to be announced by the master of ceremonies were the Lady Sockamore and her maids. The assembly turn their heads as one, as the Lady Sockamore appeared in the doorway. Clothed in the dress the hags had given her to wear, she shimmered her way slowly forwards, head proud, breasts prominent, her perfect skin revealed by the cut of the dress that pulsed in a sensual manner. There was a stunned silence. The women envied her looks, her style, her elegance. The men were just transfixed. As she seemed to glide across the stone floor, the vacuum of silence was strangely punctuated by the sound of leather stretching. At first just odd hints of it, but as she moved forwards, there was a definite creaking in the air. The Lady Sockamore wondered what could cause such a strange sound, failing to recognise the stretching of a hundred cod pieces trying to keep hold of their errant charges. Wives looked down with distain, some elbowed their husbands, whilst others took hold of the offending codpieces, giving them a heartily discouraging wrench. The hags smile graciously, as though they had no idea what seeds the enchanted dress has already sown, but inwardly smirk, knowing the soup hadn't even arrived on the tables.

'Oh, what fun,' they both thought.

The top table, having been announced, and everyone in place, the King announced the beginning of the meal, at which point the servants came in with the first of the many courses. The King who, like his Knights, was similarly entranced by the Lady Sockamore leant over towards her.

'How delightful you look my dear. I am at a loss for words at your remarkable appearance. Surely there cannot be in all of nature's beauty a creature more admirable than yourself this night.'

The Lady Sockamore flinched. The thought of the King talking to her in such a way was disgustingly disconcerting. What could she say? She decided to deflect him.

'I am humbled by your words Sire, but surely you are wrong when at your side is your daughter who indeed deserves such words. Who could possibly compare with the Lady Gossamer's beauty?'

The King smiled and raised his glass.

'Indeed,' he replied, 'and you are quite right, this is my daughter's night, and I must not say ought to diminish her joy.'

The Lady Sockamore looked past the King towards the Lady Gossamer and saw no joy upon her face. She was in conversation with the Bludgeoner, and it did not appear to be going well.

'Forgive me for being blunt my lord,' said the Lady Gossamer, 'but you seem less than enthusiastic with our planned betrothal?'

Catlin stared at the Lady Gossamer. He grunted.

'How would you feel if one minute you were in control of your fucking world and the next you woke up and found yourself in a damp hole of a forest, naked, unsure of where you were? Then as if this were all planned, everyone you come across continues to trick you into thinking you are going crazy? Someone is behind what happened back in the forest, and what has happened since. I think I know who it is. But what you need to understand is that whatever happens next, I won't forget. I will remember every last one of you and the parts you have played in this fucking shit show.'

The Lady Gossamer shifted uncomfortably in her seat. His words were too close for comfort. Did he know it was at her bidding that Sir Sockamore attacked his entourage?

'I am unable, as a woman, to imagine what you have undergone, but I can assure you, I have played no part in this other than being faithful to my role as the daughter of the King.'

'Listen sister, I know you are acting out a part. You don't have to mention your 'role.' You think I don't know what's going on? You think I don't realise that before I get to bed you, something will happen? You aren't going to go through with that, not unless you are being paid extra for the bed scenes on top of the acting?'

The Lady Gossamer frowned deeply. She was shocked that the Bludgeoner seemed to know about her conversation with the Bishop of Nantes. He knew everything! She had underestimated him. He was indeed as wily as they said, his animal cunning enabled him to see beyond the obvious. She was undone. In a last ditch attempt at saving herself she whispered to him.

'I know who really is behind what is happening. I will tell you all after the meal. I cannot say more with my father at my side.'

The Lady Gossamer had no intention of suffering Moredeath's wrath. The betrayal of Sir Sockamore, should he ever return, would be an easy price to pay in order that she was not the subject of Moredeath's revenge. Kenny Catlin stared at her, examining her closely. Was she really going to spill the beans? Was someone finally going to confirm all of his suspicions? He leant across to her.

'If you tell me what is going on, I will make sure you live like a queen forever,' he whispered.

The Lady Gossamer took a deep slow breath. Was she misunderstanding what he had said? The implications of his words were immense. If she were to live like a queen forever, then what of her father? Did Moredeath intend getting rid of him? There was no other way she could be queen. She turned and glanced at her father who was deeply engrossed in conversation with the Lady Sockamore. If, as she suspected, he intended to marry the lady, then she would be denied the crown, possibly forever. A cold mercenary feeling damped her bones. He would have her marry Moredeath and suffer the consequences of their alliance so why should she care what happened to him?

'I promise you, you will not regret telling me what is actually going on' continued Catlin. 'I will protect you, and then leave you in peace, you have my word.'

Chapter Thirty Six

The soup arrived and was put in front of Lady Sockamore. She stared at it. Her aversion to soup was intense, following her experience in the Greer Swamp. Everything about soup now shouted castration. She felt her private parts sucking in, like a snail withdrawing into the safety of its shell.

'Eat up my dear,' said the King seeing her reluctance, 'a woman needs to ensure she is properly nourished if she is to fulfil her obligations to a man. Full bodied on the bedstraw, then ripe for childbearing and suckling.'

Sir Sockamore felt a snarling rage at the images the King was projecting onto his alter ego, the Lady Sockamore. There was no way she wanted to be 'full bodied on the bedstraw then ripe for childbearing and suckling.' The thought repulsed her.

'The King is right my lady,' said one of the hags, 'you need proper nourishment. I would encourage you to partake of the soup.'

Under the table the Lady Sockamore felt the hag kick her and she almost let out a painful yell. She picked up the spoon and, using all of her courage, took a mouthful.

'There you are,' said the King, 'that's better. You don't need to eat it all, you must leave a little room for the roast boar, the duck, the fish, the rabbit and of course Mistress Jupp's famous pies. Once tasted, never forgotten, as they say.'

It was not long before everyone in the room had finished their soup. The hall was ablaze with the fire of conversation. There was so much to talk about. Moredeath, the Lady Sockamore and her missing brother Sir Sockamore, Sir Godfrey, the Bishop of Nantes and even the Magician whose whereabouts were still the subject of intense speculation. There was not one topic of conversation that did not lead on to another as assembled guests voiced their opinions on each subject with equal vigour. How was it that Moredeath had turned out to be the least impressive marauder they had ever seen? Was it true the King had demoted the Bishop of Nantes to a lower table in favour of the Lady Sockamore and if so, was it also true he had designs upon her? How had a beauty such as the Lady Sockamore been hidden from view all of these years when Sir Sockamore could have easily brought her to court? What had happened to Sir Godfrey to make him appear so old and fragile? Most of the wives however were

184

not talking to their husbands after the incident of the creaking codpieces. Such things were hard to forgive and they spoke to each other instead.

The Bishop of Nantes was deep in conversation with his arch-deacon when something strange occurred. He tried to think of what it was he was saying when his mind went totally blank.

'Forgive me archdeacon, what was it we were discussing?' He said. The archdeacon looked at him with confusion.

'Why your eminence, we were talking about what you were planning on saying at the ceremony tomorrow.' The Bishop smiled weakly and said 'yes indeed.'

'I think you were going to say that as a gift to the couple you were going to build a monastery in their honour.'

'Quite right,' said the Bishop, 'yes that was what I was going to say.' And then he stopped and just stared into space.

'Your eminence, are you feeling alright?'

The Bishop was not feeling alright. Without warning it was as if parts of his mind had gone missing. He had never experienced such a thing in his life. He looked around the great hall and asked himself what he was doing there and who all the people, were but instead of an answer he found the question wandering in a great emptiness.

'Your eminence?'

A terrible fear came over him, such as would a lost child. Something was dreadfully wrong. He found his hand wandering into the pocket of his tunic and he pulled out the note left on the Magician's door. He read the words, but they didn't make any sense anymore.

'To whoever reads this. From this day forth you will be free from the past and the future will come to you as though you were a newborn. Nothing will ever stay with you long enough to warrant your discomfort.'

'I think I need to go to my room,' said the Bishop, who couldn't remember where that might be.

Not long after the Bishop's exit, it became apparent that the eyes of all of the men in the room were fixed upon the Lady Sockamore. Try as they might, each man seemed transfixed, other than those of Sir Godfrey, who had declined the soup on the grounds of potential flatulence, and Kenny Catlin who, though he had eaten it, seemed unaffected. The King had fallen deeply in love with the Lady Sockamore within moments of tasting the soup, and was staring into her eyes in a most disconcerting way.

'Why are you looking at me like that,' asked the Lady Sockamore. The King put on a sickly grin and muttered, 'I am in love.'

'With whom?' asked the lady.

'With you my dear.'

'No, you are not!' said the Lady Sockamore.

'How could I not be? asked the King, 'when your eyes are like the deepest of woodland pools, yet reflecting a brilliant summer's sky, and your radiant hair falls over your soft pale skin like......'

'For the love of Moyen behave yourself,' hissed the Lady Sockamore and turning to the hag at her side whispered, 'This wasn't supposed to happen, what's going on?'

The hag turned to her sister.

'Sister where did you put the potion?'

'In the soup sister.'

'Whose soup?'

'Oh, just in the general soup cauldron in the kitchen.'

'Whoops,' said the other hag.

'You've done this deliberately,' hissed the Lady Sockamore, 'you told me it was Moredeath you were going to enchant. You didn't say anything about the King!'

The hags smiled the type of smiles that openly reeked of their deceit. What the hags had failed to say was that not only did the love potion make any man who drank it fall desperately in love with the Lady Sockamore, but it also compelled the victim to be brutally honest about their feelings. As the Lady Sockamore had just discovered. The King leaned over once again.

'My lady, you cannot be so cruel as to deny my love for you, you would be wicked and heartless to do such a thing and beauty such as yours could never exist alongside a cold heart,' he said, pouring more wine into her glass.

'Help me,' hissed the Lady Sockamore to the hag.

'But you wanted every man in Naze to admire you, don't you remember? We have done no more than to present you with your wish.'

'That wasn't what I meant. I was talking about combat and Knightly pursuits, not this. I will not be spoken to like this. What makes the King think I am open to such blatant advances?'

'Oh my dear, you have much to learn about men if you do not see that that is how men are when they are temporarily unleashed from the confines of courtesy.'

'But I am Sir Sockamore of Stotesbury, not some common Inn keeper's daughter who suffers such nonsense in order to earn a shilling or two.'

'Tell me, sir Knight, have you not spoken such words to a woman to gain advantage for yourself?' whispered the hag.

'That's not the point and you know it. To joust for the court is not the same as a common roustabout on the village green. A man may do both. For indeed, one is good practice for the other, but the protocols expected of the court do not apply to common women.'

The hag's eyes went cold, and her face stiffened.

'Well, sir Knight, perhaps this evening will change your mind.'

All the while this conversation was in progress, the second hag was watching Moredeath. He had partaken of the soup but was showing no signs of ardour towards the Lady Sockamore. She nudged her sister.

'Why hasn't Moredeath shown any signs of expressing his love for the Lady Sockamore?'

Her sister looked down the table toward Moredeath and it was clear that he was more interested in the Lady Gossamer. They were deep in conversation.

'I don't know sister,' replied the second hag.

'Every man in the hall is staring at Lady Sockamore, all except Moredeath and Sir Godfrey, it is most peculiar.'

'Something is not right, and if Moredeath doesn't fall for our protégé, then our plan will not come to fruition.'

'We must do something to encourage him, sister.'

The hag next to Lady Sockamore nudged her sharply in the ribs. The Lady yelled.

'You need to go to the privy,' said the hag.

'No, I don't thanks, I'm fine.'

'You need to go to the privy,' repeated the hag, kicking the lady's shin.

The Lady Sockamore's face darkened. She didn't like being given orders and she certainly didn't like being kicked.

'Go!' hissed the hag.

With great reluctance, the Lady Sockamore stood up, and leaving the top table, shimmered down between the great tables. As she did so, the conversation in the hall stopped and the eyes of all the men were fixed upon her. The eyes of the women jealously scanned her, and then noticed their husbands and partners and realised what they were looking at. The whole room stopped whilst she walked its length, all apart from Moredeath who seemed impervious to her charms and Sir Godfrey who had fallen asleep during the roast duck.

Once at the privy, the Lady Sockamore decided it was actually too good an opportunity to waste, and so sat for a moment brooding on the events of the evening, and wondering what would come next. It did not take long for that to happen. On the wall outside the privy door was a mirror and, as she passed it, she could not help glancing at it, and there for the first time in her life, she truly fell in love. Oh, she had loved the Lady Gossamer when she was Sir Sockamore, or rather she had mistaken it for love, but this was something else. Who was this glorious creature wearing such a mesmerising dress? For a fleeting moment the words 'still a man inside' and 'soup' collided, then they disappeared into the ether of the mind. The Lady Sockamore had fallen deeply in love for the first time, with herself.

On her return to the hall, she was going to tell the Bloodly Sisters what they could do with their ridiculous plan. She was not going to be some feast for a hall full of uncontrollable men with their errant cod pieces and angry wives. She would go back to her room and spend the rest of the night admiring herself in the mirror instead. Furthermore, she had decided she did not need those ridiculous appendages Sir Trusty and the Knaves, the witches could keep them. What use could they be to such a beautiful, glorious woman such as she? She stroked the dress, and it felt good, clinging as it was to her unbelievably mesmerising body. She stepped through the door to the hall and stopped in her tracks. There was not a single sound to be heard nor a single person to be seen. The room was empty, the revellers gone. It was as if they had been taken as one to some other place.

Chapter Thirty Seven

In the garden of Rick Facile, his manager, Dick Friendly, and his solicitor, Max Moran, had been discussing the minor problem of a few million that they had sequestered, to invest in a film Kenny Catlin was supposed to be producing. Unfortunately for them, the money disappeared with Catlin, who was now being sought under an International Arrest Warrant. Standing by the statue of The Stinger, they had reached the conclusion that drastic action had to be taken before Facile found out.

'Is that Insurance policy still paid up?' asked Moran.

'What, the one on Rick's life?'

'Yes, that's the one.'

'Why are we talking about that now?'

'I just wondered how much it was for, that's all,' said Moran.

'I don't see what it has to do with the money we are talking about.'

Moran stared into the distance as though he was considering something deeply.

'Well, you never know what might happen in the future, that's all. I mean we have to protect our interests. I am just being prudent.'

'It's a bit late to be prudent, isn't it? I mean if we'd been prudent, we wouldn't have lost a shitload of Rick's money at the worst possible time. He's got a world tour coming up that needs financing and I haven't enough money to hire a fucking coach trip to the nearest cinema.'

Dick Friendly took a deep drag on the spliff he'd been smoking and coughed heavily.

'You should give that up,' said Moran, 'or take out a policy on yourself.'

'Thanks. So good of you to be so interested in my fucking health. I wouldn't have to smoke this stuff if I wasn't up to here with nerves.' He pointed to the top of his head. Moran threw him a cold look.

'You need to get yourself together Dick. If there's one thing I've learned in life, it is that thinking instead of action leads you nowhere. It's at times like these that the man of action succeeds.'

'Well, I'm not fucking Rambo or Jack Reacher and neither are you. What we need is money.'

As they were talking, the familiar guttural voice of Rick came from behind the bushes. He was talking to one of the party goers, telling them he was going to find Deloris, who had disappeared.

'Speak of the devil,' said Moran, caustically, just before Rick appeared around the corner.

'Rick! What are you up to?' asked Dick Friendly.

'Fuck me if it isn't the 'A' team,' said Rick sarcastically. 'Have you guys seen Deloris anywhere? She fucked off when I said I was going to show my art off. That's the trouble with women, so fucking unpredictable.'

The two men said they hadn't seen her.

'Well, I'll find her eventually,' he looked at The Stinger. 'I see you are admiring my latest acquisition. Can't beat a bit of art, can you?'

'It's very realistic,' Dick replied. Without asking Rick Facile filched the joint out of his manager's fingers and drew on it.

'It's a giant crab,' said Facile.

'It's a scorpion actually,' said Moran, in a demeaning manner.

'It's a scorpion actually,' repeated Facile in the sort of voice a schoolboy might use to annoy another.

'You know what Moran, you can be a real smart-arse prick sometimes. Just because you went to Eton or somewhere. It gets right up my fucking nose.'

'Come on Rick,' said Dick Friendly, 'there's no need to be like that. Max has done a lot for you. You know, contracts and deals. He's helped your career more than you know.'

'We'll he can fucking do it for someone else in the future because as of now he's fired!'

There was a moment's silence as Facile stared menacingly into Moran's face, taunting him, and then, without a word, Moran's arm shot forward, pushing Facile backwards. Facile flew through the air and landed on The Stinger, at which moment the menacing tail flicked into action and its long lethal sting embedded itself into his body. He called out a surprised 'fucking hell', before breathing his last.

'Jesus Max!' shouted Dick Friendly, 'what have you done!?'

'It was an accident Dick, you saw it.'

'Well...'

'How was I to know that Scorpion thing was going to do that? I just pushed him away from me, that was all. He was threatening me.'

'But you've killed him!'

Max Moran grabbed Dick Friendly by the throat.

'You listen, and listen well. If you accuse me of anything I will make sure you regret it. What happened here was an accident and nothing more. Now we are going to walk away and pretend it didn't happen, and on Monday morning you are going to get in touch with the insurance company and make a claim on the policy. I am going make sure that all of Ricks assets are protected from his creditors, and you and I, as co-executors of his will, are going to make sure that we are the beneficiaries.'

Moran released Friendly's throat. He started coughing hard. Between bouts of coughing he said, 'but shouldn't we call an ambulance? Do something to help him?'

'He's dead, can't you see that? You went with him to buy that monstrosity. If there are any questions asked then who's to say you didn't plan the whole thing right from the start?'

Friendly muttered a resigned 'shit.' He knew he was trapped.

'Now come on, before anyone finds this.' Moran guided Friendly back towards the house, leaving the impaled Facile where he lay.

Five minutes before and not one hundred yards from where Rick Facile lay dead, Whattlewherrit had entered the house and was trying his best not to get the shard to take him back home. The lights, the noise, the general hubbub of an alcohol and drug fuelled party were more than his senses could bear. It was as if he had been placed in a barrel full of bells and rolled downhill. His mind was unable to think, his feet were uncertain, he felt totally overwhelmed. Even the fiercest battle could not compete with the mayhem before him.

He clutched the shard silently, asking it instead to take him to Moredeath. It did not seem to hear his thoughts. No wonder, in this cacophonous den of debauchery. For all the times he had wished he could experience the What Will Be, he now regretted it bitterly. If this was what the What Will Be represented, then he wanted none of it. Uncertain as to where to go, he wandered into rooms where people were being pinklarried but who did not seem to care who saw them. He walked into several cupboards and a huge space in which waterless boats were parked, but nowhere was Moredeath to be seen. Everywhere he went, people seemed to want to speak to him, and tell him they 'loved how he had downplayed his costume', which made no sense to him whatsoever. He asked after Moredeath but to no avail. He was about to give up when a man ran through the crowd shouting that 'Conan the Barbarian' had stolen his girlfriend, and had locked himself in a room with her. Whattlewherrit clutched the shard. It was all too much for him. The lights, the noise, the mayhem, the thought of another poor girl, this time trapped in a room with Moredeath. He just wanted it all to go away! Go away. And so, it did. Silence reigned. There was no one to be seen. No music played. He stood alone in the eerie quiet of Rick Facile's mansion. Wondering what had happened. A terrible feeling struck him like a blow to the body. What had he done! Had he repeated his mistake again only this time with hundreds of people? He was contemplating this thought in the ominous silence when there was a creak of a door on the upper floor. He looked up at the elaborate staircase and waited. Whoever it was, was slowly moving towards the top of the stairs. It did not take long for him to see who it was. Moredeath! The Bludgeoner reached the top of the stairs, his axe in his hand, and turning the corner of the bannisters, stared down. His face creased, his angry eyes narrowed, and the knuckles of his huge hands went white as he shouted 'You!!!'

Chapter Thirty Eight

Mistress Munn had no option, at least that was what she told herself. Things had got out of hand, and she had to get the imposter out of the great hall. If the wedding went ahead, then all would be lost, and she hadn't heard anything from Whattlewherrit. She knew things were amiss from the minute the Lady Sockamore and her maidservants appeared. That dress, the way the men all looked at her after the serving of the soup. Why anyone would think it was cast with a spell.

As soon as the Lady Sockamore left the room there was mayhem. Fights broke out between men and their wives. Men fought with men, shouting at one another and saying such truths that even a priest in a confessional would never want to hear. It was as if they had all gone mad. That was when she thought of her plan. It was simple, and might not have worked, but as she saw it, there was no other option. She went to see Gladwell Jupp and borrowed her voluminous hooded cloak. She also borrowed a long staff and finally the bell used to call in the wash pot boys.

'What on earth do you want those things for?' asked her friend.

'If you knew Gladwell, you wouldn't lend them.'

'Well I wants them back, so don't you go losing them!'

Mistress Munn reassured her they would return, but did not say when that might be. Making her way to the hall, she hooded up and then flung open the doors shouting, 'make way, the plague, make way, the plague.' At first no one seemed to hear but soon people started to turn from their bickering, hearing the bell and her mournful cry. The noise in the hall slowly decreased. The assembled guests looked on in horror as the plague carrier made their way into the room. People gasped, they cried out, they went to clutch their pinklarry brooches but of course none were wearing them. They were in their finest garments. No one would pin a pinklarry badge to their best clothes.

The further into the room she went ,the more they scattered behind her, running out of the great oak doors. This was when Mortimer made his appearance. As if it had been planned, though it had not. He scuttled out of Sir Godfrey's frayed tunic and walked slowly towards the hags, the King and the Lady Gossamer. The hags shrieked, the King cried out, and the Lady Gossamer feinted. Sir Godfrey, who was still suspended above his seat, trapped by his rusted armour, just accepted this was all part of his punishment by the Great Moyen.

'Swollen armpits, painful puss filled buboes, dreadful agonies, I deserve it all,' he said to himself. Apart from Kenny Catlin, the top table fled as Mortimer sauntered towards them and Mistress Munn came ringing her bell.

Catlin sighed.

'For fucks sake,' he muttered, 'what next?'

So it was that Mistress Munn approached him and he took it all as if it was just another episode in the Truman show.

She lifted her hood and spoke.

'It's time,' she said, 'you have to come with me.' Catlin frowned as he stared at her.

'If you don't come now, then you will be here forever' she said. For the first time in his life, he knew he had to trust someone.

'If you say so,' he said nonchalantly.

She then went to Sir Godfrey.

'Beth,' he said, 'you've got the plague?'

'No, I have not but I can't explain. You have to come with me.'

'I can't', he said

'But you must' she insisted.

'I can't'

'Why not?'

'My armour has locked tight and I can't move.'

Mistress Munn looked down and saw what had happened.

'Moredeath, come over here and help me. We need to free Sir Godfrey.'

Chapter Thirty Nine

'So, there you are,' said the Lady Sockamore entering the bedchamber to find the two hags. 'I went to the privy as you told me and when I got back everyone was gone. What happened?'

The hags both looked dejected.

'The plague, that's what happened.' said one.

'The plague? What are you talking about?'

'A plague carrier came into the hall leaning on a staff, head covered, ringing the plague bell and everybody scattered.'

'Including you,' said the Lady Sockamore.

'There was a rat,' replied the hag, 'don't forget the rat, sister.'

'Well, there may have been a rat,' replied the Lady Sockamore, 'but if you ask me, its name was Mistress Munn, the Magician's house maid.'

'What are you talking about?' said the hag.

'Well, when I was making my way back from the privy, I saw Mistress Munn taking off a long cloak she had been wearing, and she had in her hands a bell and staff. Not only that, she was with Sir Godfrey and Moredeath. They looked like they were heading somewhere, presumably out of the castle.

The hag's faces were like thunder.

'She's tricked us!' shouted one of the hags.

'She's taken Moredeath,' shouted the other.

'It's the Magician again, he has put her up to this,' said the first.

The Lady Sockamore was delighted though she did not say as much. No Moredeath, no seduction, no bedstraw. What could be better? 'So, ladies, where do we go from here?' she said cheekily. The hags just scowled.

In his chamber the King was recovering from the shock of the evening, and poking out his tongue to examine it, to see if he had contracted the plague. There were no immediate signs, but that rat had come very close before he had made his escape. You could never be too sure. What he could be sure of was that he loved the Lady Sockamore. His every other thought was of her beauty and her charm. The way she walked, the way she smiled, even the way she told him off for telling her how much he loved her. Actually, especially the way she did that.

There was a hint of his nanny when she used to tell him off as a small boy and threatened to use the hairbrush to beat him. Oh, such memories.

Could a woman promote more desire in a man? She would be his queen. There was no question in his mind. They would create a dynasty of beautiful children together to rule over Naze for the next hundred years. He was contemplating this when his daughter arrived.

'Father, what shall we do? The world has gone mad. People are fighting one another in the street, saying such things that only madmen would say. I blame the Lady Sockamore. Something is not right with her. I mean wearing such a provocative dress was bad enough, but look at what she has done, setting husband against wife, brother against brother, friend against friend. The woman is poison.'

'Calm yourself daughter. We cannot blame the Lady Sockamore for the unruly behaviour of our wedding guests. After all she did nothing to provoke them.'

'Am I to believe you did not hear the creaking codpieces upon her arrival?'

The King drew breath.

'Well, that was slightly disturbing, but can you say it was her fault?'

'Indeed, I can father. The woman looked as though she were wearing nought but painted skin.'

The King's eyes glazed for a moment as he recalled her entrance.

'Yes, I suppose one might, if one was to use one's imagination hard enough.'

'And you are telling me you did not?'

'My child, you must understand men are driven, like helpless swine before the rod of a swine herd. Beaten forward by the relentless demands of...'

'Their loins?' interjected the Lady Gossamer.

'I was going to say the Great Moyen's demand that they go out and produce progeny.'

'Tush!' replied his daughter. 'What excuse is that you use? I am well acquainted with what drives men and it is not the wishes of the Great Moyen. Indeed, you are right, they are like swine. However, they are more like those rooting about in the undergrowth searching for truffles to quaff. Always hungry, never satisfied and seldom in control of their urges.'

'What makes you speak so, daughter, when you are still a maid? How can you, such a delicate flower, know anything of men?' The King chuckled to himself.

The Lady Gossamer realised she had gone too far. Her father must never know the truth about the needlework she had just finished.

'We must hope that by the morning, things will have settled for the wedding ceremony,' said the King.

'She must not be there,' said the Lady Gossamer firmly, 'nor those two strange maids of hers. There is something not right about them.'

After Mistress Munn's appearance as a plague carrier, the small party made their way through the silent hall and out of the castle into the night. Sir Godfrey, Kenny Catlin, and Mistress Munn. There was turmoil in the castle courtyard as the guests shouted at one another about the plague. Due to their love for the Lady Sockamore, the men shouted 'a plague on you, may your pinklarry shrivel' and other such insults, whilst the women cursed their men for falling in love with 'that woman!' Wishing she would contract the dreadful disease. For this reason, it was easy for the party of three to make their way unnoticed into the night. The air was chilled by a cloudless sky in which hung a half-moon, providing light for the travellers as they trekked away from the castle, and out towards the South.

'Where are we going Beth?' asked Sir Godfrey.

'To Merrelay,' she replied.

'To Merrelay?'

'I cannot think of a better place at this time.'

'But the wedding? What about the marriage?' asked the old Knight.

'There is not going to be one,' replied Mistress Munn.

'How so?'

'It is a complicated story and Whattlewherrit would be the one to tell it in its entirety but he,' and here she pointed at Kenny Catlin, 'is not Moredeath.'

'Not Moredeath? But how can that be?'

'Whattlewherrit got himself into a little tangle with his spells and this one got exchanged with Moredeath.'

'Exchanged?'

'Well I don't rightly know the ins and outs of it, but it comes down to Whattlewherrit looking into the What Will Be for the King. Something happened as a consequence, and he has been trying to put it right ever since.'

197

The old Knight shook his head.

'Cornelius always said something would happen with that boy. I remember him saying that there was something different about him. 'He is not as we are." He used to say.

Mistress Munn nodded and sighed.

'You can stop this,' said Catlin. 'All of this crazy talk. If you think it impresses me, it doesn't. You said you would get me out of this, so just cut the crap, tell me where we are going, and when I can get back to reality.'

Mistress Munn scanned Catlin. She was furious with his belligerent behaviour.

'You don't belong here,' she said. 'You come from another world. I saw it. I saw you naked with your pinklarry stiff as a pikestaff, with that young girl. I saw the writing on your belly and when you arrived here at the castle I saw it again. You may think this is some game we are playing with you, but the truth is stranger than you could ever know. You needs to go back and the only person what can get you back is the Magician, and he is not here. You needs to pray he will return, or you will never get home again.

By the time they reached Merrelay they were all exhausted. Catlin was fed and given a room in which, not for the first time, he considered he was going mad. Plagued by questions and doubt. his mind would not settle for a single moment, but the more he thought, the more restless he became. He paced the floor muttering to himself, his volcanic frustration building steadily, ready to erupt.

Downstairs in the dining hall, Sir Godfrey sat with Mistress Munn. The dim candlelight, and the gentle crackle of the fire, created a soft background to their conversation.

'I am sorry Beth, for all that I have done to you.' said the old Knight.

'Hush Arthur it is all in the past now,' replied Mistress Munn.

'That's just the point Beth, it isn't. It is right with us here and now. You and I, we are doomed to live forever. Always regretting the past, never able to put right the wrongs I have done. I find a burden so great, it rusts my soul so deep that the flakes of it are forever corrupting my mind, reminding me. I shall never be allowed to forget.'

'But you did nothing with a bad heart, my dear,' said Mistress Munn, 'for when you drank the wine it was to save yourself. Who would not have done so had they found themselves in just the same position? And when you gave it to me, it was because you wanted me to live forever. Who would not want such a man's love?'

'You are generous Beth. If only the Great Moyen saw things your way. And you say nothing of the fact I took myself away and left you? How could I have done such a thing? I pledged my love to you, I offered you eternity and then I fled. I feel such shame.'

Mistress Munn stared at the flames for a moment.

'I did hope you would return Arthur, but I knows it was your torment took you from me. It broke my heart, I cannot say different, but I also knew you was a landed gentleman, and I was a Magician's maid. What was I to expect, that you would suffer not only the shame of your deception, but on top of that to marry a serving maid? I should have said no when I said yes instead. There is no bad decision in love, but it takes two to make it.'

'I have always loved you Beth. If you think that for a single moment of a single day I have not borne you in my thoughts, then you are mistaken. The Great Moyen has punished me more with our separation than he could any other thing.'

'Well, he shall punish you no more my dear. I do not know what may happen next, but whatever that may be, we shall face it together.'

Sir Godfrey sighed.

'You are generous beyond any expectation Beth, and I will see to it that what is left of me shall be yours forever. Not that there is much to be had but conversation. Time has whittled down the woodpile. The once heaped fire of youth has given way to the ashes of old age.'

'Don't you worry Arthur, I was always good at rekindling a reluctant fire!'

Mistress Munn laughed heartily and slapped her love on his swollen knees. The ones that had been trapped in his rusty armour at the wedding feast. He held back from yelling from the intense pain she had inadvertently managed to deliver and thanked the Great Moyen once more for reminding him he was a sinner.

Chapter Forty

Morning came to Naze with the cock crow. The castle wardens were waking after a hard night of being on guard. It was a crisp though misty autumn morning, and the sun struggled to bring warmth to the parapets where the men blew on their frosty fingers and stamped their frozen feet. A smattering of coughing and blowing of noses could be heard through the thick damp air alongside coarse words expressing their discontent. It had been a long night, one that started with a riot in the courtyard below. What had been billed as a pre-wedding feast had turned into a rout in which the Knights and dignitaries of Naze had set upon one another, for no apparent reason, and had ended up in an all-out battle with no obvious winner.

'I 'spect there's a few sore heads down there this morning,' said one warden to the other.

'Serves em right,' replied the other. 'I have no sympathy for them as can't keep their drink. They was like a pack of animals punching and gouging one another.'

'I tell you what Will, it was the women what was the worse. I don't know as what they was fighting over, but whatever it was, it had put a rat up their arses.'

'Jake was saying it was that woman, the Lady Sockamore what started it.'

'How so?

'Well, according to Jake she come to the feast wearing nowt but her tits painted in all these colours what dazzled the eye, and a skirt what made it look like she was afloat above the ground.'

'Oh, come on Jez, you know what Jake is like. He would tell you a horse was a pig if it suited him.'

'No, I believe him Will. You should have heard what some of them there dignitaries was shouting to one another. They was professing their love for the lady, out loud mind, and in front of their wives an all. It was shocking to hear. And their wives in return was telling them the truth about how useless they was on the bedstraw. I have never heard such in my life. I tell you something peculiar was going on and I don't think it was all down to the mead.'

The sound of pee trickling down the wall below caught the ears of both men who looked over the parapet.

'Well, someone's up,' said one to the other.

The King shook his pinklarry and tucked it away from the cold morning air. The chill he felt from the draughty privy brought his mind into focus, reminding him of the disaster of the night before. What should have been a celebration, the bonding of his daughter to Moredeath the Bludgeoner had turned into a plague-ridden battle of the sexes. He looked in the mirror and put out his tongue, then he felt under his arms for puss-filled lumps. There were none. Well at least that was something positive amongst the dreadful fallout of the feast. What had happened was inexplicable. Every man in the great hall falling in love with the Lady Sockamore. Every one of the guests saying such brutal things to one another and insisting they were true, and on top of that, the plague teller! Were it not for love, he would have been in an ill humour. Love, however, was still a potent force within him, despite such a restless and tormented night, and the thought of the Lady Sockamore filled him with the very essence of youth. He felt a young man again, vibrant, his head full of the excitement of life. Anything was possible when you were in love, and nothing mattered, for love itself was enough. It bathed the mind in the sweet oils of expectation, so that all else fell away. His thoughts drifted on her eyes, on the dress, on her walk, and yes, the tantalising way her breasts bounced, causing his heart to bounce along with them. He rang the bell for his servant to come and dress him. A hearty breakfast was called for. He would need to build his stamina if he was to court the Lady Sockamore. There was no doubt in his mind she would be boisterous in the bedstraw!

'I have never known such behaviour in my life' said Gladwell Jupp as she looked around the battleground of the kitchen.

'Look at all this fine food gone to waste. Barely a thing eaten after the soup course. It is shameful.'

The kitchen maids stood looking around them, not knowing what to say.

'And those pantry boys. What came over them? Why I am flabbergasted at their antics, saying they was in love! And with a fine lady and all! Why, I would imagine I had gone mad had I not seen it with my own eyes. The wooden spoon awaits their impudent arses when they gets back here, there is no doubt about that!'

Gladwell stared at the chaos and shook her head.

'Well, there is nothing for it but to pick up our skirts and set too,' she said. 'No doubt we shall have to go through the whole thing again tonight, we have the wedding to get through. Lord save us.'

No sooner had she sent the kitchen maids to their tasks, when the Kings servant arrived.

'His Majesty is requiring his breakfast Mistress Jupp,' he said.

'Is he indeed. Well, there's a surprise. Given that he hardly touched the goose I had specially prepared for him, nor the rabbit.' She took a deep breath in. 'I suppose he is in love with the Lady Sockamore too. Lawks a mercy what is the matter with all you men? You are nought but boys with a handle as far as I can see. Not a thought in your heads lest it comes via the codpiece.'

The King's servant coughed an embarrassed cough.

'Well, I shall put together a plate from last nights unfinished meal and he will just have to make do with it. I am not cooking anything special for him this morning. If he can't eat my victuals when they are hot then he shall jolly well eat them when they are cold.'

She plopped a few slabs of meat and some pickles on a plate and handed it to the servant.

'There you are. If he has any complaints, then tell him I've fallen in love and can't think straight.'

The servant nodded and left before Mistress Jupp said anything else.

The servant returned to the King with his breakfast but decided that he would not mention Mistress Jupp's observations. As the King tucked into his cold goose, he told the servant he wished to see Moredeath as soon as he was up.

'I am afraid that won't be possible Sire,' replied his servant.

'How so?'

'Moredeath is no longer at the castle.'

'What are you talking about man? Of course he's at the castle, he gets married today!'

'Apparently, he left last night in the company of Sir Godfrey and a serving maid.'

'He what!? Well, where did he go?' demanded the King.

'No one seems to know Sire, apart from the fact he was heading south.'

'The Bloodlands! He is heading back home,' said the King, his voice edged with a hint of desperation. 'This has all been too much for him. First the attack, then the Magician shrinking and ageing him, then last night and the plague carrier. By the Great Moyen we have lost him.'

The King put down his goose and sighed. All of his plans had gone to pieces. His daughter's future, thrown away by a careless Magician, and a wandering plague carrier. The King sat for a while, weighing up the situation.

Something had to be done. After a time, he looked up and said, 'We shall have the joust as planned, and whoever wins will marry my daughter. We don't need Moredeath, he is but a shadow of the man he was, there is no way he will protect the Kingdom. Spread the word that the Knight who wins the garland shall wed the Lady Gossamer this very night'.

On the other side of the castle, in the chambers of the Lady Sockamore, the hags were brooding. Their plans had gone sadly adrift. Despite the riot in the castle courtyard after the plague bearer had left, and the powerful love potion which turned every man into a whimpering fool, Moredeath himself seemed totally immune to it. Never once did he even glance at the Lady Sockamore. The man was impervious to the strongest potion they could devise.

'I cannot understand it sister. I had heard rumours of his remarkable constitution, but it seems beyond belief that he could withstand our spell.'

'Perhaps he didn't eat the soup,' said the other.

'Oh, but he did, I watched him. Something about him is not right.'

The Lady Sockamore said nothing. In another life, in another body, she had been there when the real Moredeath escaped his fate, saved by the Magician. She had seen the man he was and the man the Magician had turned him into and she was not at all sure they were the same. Perhaps, like herself, Moredeath's body had changed and inside was the Bludgeoner of old. Somehow, she doubted it. Her intuition, which had grown stronger in her new body, told her it was a different man. Though she said nothing, she was beginning to believe the Magician had tricked them all by replacing the real Moredeath with an imposter. In which case where was the Bludgeoner?

Perhaps the least said the better. After all, handling the imposter would be easier than trying to cope with the giant of a man who had disappeared. There was another matter to consider. Since falling in love with herself the previous night she had no wish to become Sir Sockamore again. How could he compete with her beauty, her power? The hags were right, they had given him the ultimate weapon, to entrance and be the object of adulation without having to do anything other than be who she was. She thought back to the previous night and how once she had left the empty hall in search of everyone, she found them fighting over her, swearing she was the only thing they lived for. Who wouldn't find that intoxicating? Who wouldn't want more? She could keep them all at arm's length well enough, it would just require practice.

'We need to find the Magician,' said the first hag, 'to destroy Naze was only a distraction, the shard is what we came for.'

'I agree sister, but where is he? No one seems to know his whereabouts.'

'What about that shifty little maid of his. Mistress Munn. Do you think she knows?'

'If anyone does it will be her,' said the Lady Sockamore joining in the conversation. 'She is like a mother hen to him.'

'Where is she now?'

'I have no idea, unless she has gone back to the island.'

'Then that is where we shall go. If she is there and knows where the Magician is she will not be able to stand up to us. We will get the answer out of her soon enough.'

Chapter Forty One

The hags crossed the water for the second time to the Magician's island. Their plans had not gone well. Moredeath had not fallen for the Lady Sockamore, the Lady Sockamore was far too content with her status as the most desired woman in Naze, and the Magician was nowhere to seen. Something was dreadfully amiss. As the prow of the boat pushed forwards into the dark waters of the estuary, they sat brooding and plotting their next move.

'What if he did come back to the island and opened our little gift to him?' asked the first hag.

'We shall see when we get to the island whether he found the note we left him. If so, then it is possible he has already lost his senses and then the shard will be ours. He may well be tucked up like a baby, all memory gone, all desire departed, just an empty shell. How satisfying that would be.'

The hag cackled softly.

'In which case,' said the second hag, 'all we have to do is to overcome that interfering maidservant, Mistress Munn.'

'She will be no problem. We will destroy her. That old woman is no match for us. After all, we captured Cornelius didn't we, and she is just a maid. Once we have the shard we will be invincible. No one will be able to stand in our way.'

'What about our protégé, Sir Sockamore's sister? What do we do with her?'

'Oh, I am sure we can find some use for her in our plans.'

'But she seems too fond of her new role for my liking. We can't have her being happy. That wouldn't do at all.'

'Then we shall turn her back into her former self, just as we promised, and he will be forever longing for what he has lost. The same as he was when we took away his manhood! He will never find satisfaction in who he is ever again.' The hag laughed.

'How perfect,' said the other.

'Am I to wait,' called out the boatman interrupting the hags. The boat lunged against the mooring.

'We shall be done within a matter of an hour or so, when we will return to Naze. See to it you are here to take us back.'

The boatman withdrew his oars and muttered to himself about wasting his life sitting around waiting for other people and then said, 'very well.'

When they reached the door the two hags were pleasantly surprised to find the note they had left for the Magician had gone. He had taken the bait and read the spell! Without hesitation they rapped on the huge door to the tower and called out. There was no reply. They tried again. Still no one answered. One of them was about to try again when the second one said, 'have you tried the handle?' The door opened. The hags went in.

Being inside the home of the Magicians of Naze was something the hags had dreamt of for so long they had to stop for a moment in order to fully comprehend where they were. The walls were whitewashed and there were windows, so that instead of the dark interior they had anticipated it was surprisingly bright.

'Oh I don't like this sister,' said one to the other.

'Far too light,' said the other, 'makes you feel like those horrible sunrises when everything is soft and lit up. Give me a grey day any day of the week.'

'I've always said if you want to feel comfortable with yourself you can't beat a good cave,' said the first.

'It just shows you how warped the minds of Magicians are. There's not a hint of mould, or damp in the place. Makes your blood run cold.'

'We must just suffer it for a short while, until we find the Magician.'

The hags searched every room but one and found no trace of the Magician, nor Mistress Munn. Finally, upon reaching the top of the tower they walked into the Magician's study. This room, like the rest of the tower, was light and bright. The walls were lined with shelves, upon which books sat in rows. Books about medicines, herbs, the stars, trees and plants, all manner of things that might be of interest to an educated man. There were sets of scales and a telescope, and a strange glass orb held suspended on copper wire. Objects of all sorts fought for space with the books, objects the hags had never seen before. From the ceiling hung a chandelier made from the discarded antlers of a deer and on the walls candle holders in the shape of branches, with leaves protruding, giving one the impression a forest was in the process of enveloping the room. As for the floor, it was polished wood and in the middle was placed a circular rug, the edge of which was elaborately decorated with the figures of animals following one another around the circle.

'What a horrid place,' said one hag to the other.

'Gives me the creeps sister.'

'Can you imagine the sort of warped mind that would spend time in such a room?'

'I cannot sister.'

'Well, he's not here, is he?' said one to the other as they both stepped onto the rug.

'We must look elsewhere. He took the spell we left, so he must be close by.'

The sisters agreed they would go back to Naze and find Mistress Munn. As both stepped forward something unexpected happened. Neither of them could put a foot outside the perimeter of the rug. They looked at one another and hissed as only hags could.

'What has happened?' said one to the other.

'It's a spell!' said the second sister.

'A spell?'

'Someone has set a spell, we are trapped!'

'The Magician! Curse him!' cried out the hag.

'What are we to do?' said her sister.

The other hag bent down and lifted the edge of the rug, and underneath it saw what she had suspected. Written in chalk were the runes casting the spell. She bent down and tried to rub them away, but they would not budge. Her sister joined in but it was no use. Lifting the edge of the rug all the way round, they found the runes formed a complete circle, entrapping them. It was a good hour before the boatman's voice could be heard shouting from below. The sisters called out and he eventually made his way into the room. Seeing the sisters standing on the rug, he assumed they were just wasting his time by loitering in the tower.

'I'm going back to Naze,' he said, 'I have a living to make.'

'Stop,' said one of the hags, 'we need your help.'

The boatman looked confused.

'What sort of help.'

'We need you to lift us off this rug.'

The boatman laughed. 'You are pulling my pinklarry aren't you,' he replied.

'Not at all,' said the frustrated hag. She lifted the rug and showed him the runes. 'The Magician has cast a spell, and we cannot move.'

The boatman drew breath. There was no way he wanted anything to do with magic, but on the other hand was not inclined to leave the two paying passengers stuck in the tower.

'We will pay you twice your usual fee if you will lift us over the spell.'

The thought of earning so much in a day tipped the balance for the boatman and he agreed. He stepped forwards and put his strong arms around the first hag. He gauged her weight to be not much more than a large sack of corn and he had shifted plenty of those in his day. He lifted, or rather he didn't. No matter how much effort he put in there was no way he could move the hag. He tried lifting the other, but the same thing happened.

'What's the matter!' said the hag.

'I can't shift you. It is as if you weigh the same as a horse or a cow. I am strong but not that strong.

'Well you can't leave us,' said the second hag.

'Seems to me I have no option, ladies. I am not strong enough to move you and I am not skilled in magic. Whoever did this will have to undo it.'

A dreadful thought came over the hags. If it was the Magician who had cast the spell, and if he had read the note and was now no more than a baby in his mind for loss of his memory, then he would not be able to undo the spell. They were trapped forever!

'I must catch the tide ladies,' said the boatman. 'When I get back to Naze I shall enquire after the Magician, but more than that I cannot do.' And with that, he left the hags.

Chapter Forty Two

When the hags did not return, the Lady Sockamore became restless and ordered a bath to be drawn for her. She would spend her time preening herself so that when the joust took place that afternoon, she would look her best. After all, she had to live up to her admirers' expectations, and there were many admirers.

It took a while for the water to arrive from the kitchen cauldrons but once it did, she dropped her clothing and slid into the bath, feeling its soft, buoyant warmth surrounding her. It was the first bath she had ever had, and certain things struck her immediately. For one thing her chest was floating in a most entrancing way. She shifted her body and sure enough they bobbed like two pink islands in a most satisfactory manner. This was indeed unexpected and a source of great amusement. She pushed one underwater, but it bobbed up again when she let go. She tried the other. Sure enough the right was the same as the left. How satisfying!

It was as she was bobbing them that she noticed their pink caps hardening and as they hardened, she noticed that as she touched them, not only did they feel excited but so did her twixt and in-betweens. This was curious.

She ventured a hand down towards her twixt and in-betweens, and upon doing so, felt a jolt of something unexpected gush through her whole body. What was this? What was happening? She felt around in places she did not know existed and found the most curious thing, not only curious but breathtakingly exciting.

What was this thing she had chanced upon? Every tiny movement made her feelings dance, and as they did so, the strangest thing occurred, she began to think of the Lady Gossamer. To her mind came the vision of that lady bathing just as she was, and doing exactly the same thing as she was. As she twiddled her twixt and in-betweens, so in her mind's eye did the Lady Gossamer. It did not take long before she cried out, with an enormous burst of pleasure, and lay transfixed.

Then, as if these revelations were not enough, a further stunning realisation came upon her. Maidens, like men, were able to find pleasure in themselves. They did not need men! This could not be so! They were not equipped with a pinklarry so how could this possibly be? The Lady Sockamore lay back and considered this momentous discovery before deciding she had to check it all out again in case she had made a mistake.

There was a knock at the door. Fortunately for the Lady Sockamore, she had already had time to test out her theory sufficiently.

'Who is it!?' she called out, 'I am at my bath.'

'My Lady, I am sorry to bother you,' said the voice of one of the serving maids, 'but I have a message from the boatman.'

'The boatman? What boatman?'

'The one what takes people across the estuary my lady.'

'And what does this boatman say?'

'He says that your maids went across the water to the Magician's island and have got themselves stuck.'

'Stuck? How so?

'My lady, they says they have been trapped by a spell.'

'A spell?'

The Lady Sockamore's mind, distracted by matters of the bath, soon focused on the news the hags were caught, and could not therefore cause her more distress.

'Tell the boatman I will deal with it, and thank him with a coin.'

The Lady Sockamore was overjoyed. Could life get any better? The hags were out of the way, she was feeling much better about the body she had been given, and to her great surprise she found that she was in love once again with the Lady Gossamer. She decided, that very afternoon, as the men jousted for the Lady's hand, she would tell the Lady Gossamer exactly what she felt.

The King looked down upon the fields beyond the castle. The tents had been erected, the armour stacked, the flags were flying, and the remains of the great feast were put out for all to eat. The King had insisted his Knights participate, despite their apparent feelings towards the Lady Sockamore and, in many cases, severe bruising from the riot the night before. He was having nothing of it. The lady would be his. The Knights should be grateful they had the right to fight for the hand of his daughter. Why, not one night ago any one of them would have fallen on his knees in front of him at the thought his daughter might grace their bedstraw. Once his daughter was married. he would propose to the Lady Sockamore and she would of course accept. What maiden would not want to be the Queen of Naze? As for Moredeath, well he could go back to the Badlands as far as he was concerned. Good riddance. It had been a lesson well learned. He decided he would call on the Bishop of Nantes in order to make sure he was up to date about the situation. After all, he did leave the previous night in somewhat of a hurry.

The Bishop was sitting in his rooms, the arch deacons standing by his side when the King arrived.

'Bishop I just called in to say....' He stopped in his tracks. 'Why have you got the eternal underpants on your head?'

The arch deacons looked horrified. They knew what was coming.

'Why don't you stuff your pinklarry up your horses arse!' Shouted the Bishop.

The King stepped back.

'What did you just say?'

'He said....' offered one of the arch deacons but was cut short by the King.

'You are talking to your King, Bishop, have you gone mad?'

'You sir are an arsehole. No one likes you and your daughter has been in the bedstraw with every Knight in the realm!'

The King's eyes widened, his jaw dropped and he went the colour of a cockerel's comb.

'What on earth.....' stuttered the King.

'Your Majesty, the Bishop is not well,' interjected the arch deacon.

'And the Holy Wine tastes like horse piss!' shouted the Bishop. 'Damned horse piss.'

'Is he saying he has drunk from the bottle of Holy Wine?' said the King.

'I am sure....' began the arch deacon.

'Indeed I did, and I can tell you now the Great Moyen's vineyard must be one giant privy, the way that wine tasted. And nothing happened. Not a single thing. I wasn't surprised of course. The whole thing is rubbish, the Wine, the Book of Words, the Eternal Underpants. Tell me this if you will. Who else, apart from the Sisters of Irreverence, ever saw the Angel Debbie? Eh? Tell me that. They said she appeared before them, but anyone could say that. If you ask me, if it wasn't for the money it generates, religion would be a total waste of time.'

At this comment one of the arch deacons passed out and hit the floor with a thud.

'He's gone mad!' said the King. 'What dark forces are at play here?'

'I am sorry your Majesty, I fear he has been possessed,' said the remaining arch deacon.

'That note was untrue as well. A pox on whoever wrote it,' said the Bishop.

'Which note?' asked the King.

'Sire,' interrupted the arch deacon, 'the Bishop ventured onto the Magician's island with a view to the possibility of the church building a monastery there and when we arrived on the door of the tower was a note left for the owner of the island. The Bishop felt that perhaps you would accede to his request and donate the island to the church so he assumed the note to be his. Since that time things have been greatly amiss.'

The King grunted.

'That damned Magician. First Moredeath and now the Bishop. I will have him hung at the castle gates if he ever sets foot in Naze again!'

Chapter Forty Three

The day had turned into a bright but crisp one. Clouds scattered across the sky as soon as the early morning sun had melted away the mist. All stood fair for a fine tournament, albeit not the one originally planned. There had been no word of Moredeath, or of Sir Godfrey. The assumption was that the pair had travelled South together, but why Sir Godfrey had left when he did was a mystery. The King, in Sir Godfrey's defence, said that being so frail, his fear of the plague must have overwhelmed him.

'I don't expect we shall see poor old Godfrey again,' he said with genuine, and for him, unusual feeling, as he and his daughter discussed the disappearance.

'Well at least he won't have to joust for your hand my dear!' He joked.

The King made sure the Lady Sockamore was seated one side of him and his daughter the other. The stand in which they sat was filled with dignitaries and their wives, most of whom were nursing hangovers and bruises from the night before.

The church was represented by the arch deacons. The bishop had been secured in the castle dungeons for preaching dissent. His madness was getting worse. In between his rants about anything and everything, he would ask where he was, and what he was doing there. The King could not afford an outburst at the joust. Nothing could be allowed to ruin the smooth running of the afternoon, given the disaster of the night before. The Lady Gossamer, not knowing about the bishop's descent into madness, asked after him.

'Oh, do not worry your pretty head about the bishop my dear, he is suffering some form of ill humour, and cannot be here this afternoon.'

'What is the matter with him?' she asked.

'Oh, he has suffered a form of madness my dear,' said the King, hoping his honesty would deflect his daughter from asking more. It did not work.

'What is he saying father?' she asked.

'Oh, he is confused about the Great Moyen's plan for us all.'

'The bishop? But surely, he knows more than anyone about the Great Moyen?'

'Indeed daughter, that should be true, but as I say, he is afflicted by some strange humour that has twisted his mind.'

'Could it be demons?'

'Unfortunately, it could, my child.'

'And what else is he saying?'

The King felt a pang of uncertainty cross his mind as he told her there was nothing else. How could he tell his dear daughter what the bishop had said about her sharing her bedstraw with all of the eligible Knights of Naze? It was unthinkable that any father could repeat such a thing.

'I am sorry, I appear to have listened into your private conversation, your Majesty,' said the Lady Sockamore, leaning towards the King, 'but I couldn't help overhearing what you were saying about the bishop? Am I to understand he is in some way afflicted?'

The King, who would normally have been annoyed at anyone else interfering, turned to the Lady Sockamore, smiling.

'You are correct my dear. Such a sad state of affairs. Apparently he has not been right since visiting the Magician's island. I blame the Magician of course. Whattlewherrit has been nothing but trouble since his father Cornelius disappeared.'

The Lady Sockamore nodded and smiled. The name of Whattlewherrit gave her a deeply uncomfortable feeling. They had never seen eye to eye when she was Sir Sockamore, and she still maintained a deep dislike for the man, however if it was he who had trapped the hags, then, she had to admit, he had gained at least some merit for ridding her of the two harpies.

'My brother spoke of him often, and was never complementary.'

'Well,' said the King, 'if I am honest, there was no love lost either way. The Magician called your brother a self-centred popinjay and worse. He did not suffer vanity in any form. Magicians, by their very upbringing are inclined to a rather austere approach to life.'

'We have not spoken of my brother at all since my arrival,' said the Lady Sockamore. 'Have you word of him?'

The King sighed and shook his head.

'Not a thing my dear. I am sorry to say that we believe he entered the Greer Swamp and may have fallen victim to those hideous hags the Bloodly Sisters. Why he went there no one knows. Sir Bloatmore, who accompanied him to find Moredeath, believed he was seeking a way to combat the spell the Magician had put upon Moredeath. I am afraid to say, if true, his idiocy may well have led to his own destruction.'

'You think him a fool then,' said the Lady Sockamore, 'and not valiant for trying to put right the Magicians wrongs?'

The King shrugged.

'You will forgive me for being frank my dear, but your brother was always of the opinion that he was better than everyone else. Whereas he could be particularly stupid. I believe he even thought I would give the hand of my daughter to him.'

The King chuckled.

'Imagine that, Sir Sockamore eventually ruling the land. He would begin by installing mirrors in every room so that he could see his own reflection as he walked by,' interrupted the Lady Gossamer.

The King laughed out loud. The Lady Sockamore grimaced. She tried to hide her anger. Inside she was snarling and already planning her revenge.

'I have to say my dear, I see little resemblance between yourself and your brother. It is so peculiar that he never mentioned you at all.' remarked the King.

'Well, we were not really close,' replied the Lady Sockamore. 'In fact I feel I hardly know him nowadays.'

'Sadly, I believe you may never get to renew your acquaintance.'

'I believe you are right, your Majesty. I shall just have to remember him as he was.'

'Quite so.'

The joust began with a loud fanfare. Along the lists, where the Knights confronted one another, crowds had arrived to watch the contest. A loud cheer went up as the first of the contestants arrived. Sir Sullimore and Sir Petmore took their ends, ready for the King's signal.

'Get the less experienced Knights out of the way first,' said the King to the Lady Sockamore. 'This will be a short session.'

The Lady Gossamer looked at her father and then at Sir Petmore. She would never have called him 'less experienced' or one for taking part in a 'short session'. Sewing his coat of arms on the tapestry she had recently finished, took a long time, because she found him very experienced indeed.

A mile away on the island at the very same time, the two hags were still trying to rub out the chalk marked spell. It was no use. It was clearly part of the spell itself, that stopped anyone caught by it, rubbing the runes out. The hags were at their wits end.

'If we ever get out of here, I shall boil that Magicians head in his own blood,' said one to the other.

'If we ever get out of here, I shall do the same to the Lady Sockamore. She knows we are here and has done nothing to save us.'

'This is unbearable,' said the first, 'and I am dying for a piss.'

'Well sister you will just have to do one then, and I shall join you. It's been hours since I last had a decent squat.'

The two hags lifted their skirts, squatted down, and pissed a stream that wormed its way across the floor. Upon reaching the runes, it hissed like a snake upon contact, at which point the markings vanished.

'Did you see that sister?'

'Strong urine sister, I have been holding it in for quite some time.'

'No, I mean they've melted away! We are free.'

The two hags stepped forwards, and sure enough they were able to walk away unhindered.

'There is a boat laid by the tower. The Magician must use it when the boatmen is not available. We will be able to get back to the castle and finish our plan.

Back at the joust, Sir Petmore was still in the saddle, having defeated Sir Sullimore on their second run. The Lady Gossamer clenched her fists tightly, hoping he would be her champion. If she had to marry someone chosen for her, then he may as well be good on the bedstraw.

'A fine run I must say,' said the King, 'that young man has stamina.'

'Indeed he does, father,' replied the Lady Gossamer.

'He lacks accuracy,' said the Lady Sockamore, 'his lance was too low the first run.'

'Oh, my dear, much though I am pleased you wish to enter into the spirit of the joust, what would a maiden know of such things?' The King chuckled to himself.

The Lady Sockamore growled softly but held back on what she was thinking.

'Perhaps the Lady Sockamore has watched a joust or two father. After al, Sir Sockamore, whatever one might say about him in other ways, was certainly the finest Knight in Naze when it came to the joust.'

The Lady Sockamore smiled and acknowledged the Lady Gossamers remark.

'Well, you just have to think yourself lucky he's not here today then or you would have ended up with the poetic popinjay!' laughed the King. At this point the Lady Sockamore could hold back no longer.

'I must protest at what your Majesty has just said, whilst my brother and I were estranged, the name of Sockamore is at stake when you make such derogatory remarks.'

The King, surprised by the Lady's response, apologised and said, 'it was but jest.'

'Jest can be a harmful thing, your Majesty, when it leads to the derogation of a family name.' Then, as if the subject was suddenly over, she said, 'tell me Sire, am I correct in saying that this competition is open to all comers?'

'Indeed it is, my Lady.'

'And that the winner, whoever that might be, has the hand of your daughter'

'I have pledged as much, and a King does not go back on his word,' replied the King.

The Lady Sockamore turned to the archdeacon sitting on the other side of her.

'You heard as much?' she asked. The arch deacon replied that he had heard the King pronounce it so.

'Good,' said the Lady Sockamore, 'then we are all of the same opinion.'

'My dear you seem slightly heated on the subject. Pray do not get yourself into an ill humour. Enjoy the competition. It should not take long.'

The King was right. The competition was swift and brutal, and to the Lady Gosammer's delight, Sir Petmore was still in the saddle, four Knights in.

'How many men are left?' shouted the King to his equerry.

'There are three unwed Knights remaining Sire if we are to discount Sir Sockamore and Sir Godfrey.'

The King laughed out loud.

'Well, we can assume that Sir Sockamore will not turn up,' and seeing the Lady Sockamore's discouraging look added, 'unfortunately,' as an afterthought.

'And as for poor old Sir Godfrey he is hardly likely to make an appearance. It is for the best he does not know, for though I have respect for the man, I do not think he would fare well either in the joust, should he win, nor in the bedstraw! Eh daughter?' The King laughed heartily. The Lady Gossamer did not give her father the courtesy of a response. Being put up for the highest bidder was bad enough, without making merry about being in the bedstraw with an old man.

It was not long before to the surprise of everyone assembled, Sir Petmore had downed the last of the unwed Knights. The King, though surprised by the result, took it as divine confirmation that Sir Petmore would be his son in law, and was about to announce him the winner when something unexpected happened. A single dark cloud issued across the sun, temporarily turning the field cold and grey. For a moment it was almost as dark as night. All eyes turned towards the vanished star but only the vaguest glow could be seen and then when the crowd thought it would never return, the cloud dispersed and slowly the light returned.

'Hello dearie,' said one of the hags to the Lady Sockamore. The lady Sockamore jumped.

'I don't expect you thought you would see us again, did you? Perhaps you thought we had returned to the Greer Swamp, disappointed at how things had turned out?' She shook her head and went to answer but the hag continued.

'You will be pleased to know we are far from finished.' The hag cackled 'In fact here comes the next part of our plan.'

Looking down the field, to the amazement of the assembled crowd there stood a black horse, as dark as a dragon's eye, and upon the horse sat a Knight whose armour robbed the light from around it, so that it was darker even than the horse. The King, who was in mid speech about how Sir Petmore had done so well, was nudged by his daughter and looked across the field himself. For a moment he said nothing but then asked his equerry what was happening? The equerry, none the wiser, suggested it must be a Knight from beyond Naze.

'Is this allowed?' muttered the King. The equerry consulted the proclamation the King had made.

'It appears so your Majesty. It does say to all comers.' The King huffed uncomfortably and reluctantly said,

'Well if that be the case then I suppose we must allow the joust to continue.'

He raised his hand and Sir Petmore took his position, as did the dark Knight. There was a deep thrum of hooves as the ground shook beneath the feet of the crowd, and the two Knights headed toward one another meeting with a dull thud, as the lance of the black Knight hit Sir Petmore straight in the breastplate and knocked him to the ground. The crowd gasped. The Lady Gossamer moaned, and the Lady Sockamore took her leave, telling the hags she needed to go to the privy. They said nothing but both were grinning from ear to ear. The King was perplexed and didn't know what to say. One of the hags leaned towards him and said, 'aren't you going to declare him the winner?'

Chapter Forty Four

It had taken Sir Godfrey two days to get back from Merrelay castle and he was saddle sore. His love plums, though not much to speak of nowadays, felt as if they had been spent time in Mistress Jupp's mortar and pestle. Whilst she was grinding chillies at that!

His beloved Beth, Mistress Munn, had begged him to stay away from Naze but he would have none of it. Once he realised he had left Mortimer in the great hall on the night of the wedding eve, he knew he had to go back. How he could have overlooked his best friend and companion in the chaos he did not know but there was no way he could leave him to his fate in the castle.

As he approached Naze castle he heard an unfamiliar roaring. Voices shouting and cheering and he wondered what it might be, and then he remembered the joust. It was to be a celebration of the wedding. This came as a surprise to the old Knight. He was sure the joust would not go ahead as he had left Moredeath at Merrelay with Mistress Munn. He nudged Desmond, his horse, gently in the flank and Desmond trotted for ten paces before running out of steam. Sir Sockamore sighed. He could not blame Desmond, after all everything at Merrelay had begun to decay, the moment he got back with the wine. It was as if everything around him was being consumed by rot. The castle itself was falling into the moat and had nearly killed Whattlewherrit during his visit. He nudged Desmond again and his faithful horse huffered, and began to trot once more.

Within the hour he was approaching the jousting field with its striped tents and merry flags flying. The day had been a bright one and so it was to his consternation that, as he finally reached the back of the field, everything went dark, and the temperature dropped. It was only for a short moment, but it was enough to send a chill through him. Something felt wrong. As the light reappeared, he saw the strangest thing. In front of his very eyes, out of view of the crowd, a black Knight appeared as if from thin air, and proceeded to approach the jousting field.

'Something is very wrong here Desmond,' said the old Knight, 'we need to find out what it is.'

So it was that, instead of going straight to the castle, he gently pulled his horse's head towards the armoury tents where the Knights equipment was stored. By the time he had reached the tents and had ascertained from a young knave what was happening, he knew there was only one thing for him to do. Just as Sir Petmore was knocked from his saddle Sir Godfrey picked up a lance and a shield, and, remounting Desmond, rode out to face the Black Knight.

The King was still summoning up the courage to give the unknown Black Knight his daughter's hand when a gasp went up from the crowd. He turned to look down the field, and there saw Sir Godfrey, lance and shield in hand. The hags stared beyond the King, to where he was looking and then back at one another. They laughed such a wicked cackle that both the King and the Lady Gossamer peered at them in dismay. Those sounds should not have come from the throats of attractive serving maids.

 The King shouted out, 'Go back Sir Godfrey leave the field for your own sake!'

 The crowd shouted similar things, desperate that the old Knight would not lose his life. It was clear the Black Knight would make short work of him, but Sir Godfrey stood his ground. The Black Knight turned to face him. The crowd went quiet as the Black Knight dug his heels deeply into his horse's flanks. Sir Godfrey gently nudged Desmond's flanks and whispered, 'come on old boy, we can do this.'

 As the Black Knight thundered down the field Desmond trotted toward him like a donkey on a beach. The heavy thud of the black Knight's horse approached. The Black Knight had travelled three quarters of the field to Sir Godfrey's quarter. Sir Godfrey braced himself. In truth he did not manage to see the Knight coming soon enough and with a sickening blow the black Knights lance pierced the old Knights armour and he was skewered like a pig on a spit.

 The women in the crowd shrieked, the men held their breaths, as the old Knight, beloved by all was hauled up on the end of the Black Knight's lance, and thrown, like an apple on a stick, to the back of the field. Desmond turned around and clopped as fast as he could after his master. In the Royal stand the two hags grinned widely, whilst the King and his daughter sat bereft.

 Even though the Lady Gossamer would not have wanted the old Knight as her husband, none the less she did not want to see him die in such a horrible way. Once again, the King stood to unhappily announce the winner of the joust, but he had no sooner begun to do so than the crowd shouted out, as they had when the old Knight originally took to the field. The King looked, the hags looked, the Lady Gossamer looked. To everyone's amazement Sir Godfrey had remounted his horse and was making this way back up the field.

'How can this be?' exclaimed the King, 'he was stuck like a pig.'

'What's happening,' muttered the hags, 'it's not possible.'

It was the first time since drinking the Holy Wine that Sir Godfrey had welcomed his immortality. Despite the lance piercing him and a fair deal of blood gushing from the wound, he was still alive. His only regret was that immortality did not bring with it endless stamina. Far from it. He was tired just rising from the bedstraw these days, and jousting was not something he had done for many a year. As he found himself confronting the black Knight once again, it was only the cheering of the crowds that gave him the energy needed for a second run. The end however was swift and not at all pleasant, as once again he was pierced and thrown. This time, as he lay on the ground, he had to admit he would be unable to rise to fight a third time. His strength was gone. The Great Moyen had once again punished him for his indiscretion with the wine, and he would have to suffer the humiliation of defeat. He staggered to his feet. The crowd cheered as he led Desmond off the field, none of them able to believe he had survived at all.

'Well, that's that,' said the King to the Lady Gossamer, 'I am afraid I have no option but to give your hand to this intruder whoever he might be. The Lady Gossamer wept silently.

'There you are sister, I told you we would win in the end,' said one hag to the other.

'Not so fast sister,' replied the other as yet another Knight appeared.

'Oh, for goodness sake, what now,' said the second.

'I think our protégée, Sir Sockamore, has reappeared,' answered the first.

'But how can he? We haven't undone the spell?' The two hags stared bewildered.

'Are those the arms of Sir Sockamore?' said the King in disbelief.

'I cannot believe it father,' replied the Lady Gossamer, 'but he is back!'

The Lady Sockamore felt uncomfortable in her armour. It no longer fitted. It was way too big, but there was no option. She knew the hags were behind the black

222

Knight and she also knew if she was to let him win, the hags would finally rule Naze. The black Knight would despatch the King once the Lady Gossamer was married to their creation. She kneed her horse's flanks and lifted her lance and shield. They were heavier than she remembered, but of course, she now had only the strength of a maiden. Like so many things, it was something she had never considered whilst a man. Women were not weaker than men from lack of effort but only from design, and of that they had no choice. The Great Moyen had not made them for battle, lest it be the battle of childbirth. How strange that she should be made to recognise this at such a moment, when, though she knew she had the skills to defeat the black Knight, she was not at all sure she had the necessary strength. Despite her reservations she galloped on. Using all of her concentration, she pitched her lance at the black Knight's most vulnerable place. They clashed. The Lady Sockamore managed to parry the black Knights lance aside, but in so doing missed her target. They passed one another and turned. Once again, to the thunder of hooves, the crowd held their breath as they rode towards each other once more.

Chapter Forty Five

Whattlewherrit stood at the bottom of the stairs looking up at Moredeath the Bludgeoner. Rick Facile's house was eerily silent, the partygoers having disappeared. Despite Whattlewherrit's fear that he had somehow magicked them away he had no time to dwell on the possibility. Moredeath had to be his focus, or he would inevitably find himself in even deeper trouble. It was as he was considering this, that Moredeath's axe flew past his left ear, and embedded itself in the polished hardwood floor just feet behind him.

'You've got to stop that Moredeath,' he shouted, 'if I die then you are stuck here forever.' The Bludgeoner was in the process of unsheathing his sword when he stopped. The Magician's words had fought their way through his anger and resonated. Whattlewherrit could see him fighting his natural urge to kill him. The Bludgeoner's face contorted into a solidified mask of vindictiveness. He did not need to reply to the Magician, his look was enough. It was as if someone had rolled a huge rock over the mouth of a volcano that was about to explode. He might have paused momentarily but there was no doubt what was building inside would come out and come out soon. Whattlewherrit held the shard fast and trusted himself to a deeper being. He asked the shard to send Moredeath and himself back to Naze and the imposter back to the What Will Be. Adding, 'by the way, can you bring all the disappeared partygoers back please.' He felt the ground shift and a strange sensation not dissimilar to dropping into water from a great height, and then it was over.

Not for the first time Moredeath, found himself in an unknown tent, on a combat field, feeling incredibly angry. This time it was back in Naze and a joust was in progress. The two riders were confronting one another. One was a Black Knight, whilst the other wore the coat of arms of one of the Knights of Naze. They raced towards one another and the black Knight, without too much effort managed to dismount the Knight from Naze. The crowd groaned as the Knight fell. As they did so, the Knight's helmet flew off and revealed to everyone's amazement that the rider was not in fact Sir Sockamore, but instead his sister. There were shouts of dismay when it was discovered a woman was competing against the black Knight.

Moredeath pushed the crowd apart and stepped onto the jousting field. He grabbed the reigns of the Lady Sockamore's horse, picked up her shield and

224

lance and aimed the horse at the black Knight. In the stands, the hags stared down at the black Knight. The black Knight looked up at them and lifted his hands as if to say what do I do now? Without regard for where she was, one of the hags shouted out 'Kill him!!' At which point the black Knight lifted his lance, kicked his horse and charged at the Bludgeoner.

The collision, when it happened, was like the meeting of two trains crashing head on. There was a moment when time stood still, as both lances smashed into the other's shields and shattered into splinters. The opponents rode on past one another and picked up new lances at each end of the field. The shock had obviously damaged the Black Knight. Suddenly the young faces of the hags flickered and for a second or two a ghastly old face momentarily appeared. They looked at one another.

'Are you alright sister?' asked one

'As well as you are sister I think.' The fight was draining their energy. They hadn't planned on so many jousts, or such stiff opposition.

The joust commenced. Moredeath was seething with rage. All of the pent-up energy and frustration he had felt since first arriving in Naze was boiling beneath the surface. His head was pounding with one word and that word was death! His face set in stone like a fierce gargoyle, he charged down the field and when the two opponents met, he planted his lance firmly into the breastplate of the Black Knight. The Knight visibly shuddered before falling off his horse. Once again the Bloodly Sisters true faces began to emerge from beneath their masks, but this time they did not vanish. Not only that but their beautiful bodies began to noticeably shrivel, their skin wrinkling before their very eyes.

Down on the field, the Bludgeoner dismounted and drew out his broadsword. The Black Knight got up and drew his. A fierce sword fight ensued but the Black Knight was no match for Moredeath. The Bludgeoner swung with such force it shattered the Knights armour and severed his arm, leaving him defenceless. The Bludgeoner was in no mood to take prisoners. He swung again, and in one move, despatched the Black Knight's head. That very moment, as if someone had sliced open a pig's bladder full of air, the Bloodly Sisters began to deflate. Their very essence departed their bodies, leaving only the garments they sat in. The crowd cheered heartily. Moredeath grunted, whilst looking around for the Magician. He stomped off in the direction of the river and the Magician's Island.

'Come back!' shouted the King, 'what about my daughter?'

But it was too late. Moredeath was gone.

As soon as the Lady Gossamer was able, she rushed from the stands to where the Lady Sockamore lay.

'Oh my dear, how brave you were to fight for me,' she cried as she leaned over her. The Lady Sockamore groaned. She had been knocked out by the fall.

'Where am I?' she asked as she opened her eyes, and saw the Lady Gossamer.

'Why you are at the jousting field in Naze,' replied the Lady Gossamer, 'don't you remember?'

'I don't remember anything. Who are you?'

The Lady Gossamer frowned. 'Why, I am the Lady Gossamer,' she replied.

'You are very beautiful,' said the Lady Sockamore and without further thought, leaned up and kissed the Lady Gossamer full on the lips. The Lady Gossamer felt the kiss and it was like no other. Soft and gentle and loving. She blushed.

'Madam!' she cried, you are not well.

'I shall remain this way until you promise me your love,' replied the Lady Sockamore.

The Lady Gossamer was shocked but as she looked into the eyes of the woman in her arms, she found herself strangely attracted to this beautiful, damaged woman. She stood up and commanded her servants to take the Lady Sockamore to her own rooms where she should be given the utmost care until she could get there herself. Having done so she returned to her father the King.

'I despair daughter. I think I am suffering the same ill humour the bishop is suffering. The whole world is going mad. A mysterious Black Knight. Sir Godfrey stuck like a pig and yet still alive. A maiden jousting! Is there anything more fantastic that a once stable mind could imagine? Did you know her maids have departed leaving nought but their vestments. Unfortunately, I didn't even see them go. I believe that mad bear of a man was actually Moredeath the Bludgeoner, returned to his former self.

'What makes you say as much?'

'I saw him in the What Will Be. The Magician showed him to me, riding through the woods on his way to Naze. It was the same man as just destroyed the Black Knight. He should be your husband.'

The Lady Gossamer felt a deep feeling of relief, knowing he had departed the field.

'You didn't tell me you had seen him. Why not?'

'I was afraid to describe the man to you. I thought of your tender white skin being pummelled by that beast...'

'And yet you would have had me marry him!' protested his daughter.

'Ah yes but that is politics my dear. One cannot avoid such things if one is to keep the realm safe.'

The Lady Gossamer snorted with indignation and said, 'I am going to my rooms.'

Chapter Forty Six

Whattlewherrit found himself at the drawbridge of Merrelay castle. He looked around. There was no Moredeath. What had brought him here? Why had the shard decided he needed to be in this place? He was reluctant to go anywhere near Sir Godfrey's home, for fear it would drop on his head, as it had tried to do the last time he was there. He bit his lip, then in a moment of unexpected decisiveness, strode on the planks of the drawbridge and toward the huge gates. He rang the bell. A servant appeared and enquired after the nature of his visit.

'I am Whattlewherrit the Magician of Naze,' he replied, 'I have come to see Sir Godfrey.'

'My master is not at home at present but we have a visitor from Naze here already, one Mistress Munn.'

'Mistress Munn,' replied the startled Whattlewherrit, 'take me to her at once.'

The servant closed the speaking hatch and the large doors began to rumble open in front of him.

'So, we gets here with that man,' said Mistress Munn referring to Kenny Catlin, 'and then Arthur realises he has left Mortimer back at Naze castle. I begged him not to go back. I had this premonition things were not right. Well, no sooner had he left than the imposter ups and disappears and I am left alone.'

Whattlewherrit reassured her she was not alone anymore.

'I returned the imposter to his rightful place and if the stars are with me, Moredeath to his. Although I imagine the shard must have decided for some unknown reason he should be at Naze and I here. Let us hope we have arrived at the bottom of this barrel full of mishaps. I cannot for the life of me think of worse to come.'

'You must not go to Naze, Magician, for everyone is looking for you, and should they find you, will not hesitate to hand you in to the King. He has set a price upon your head.'

Mistress Munn took a deep breath and wondered whether it was the right time to tell the Magician the news. She went ahead trusting it was.

'There is something I have to tell you Whattlewherrit.'

The Magician looked her in the eye. 'And what is that Mistress?'

'Sir Godfrey, on his way to Naze, fell upon the Greer Swamp.'

'Indeed?'

'And whilst there chanced upon the cave of the Bloodly Sisters.'

Whattlewherrit frowned as he listened intently.

'There he found.....' she caught her breath and swallowed 'Cornelius.'

'Is he alive!?' exclaimed Whattlewherrit.

'He was when Arthur found him, but he died in his arms.'

Mistress Munn watched the Magician drain of blood; his face turned as pale as fresh white linen stiffened by the frosts of morning as he fought back his emotions.

'The Bloodly Sisters were not there?' He asked.

'They were not, and by the ashes in the fire had not been so for some time.'

'Then they have left the swamp,' said Whattlewherrit.

'But that cannot be so,' replied Mistress Munn. 'There is a curse upon them that binds them there. No woman would dare enter the forest, much less the Greer Swamp for fear of releasing them.'

'This has something to do with Sir Sockamore I'll be bound. That man is........' Whattlewherrit didn't get to finish his sentence as the chandelier in the middle of the room crashed to the ground, sending splinters flying everywhere.

'We must get out of this place Mistress, it is trying to put an end to me,' he said as the dust-clouded air began to choke his lungs.

When they got outside, Mistress Munn said, 'what are you going to do Magician? Where will you go now. There is no place for you here in Naze?'

'Well, I certainly won't be going to the Bloodlands, that is for sure,' he laughed but it was a bitter laugh. 'What would you suggest Mistress?' he asked 'there aren't many places an out-of-work Magician can go.'

'I don't know. I shall miss you wherever you go.'

The Magician was touched by her words. 'I shall miss you too,' he replied, 'unless of course you want to come with me?'

'Oh Magician, if only I was forty years younger I might consider such, but it is as much as my old body can do to walk a mile nowadays. What a curse, the Holy Wine. Arthur had no idea when he gave me the last drops that we should both end up like this. Unable to die but to age nonetheless. What point is there in life if it is no more than a never-ending burden? Would that we could both put an end to this. The Great Moyen has a cruel streak. He is unforgiving.'

Whattlewherrit sniffed scornfully. 'The Great Moyen is nothing more than a myth Mistress. I have told you so before. You are all blinded by mystery and illusion. I have my suspicions as to how it has arrived at this place but even though my words would be honest and true, should I speak them, they would meet the drawbridge of your mind.'

'Let us not fight Magician. Not now. There is little time left between us. You has your opinion and I has mine, let us agree on that.'

Whattlewherrit said no more but had a plan. If he was right then he could end the suffering of Mistress Munn and Sir Godfrey. The difficult part would be getting to Sir Godfrey without being caught by the King's men.

'We need to go to Naze,' he said, 'we have to find Sir Godfrey.

Chapter Forty Seven

Kenny Catlin looked around. He was at some party and it was in full swing. This was peculiar, because not moments before he had been standing in a castle in the middle of nowhere, with a mad old woman, wondering whether he would ever see his home again. The fact he was dressed in Moredeath the Bludgeoner's clothes seemed to make no difference, because everyone else seemed to be in fancy dress. His mind slipped a gear. It was unable to take on board this new location in which he had arrived. All he could think was that he had exactly the same feeling he had when he had ended up in the forest in Naze. One moment he was in one place i.e. Klines, the next he was in the forest. One moment he was in a crumbling castle in Naze, the next he was back in the world he had left days ago. He took a second to scan the room. The house was not familiar to him, but it was definitely owned by someone with money. He tried to think which of his multi-millionaire friends might own it. It was as he was looking around trying to spot a familiar face that someone put their hand on his shoulder. He turned to face them.

'Well, if it isn't Kenny Catlin,' said the voice. It took a moment for him to recognise Max Moran who was dressed like a priest from the Spanish Inquisition.

'Max? It is Max, isn't it?'

'It certainly is Kenny. You have a good memory.'

Kenny Catlin was blessed with a photographic memory when it came to names and faces. He had met Max Moran briefly, when he and Dick Friendly were negotiating the film deal some months before.

'What are you doing here Kenny?'

Catlin tried to think of an answer, there was none. At least none that made any sense. He needed to say something. If in doubt, throw the question back to the person who asked it.

'The same as you,' he replied.

'I didn't know Rick had invited you to his party. In fact I didn't know you knew one another.

Kenny Catlin tried to work out who 'Rick' was but could not picture anyone.

'I don't know him personally,' he replied, 'I came with a friend.'

All the while he was in conversation his mind was madly trying to make sense of this new world. Part of it was still in Naze.

Max Moran smiled and said, 'Well, you should meet him' and pointing to the garden told Kenny how to get to The Stinger.

Kenny did not want to meet anyone at that moment, he just wanted to get away from the noise and the lights. To give himself time to think. If he was to stay sane, he had to make sense of it all. He followed Moran's instructions and made his way out into the garden. He would not however look for 'Rick', whoever that was. Instead, he would work out where he was, get to a mobile and get the hell out of the place. One of the things he had noticed in the party was that everyone he heard talking had English accents. Could it be he was actually in England itself? If so, where?

Out of the house, he followed a path lined by lanterns. It was red brick in a herringbone pattern and either side topiary bushes were clipped in a variety of shapes. Rose arches framed the path further, confirming his view that this was indeed England, or if not, it was a very good pastiche. Though he was by no means a garden enthusiast he had visited often enough to recognise the style. The night air had a slight chill to it but was not uncomfortable, wearing, as he was, Moredeath's heavy tabard and hose. He looked up but the lights obliterated any view of the stars, but he did catch the flickering wings of a bat after the moths dancing in the dull lamplight.

'How the fuck did I get here,' he asked himself. His remark to himself was not about being in 'Rick's' garden, whoever Rick was, but rather encompassed the whole crazy whirlwind of events of the last few days. The last time anything made any sense was when he was with Debbie Lamb in Klines, after that nothing was normal anymore. More than once he had wondered whether he had overdone the drugs he took. Or whether some new synthetic drug had been slipped into his regular supply. Anything was possible these days. His disorientation was enormous. It was jet lag on steroids, and then some. He began to feel dizzy. He was in shock. He recognised the symptoms. His hands began to shake, and he felt cold. Not from the outside but within. He needed to sit down. A few yards on and he found a bench. It was just in time. He passed out.

Back at the house Max Moran found a bathroom where the noise was not overwhelming and he took out his phone. He tapped in 999 and waited.

'Emergency, which service,' said the voice.

'Police,' replied Moran. He waited. A few moments later a second voice answered.

'Police, how can I help you?'

'I am at a party being held by Rick Facile. I believe there has been a murder.'

'What makes you say that?' asked the responder.

'I think you will find Mr Facile is dead in the garden.'

'Did you see what happened?'

'I did not, but I did see Kenny Catlin, an American citizen who I happen to know is being sought under an International Arrest Warrant for the murder of Miss Debbie Lamb. He was in the garden near the body.'

'Where are you and what is your name?'

'I am at The Manor House, Upskirting, near Cirencester.'

'And your name?'

Max Moran ended the call.

When Kenny Catlin awoke, he was surrounded by an armed SWAT unit.

'Kenny Catlin?' asked a voice.

'Yes,' replied Catlin.

'I am arresting you for the murder of Debbie Lamb.'

'What!?'

'Anything you say may be taken down and used in evidence against you in a court of law. Do you understand?'

'What the fuck is this?' replied Catlin.

'I am also taking you in for questioning over the death of Mr Rick Facile. Do you understand?'

'I don't know what the fuck you are talking about. Who is Rick Facile and what's going on? I want my lawyer.'

Chapter Forty Eight.

Sir Godfrey took a while to recover from the beating his body had taken. To the consternation of those tending him, even though blood had gushed from his wounds he nevertheless appeared to have healed to the point where he was able to stand. He looked down at his rusty chest plate, which now contained a large hole where the lance had penetrated.

'Hmm,' he said as if it were no more than a tear in fabric caught by a thorn. 'I must go to the castle,' he said.

Despite their protestations, he made his way out of the tent and up the hill to where the pillars of the castle gates stood like two sentries guarding the castle of Naze. The gates were open, and no one was to be seen. Everyone, it appeared was watching the joust. Across the cobbled courtyard and through the doors of the castle itself he creaked, holding his aching chest. His skinny legs were hardly able to hold him, bruised as they were by the fall he had taken. But despite all of his ailments, he had one thought, 'Mortimer.'

Finally arriving at the great hall he opened the vast doors and peered in.

'Mortimer! Mortimer!' He called. Mortimer did not appear. Why he thought his friend would still be in the hall he didn't know. It was the last place he had seen him, so his instincts told him why not start there. Calling several more times he finally admitted Mortimer must have moved on.

There was nothing for it, he would have to search the rest of the castle. He was making his way down the corridor that linked the Great Hall to the kitchens below when he heard a scream. Then the voice of Gladwell Jupp.

'There's that rat again! I'll have its head on my chopping block so I will!'

Sir Godfrey gasped. Mortimer, on the chopping block! He forced himself to go as fast as he could, but only managed a slow walk, all the while imagining his poor friend being beheaded. It was agony.

'Oh, Great Moyen, punish me some more if you will, but spare Mortimer,' he called out. More screams from the kitchen.

'Stop!' he called out, hoping Mistress Jupp would hear him. 'That's my friend!'

Chop! Chop! Chop! He heard the sound of a cleaver hitting wood.

'Come here you little beast!' shouted Mistress Jupp.

He finally reached the door of the kitchen and gasping for breath breathed a 'Stop!'

Gladwell Jupp looked up. For a moment she was in shock. Sir Godfrey standing at her kitchen door, a hole the size of a cooking pot in his armour and bloodied clothes the likes of which she had not seen before.

'Lawks a mercy, what has happened to you, Sir Godfrey?'

'A slight wound from the jousting field, Mistress.'

'That's more than a slight wound if you asks me. If you was a Turkey I reckon it would take more than a pound of stuffing to fill that hole.'

'That's probably true Mistress but fortunately I am not. But less of me. I have come to find Mortimer.'

'Mortimer?'

'Yes my pet rat.'

'A rat! Who would have such a thing as a pet? Just a sight of the tail of one gives me the shivers.'

'Well Mortimer and I go a long way back. It is not to be understood how such things occur, but we became good friends.'

'Friends? With a rat? I thinks you might have taken a tumble too many Sir Godfrey, such that it has affected your mind. Are you sure you don't want to sit down?'

Sir Godfrey called out Mortimer's name and within moments his friend appeared. Scuttering across the floor, he jumped up onto Sir Godfrey's shoulder, at which point Gladwell Jupp passed out.

Many miles away, across the forest, Whattlewherrit had made his mind up. There was only one way to get to Naze fast enough and without him being caught by the King's guards and that was to enter the body of a horse. Mistress Munn could ride. That way the journey would be swift and safe for all concerned. He explained this to Mistress Munn, but she objected saying she wasn't going to 'sit on a horse knowing the Magician was between her 'twixt and in betweens.' It was a matter of principle she said, it was bad enough that the Magician was going to 'do his stuff with animals', something she deeply disapproved of, let alone 'having him below.' He assured Mistress Munn he would find a side saddle, at which point she reluctantly agreed. He talked to Sir Godfrey's stable boy, took the fastest horse and had it saddled. Within the hour they were off.

For Mistress Munn, the journey was terrifying. For one thing, Whattlewherrit seemed to be in charge of the beast, so that no amount of pulling on the reigns did any good. She shouted at him, but he didn't seem to hear, or, as she thought, didn't want to.

'Slow down, you've got no thought for an old woman's bones! I shall shake apart by the time we get there, and you will find nought but my bits and pieces!'

The Magician, she thought, was ignorant of anyone else's experience. He had always been that way, and she cursed herself for allowing him to do this to her. That boy has nought but his own plans in his head, and the needs of others count for nothing.

Whattlewherrit on the other hand was feeling a sense of exhilaration he had not felt for weeks. He shared the joy of the horse's heart pounding, the blood's pumping rush, the strength of its legs, as they galloped and jumped anything in its way and the pull of its neck as it fought against Mistress Munn and the reigns in a bid to be free.

The beast was alive, more alive than anything else could be in this world full of dullards and tricksters. Tied to the demands of their pinklarry's and love plums, worshipping the Great Moyen, unable to see beyond their desires, they would never know what it was like to be in something so alive, so immediate, so real. Maybe Mistress Munn was right, perhaps he was addicted to entering the world of beasts, but it felt like nothing else. He had done it since a child and it was why he could walk the world, knowing the world of men was such a pointless thing.

In his experience, the immediacy of being a beast was the only thing that spoke of reality. All else had its edges dulled by boredom and drudgery. Beasts lived with the knowledge that at any moment life could end, and for that reason, they lived it with such a sharp sense of focus. Everything became a part of them. The slightest movement, the quietest sound, the mildest scent of something on the wind brought their senses into a point. Like focussing the sun through a lens, their entire being was centred and alert. Something he had never been able to achieve with his restless nature, his wandering mind, and dare he say it, his forgetfulness. Perhaps that was the truth of it all. They had what he had been trying to achieve his whole life. A connection with something bigger, something raw and wild, something that dared you to be completely yourself. No names, no titles, no expectations, no demands, just to live and experience life from moment to moment.

The journey took two days. They had to stop at night and Whattlewherrit suffered the harsh words of Mistress Munn, berating him for driving the beast on.

'By the Great Moyen, my nethers will never recover from this. You mark my words if you don't slow this beast down, I shall have shook my brains down into my backside by the time we reach Naze.' As my dear old mother used to say, 'why suffer a sore arse for the sake of a man wanting to go fast?' Of course, all of that coming and going down below is of no interest to me nowadays.

Whattlewherrit tried not to think about the details of what she had said. He listened politely and then reassured her he would try to go slower but that time was of the essence. This was why they eventually made Naze castle slightly later than he would have liked, but they made it in one piece. On the edges of the castle wall, Whattlewherrit left the horse's body in order to talk to Mistress Munn.

'Once we have spoken, I must return into the shape of the horse to protect myself from those who would hang me. But you must find Sir Godfrey and get him to ride out with us tonight. We shall go together to the standing stone on Hunker Down. Good luck Mistress I shall be willing your success.'

'And to you Magician. A word of advice, don't let no stallions catch you out in the stables or your nethers will be as sore as mine.'

Whattlewherrit winced. He would never in a million years have thought of such a thing. Why did Mistress Munn have to say it! He looked at the mare and suddenly his desire to enter into its body seemed less inviting.

Chapter Forty Nine

The Lady Sockamore lay with the Lady Gossamer, naked beneath the bedsheets. It had been two days since the joust and her aching body was bruised but recovering. None of that mattered though, for she was in love. Their unlikely bonding had happened without intention. After the joust, when she was taken to the Lady Gossamer's rooms on the lady's insistence, the Lady Gossamer then demanded to be allowed to tend to her wounds herself. Her actions, in bravely taking to the field to protect her from the black Knight, had deeply affected the Lady Gossamer. The Lady Sockamore had become a heroine, a champion of women. The Lady Gossamer looked upon her with such tender eyes when she first arrived in the rooms, seeing her lying on the bed.

'How can I thank you for what you did?' She asked.

The Lady Sockamore could barely remember anything herself. It was a brutal fall at the end of the black Knights lance, and she had fallen upon the ground with such force, it had knocked out her senses. Nothing in her memory seemed open for review. She couldn't even remember who she was, much less the circumstances behind her fall and why she was jousting.

'I shall have a bath drawn for you,' said the Lady Gossamer. 'We shall get you undressed and bathe you.'

She was true to her words. Within a short time, how long she did not know, for her mind came and went, the water was poured into the bath, and the Lady Gossamer told her servants to leave.

'Now, we must get you free of your clothes. No one as beautiful as you should be condemned to wear a man's clothes for longer than is necessary.' She laughed. 'After all, the last time I saw you, you were wearing that spectacular dress!'

The Lady Sockamore groaned as the Lady Gossamer tenderly eased the tabard over her head.

'There my dear, I am being as gentle as I can. Please forgive me if I hurt you at all, I am doing my best.'

'It is alright,' she groaned, 'though I don't remember when I seem to think I have suffered worse.'

Once the tabard was removed the Lady Gossamer gasped at the extent of the bruising on her body. One side looked no less than the colours of the sun breaking through a passing storm. Thick grey clouds of wounds were touched by a deep orange that then bled into the darkest blue. The Lady Gossamer softly unwrapped the cloth binding her patient's breasts and let them fall into their natural place. She tried not to look at them for fear that she might be seen to be admiring them. The night of the feast, they had been obvious in the dress she wore, and yet strangely hidden at the same time. Now they rested softly above her ribs, full, soft, and round. The Lady Gossamer, breathed deeply, catching the sweet but musty odour from beneath her patient's arms, then said, 'we must remove your leggings.'

The Lady Sockamore shifted her hips upwards so that the lady could pull them away and as this was done, felt an exciting sense of vulnerability. Nothing now was left to the imagination. The Lady Gossamer told her to edge herself to the side of the bed where she could help lift her under her good arm. This being done she manoeuvred her to the tub and, with some difficulty sat her in it. The water stung and she gasped when first entering it, but within a short time, allowed herself to experience the relieving warmth seeping through her. The Lady Gossamer smiled.

'You are so beautiful,' she said, 'even if it looks as if someone has painted one side of your body to match nature's darkest storms.'

As she spoke, she took a ladle and gently ran the warm water over her champion's shoulders. The water trickled down over her breasts and it was like the touch of the gentlest fingers. Time and again she ladled the water, and as she did so, she noticed a change in the nature of Lady Sockamore's soft skin, a familiar puckering of the breast. The Lady Gossamer's eyebrows flickered, and she softly swallowed a small lump that had appeared in her throat.

'Why don't you join me,' said the Lady Sockamore.

The Lady Gossamer stopped for a moment, ladle in mid motion.

'Why I....'

'There is room for two and it would be a shame to waste the hot water.' The Lady Gossamer felt a strong desire to do just what she had suggested, but a part of her was still trying to understand what she was feeling.

'Reward your champion with your company, it is not much to ask is it?'

The Lady Gossamer slowly disrobed. She had been bathed since childhood by her servants, so there was nothing new in being naked in front of another woman, but this was different. She suddenly felt modest, standing as she was without a stitch upon her back.

'Get in,' said the Lady Sockamore. To which she obeyed. There was a moment deciding whose legs should go where but the Lady Sockamore opened hers to save the Lady Gossamer further uncertainty. The Lady Gossamer tried to avoid looking down but did not succeed. It was the briefest of moments. The Lady Sockamore noticed but said nothing.

'Let me repay your service to me,' she said and picking up the ladle, began to do exactly as had been done to her. She leaned forward and dropping the water gently from the shoulder, she let it trickle over the Lady Gossamers small white breasts. After several ladles she deliberately began tipping it, so it was aimed directly on the most sensitive parts. She put the ladle down and leaned further forward. Ignoring her pain and without asking for permission she kissed the Lady Gossamer full on the lips. Her hand drew the ladies head towards her so that any reluctance might be overcome but there was none. And that was how it began.

After the bath they slept until daylight. The Lady Gossamer, sensing her love was awake, turned to her. Though her eyes were barely open to the light of morning, she smiled.

'What are we going to do?' She asked.

'About what,' the Lady Sockamore replied.

'This,' she said tapping the bed.' It cannot go on.'

'And why not?'

'Because I am to be married to...' she stopped and thought, 'who knows to whom. But one thing is certain it cannot be you.' She laughed but it was a sad laugh.

'Because I am not a man, does that make our love any the less?'

'Love has no place in the fortunes of a Lady. We are victims of our birth. You should know that as well as I.'

The Lady Sockamore sighed.

'At this moment I have no memory of ought before the joust. If I knew these things once, then they are now forgot. You tell me I am the sister of this Knight, Sir Sockamore but he could be someone living on the moon and I would remember him as well.'

'I am sorry my love but I am sure your memory will stir from it's slumbers given time. I shall make it my passion to reacquaint you with as much history as

I know. Although most of it will be about your brother, for your past was unknown to me but for a few days, as it was to everyone.'

'Which is his coat of arms?' asked the Lady Sockamore looking at the tapestry now hanging on the bedroom wall. The Lady Gossamer blushed.

'Oh, I didn't manage to finish the tapestry. You will not find it there.'

'Well perhaps as we are lovers you might wish to finish it?' The Lady Gossamer smiled and said she would. For her.

241

Chapter Fifty

The King was on his throne in the throne room. Flanked by his councillors and Knights he was holding court.

'I have to inform you that the Bludgeoner has returned to the Bloodlands. Reliable reports have it that he has already passed Merrelay castle and is well on his way out of Naze. Given that this is the case and that the Bishop has taken to madness, I have no hesitation in saying the planned wedding will not take place.'

The King went on to explain that the Bishop had been given his wish to own the Magician's island but instead of his planned monastery he would be kept in the tower for safety's sake and to avoid further embarrassment to himself and the church. His solitary confinement was an apt ending to a religious person's life, argued the King. There he could meditate in peace and rehabilitate himself, after his disgraceful behaviour since coming to Naze.

'Where we go next nobody knows,' continued the King. 'If that damned Magician were here, I would force him to look into the What Will Be once again before taking him to the gallows, but he is probably on the other side of the known world by now skulking around, pretending he knows what he is doing.'

No one said a word. None of the assembled councillors and Knights wanted to be the first to say the wrong thing. They knew the King was essentially talking to himself, not looking for advice.

'As my daughter remains unwed, and as Naze needs an heir to the throne, I have decided that I must provide the progeny necessary to continue the family line. It will not have gone unnoticed to anyone that the Lady Sockamore has shown me great attention lately. He stopped and looked at the members of the court. Like a slow Mexican wave, they nodded one after the other. Their faces revealed a certain doubt which the King ably managed to overlook.

'It will be a duty on my part, of course, but then that is the burden of royalty. We have to overlook our own interests in order to put matters of state first.'

Once again everyone nodded.

'So, later this morning I shall inform the Lady Sockamore of her good fortune, and preparations can be made for our betrothal.'

Whilst the King was meeting his court, Mistress Munn was in the kitchen with Gladwell Jupp. She explained that she was looking for Sir Godfrey, and before she could go further, Gladwell interrupted her in a very stern tone of voice.

'I don't know why you wants anything to do with that man Mistress. Look at what he done to my head!'

Gladwell Jupp lifted the hair on the back of her head to reveal a large round lump.

'Sir Godfrey?' Replied Mistress Munn.

'Indeed. He is a man with very bad habits.'

'How so?'

'I'm telling you Mistress, any man what keeps a rat as a friend is addled in the mind. Why the little beast shot up his clothes and stood on his shoulder as bold as brass. It was such a shock to my senses that I collapsed on the floor and when I came round Sir Godfrey was peering down at me and so was the little beast, so I passed out again.'

'That would be Mortimer,' said Mistress Munn.

'I don't care what you calls it, it was a rat in my kitchen, staring me straight in the face, and with the plague all around us!'

'Yes, well there's something you ought to know about that Gladwell,' said Mistress Munn, trying to explain about the night of the feast.

'There's no explaining to be done Mistress. A rat is a rat, and I won't have them in my kitchen.'

Mistress Munn could see she was not going to be able to persuade her friend that Mortimer was not like other rats so she took Gladwell Jupp's hands in her own and said she was sure there was no intention to upset her on Sir Godfrey's part. Then, as if she knew something was going to happen, she said,

'We have been friends these fifty years or more Gladwell. I am to make a journey that may see me gone a long time. I do not want us to part on ill terms. Wish me well, for I need to know there are good thoughts travelling with me.'

Gladwell looked her friend in the eye and told her, I't would take more than a plague-ridden rat to come between us'.

She asked her friend where she was going but Mistress Munn could not tell her, she did not know that herself.

'You know where the Magician is, don't you?' said Gladwell.

'I may have seen him in recent days, but the less you know the better my friend.'

'You are right on that account Mistress, the rack can stretch the body so cruelly that it would make the truest person betray any secret. I shall ask you no more.' And then they parted.

Mistress Munn's searches took her through the castle, across the courtyard, and eventually to the stables where, to her relief, she found Sir Godfrey.

'I have been looking for you everywhere,' she said as though she were scolding a child.

'Well, I have been here Beth, all along,' he replied innocently.

'Yes, well I knows that now, but I didn't before! Oh, never mind, it is done now.'

She drew in close to Sir Godfrey and whispered.

'The Magician is here, in the castle grounds, and he needs us to go with him.'

'Oh, but I can't this morning, I have an appointment with the armourer.' He looked down at the large hole in his breastplate. 'He is going to do his best to put this right.'

'Forget that Arthur, there are more important matters afoot.'

'But I need it to be fixed before...'

'You listen to me,' said Mistress Munn assertively, 'where we are going you will have no need for armour. Those days are gone.'

'But I...'

'Trust me, Arthur. Whattlewherrit has a plan. I know he is a little....unpredictable...but he says he can put things right with the Great Moyen.'

She was making it up. She knew it was wrong but, in her desperation, to get him to do what he was told, she had to do something.

'How so?'

Her mind raced to find some answer.

'He has spoke to the Bishop of Nantes and is seeking a pardon. The Bishop can do that.'

'But surely....'

'In return for the pardon, we must leave Naze forever.'

The old Knight looked confused. She could see he was trying to imagine Whattlewherrit and the Bishop of Nantes in the same room, let alone negotiating a pardon.

'Do you still love me, Arthur?'

'Well of course I do,' he replied.

'Well, with love comes trust, and you say you love me, so now you can prove it by putting your trust in what I say.'

Sir Godfrey had no answer. He had to accept Mistress Munn was right.

'Saddle up and meet me at the castle gates in half an hour.'

'Where is the Magician?' asked Sir Godfrey as Mistress Munn rode towards him.

'He will be with us,' she said looking down at the horse. Sir Godfrey appeared confused but said no more.

They rode for a good half day, away from Naze castle, through the valley of Lustmore, and out towards the wetlands to the South. The day was fair for the season, although it brought with it a chill wind from the North. Despite wearing her heaviest cloak, Mistress Munn shivered. Clouds broke and reformed above them, as if restless for winter to settle its heavy bones on the land. She knew the cold months ahead would soon require the usual fasting, and would take their toll on her ageing joints. She could almost feel the weight of the frozen pail on a cold winter's morning. The aching bliss of the fire undoing the screws of nature's clamps in the evening. In winter, life was but a flicker of a candle flame for some, before the cold took them, or they fell through the ice, or met their fate in the mouth of a forest creature. But she and her beloved Arthur alone knew, for all that, they would never die. They would never die but instead would face endless winters ,suffering whatever the Great Moyen chose to send them for their foolishness, and it made her heart heavy. She was considering such things when Arthur spoke.

'Where are we going?' he asked.

'The long stone at Hunker Down,' replied Mistress Munn.

'Hunker Down?' He repeated, 'and will Whattlewherrit meet us there?'

'He will indeed my love.'

Mistress Munn, the Magician, and Sir Godfrey were not the only ones travelling that day, as the King was later to find out. The Lady Sockamore and the Lady Gossamer rode out from the castle, not long after the Mistress Munn and Sir Godfrey. They were dressed for a long ride and had saddle bags packed for more than an afternoon's enjoyment. Having discussed the ability of the Lady Sockamore to ride whilst her wounds were healing, it was agreed that they would head for Sir Sockamore's castle. It was certain there would be hospitality offered to the King's daughter, even if they did not recognise the Lady Sockamore as Sir Sockamore's sister. Their elopement would take its course from there on. They both accepted they could not predict what might happen, but they could do their best to make it their own and not that chosen for them. Fate had brought them together and fate would determine their future.

It was nearing night when Mistress Munn and Sir Godfrey reached the long stone. Said to have been brought to Naze by an ancient civilisation, it was no more than a landmark these days, by which wayfarers could tell how far they had travelled. The mystery of why and how it got there no longer interested everyday folk, which was why Sir Godfrey was bemused by their travelling there at all. He was asking Mistress Munn the reason, when Whattlewherrit appeared as if out of nowhere.

'So here we are,' he said, as if it was as natural a thing as any for them to be standing on the top of a hill in the middle of nowhere.

'So we are Magician,' replied Sir Godfrey. 'The question is why?'

Whattlewherrit looked at Sir Godfrey and then at Mistress Munn.

'A long time ago Cornelius told me about this stone'. He put his hand on it and spent a moment in thought.

'He said that it was not alone.'

'And what exactly does that mean Magician and what has that to do with us being here?'

'It means that in the What Will Be there stands a stone the exact replica of this. They are as connected as the swell of the tides are connected to the motion of the moon. As one does, so does the other.'

'But surely they just stand and take the brunt of nature's disquiet? What is it beyond that, that they do?'

'When I tried to save Moredeath I made a great mistake. I panicked. I asked the shard to take us somewhere beyond the reach of man. It took us to the What Will Be, but this was not my intention. Not to arrive just anywhere in the vastness of the What Will Be. But my wish was tangled up with the vision I had seen of Moredeath and the imposter, who I now know came from that very place.'

Sir Godfrey and Mistress Munn listened in silence.

'Somehow, without meaning to, I had managed to entangle the lives of two people from different worlds. The here and now, and the What Will Be. Try as I might, I could not disentangle them. But back to the standing stone, for that was your question. According to Cornelius, your good friend, one can travel to the What Will Be and know where one is to arrive. If we leave from here by the standing stone we will arrive at its sister in the What Will Be. There will be no confusion, no risk, no fear of things going wrong.'

He stopped and looked earnestly at his old companions.

'But I am confused Whattlewherrit,' said Mistress Munn, 'what reason would we have for travelling to the What Will Be?'

'Why, to die Mistress, to die.'

For a moment time stood still for Mistress Munn and Sir Godfrey. They stared dumbfounded.

'Think on it while I unsaddle the horses,' and with that he walked off.

Sir Godfrey was the first to speak, following the Magician's departure.

'What do you think my love? Is this what should be done? Or should we accept the will of the Great Moyen? To suffer for eternity?'

'I do not know. If I am truthful then I have to say that on the journey here, I was considering winter's advance and wondering how I was once more to endure such pain as it brings. And then I thought of an eternity of winters, and it shook me to the bones.'

'I have thought as much myself. I would wish I was stronger in my mind so that I might endure the punishment I have been sent. But on top of my own suffering, I cannot not bear to see you suffer so.'

'We should talk to Whattlewherrit,' said Mistress Munn.

Whattlewherrit returned and asked them what they thought.

'Are you sure wo will die?' Asked Sir Godfrey.

'I am as sure of it as I can be. You remember when you told me that the Lady Gossamer had administered poison to the imposter?' Mistress Munn nodded. 'How it had the opposite effect? My belief is that when you enter the What Will Be the effects of the wine will be reversed. You will become mortal once more and the lance blow you received Sir Godfrey will have its full effect.'

'What about my love? asked Sir Godfrey, holding Mistress Munn's hand.

Whattlewherrit did not need to answer for Mistress Munn interjected.

'Five year ago, though no one else knows it, I fell through the ice on Millar's pond. I drowned, or at least I should have drowned and if not drowned, froze to death, but I did not. I told no one, for how could I? Your father was away and you, well I am not sure where you were Whattlewherrit, out in the forest no doubt. Anyway, I came back and if what you says is correct then surely I will die will I not?'

'It is my belief that it will be so,' replied Whattlewherrit. 'if not, then you will have to be patient a year or two and die, as we all do, of old age. Is that not better than the eternity you now envisage before you?'

Whattlewherrit felt like an executioner promising his axe was sharp but at the same time not being entirely certain.

'And what about you Magician?' asked Sir Godfrey.

'I shall come back and look for my real father and mother.'

'You have never spoke of this before,' said Mistress Munn who was clearly shocked.

'I have never thought of it before recent times Mistress. Somehow when I heard of the news of Cornelius' death it made me wonder how I would feel if I learnt the same of my real parents. They are out there somewhere, if not alive then at least in the memories of others. I shall find a life to live somewhere in this world,' he smiled. 'Do not worry about me.'

And so it was. The decision was made, and holding the shard in his hand, without further word, he wished for them all to go into the What Will Be.

Within moments they found themselves at the top of a hill set amongst downland and standing next to a stone exactly as the one they had just left in Naze. Whattlewherrit touched it as though he were thanking an old friend.

'Where to now Magician?' said Sir Godfrey but before he could utter another word he suddenly gasped and clutched his side. Blood poured from his wound.

'Arthur!' cried Mistress Munn. She knelt down beside him, but he was already gone. Whattlewherrit was about to console Mistress Munn when, as if she had willed it herself, she fell to her side and passed away with the slightest of breaths.

Whattlewherrit stood back. A tear ran across his cheek. It was the first real emotion he had felt in years, and it shocked him to the core. He had been right about the effects of the What Will Be and yet in that moment he wished it was not so. Without him acknowledging it, Mistress Munn had been a surrogate mother to him, and now she was gone forever. An awful recognition came upon him. He was finally alone. There would be no one to criticise him but then there would be no one to console or forgive him when he could not do so himself. Mistress Munn's jibes had given him something to push against when she made them and yet at the same time something to consider when the heat of the moment had died. Would he be able to do that for himself? To tell himself he needed to rethink some action rather than blindly committing the same mistakes, over and over again? Only the future would tell. He had no time to consider it. He had two bodies to take care of.

There was a path leading down the hill, at the foot of which he could see a church. The church was built to serve the Manor House not a hundred yards away. He made for the church. If he was to bury Mistress Munn and Sir Godfrey what better place than a graveyard? He stepped through the old wooden gate into the grounds of the church and looked around. Everything was old and crumbling and he tried to read the names on the graves but to no avail. He didn't want to think of Mistress Munn and Sir Godfrey in the ground, under a worn headstone, being eaten by worms. They deserved better than that.

He went into the church, and there to his amazement he found the ideal place for them to be. There was a tomb, and on the lid of the tomb, carved finely in stone, lay the figures of a brave Knight and his wife. He would wish his departed friends into the tomb and there they could rest in peace, which is exactly what he did. As he clenched the shard and ordered it, so the two bodies faded away from the foot of the long stone and materialised in the stone coffer.

The job done, he was reluctant to leave them but knew he must. Saying a last goodbye, he left the church, walked back through the gate, and out to the road heading back to the long stone. He would return to the stone on Hunker Down and pick up the waiting horses. He was thinking about this when his attention was caught by a familiar sound. It was the creaking of the churchyard gate shutting. His head turned to listen as the shard vibrated madly. He continued walking into the road. The last thing he felt was his soul freeze before the world turned black.

The car that hit him struck like a lightening bolt. He flew into the air and rolled down the road. The driver stopped, got out, and having assessed him dead, drove off.